See
You
on
the
Other
Side

BY THE SAME AUTHOR

FICTION
Bright, Precious Days
How It Ended
The Good Life
Model Behavior
The Last of the Savages
Brightness Falls
Story of My Life
Ransom
Bright Lights, Big City

NONFICTION
The Juice
A Hedonist in the Cellar
Bacchus and Me

ANTHOLOGIES
Cowboys, Indians and Commuters: The Penguin Book of New American Voices
Wine Reads: A Literary Anthology of Wine Writing

See You on the Other Side

Jay McInerney

BLOOMSBURY PUBLISHING
LONDON · OXFORD · NEW YORK · NEW DELHI · SYDNEY

BLOOMSBURY PUBLISHING
Bloomsbury Publishing Plc
50 Bedford Square, London, WC1B 3DP, UK
Bloomsbury Publishing Ireland Limited,
29 Earlsfort Terrace, Dublin 2, D02 AY28, Ireland

BLOOMSBURY, BLOOMSBURY PUBLISHING and the Diana logo
are trademarks of Bloomsbury Publishing Plc

First published in 2026 in the United States by Alfred A. Knopf,
a division of Penguin Random House LLC
First published in Great Britain in 2026

Copyright © Jay McInerney, 2026

Jay McInerney is identified as the author of this work in accordance
with the Copyright, Designs and Patents Act 1988

This is a work of fiction. Names and characters are the product of the
author's imagination and any resemblance to actual persons,
living or dead, is entirely coincidental

All rights reserved. No part of this publication may be: i) reproduced or
transmitted in any form, electronic or mechanical, including photocopying,
recording or by means of any information storage or retrieval system without
prior permission in writing from the publishers; or ii) used or reproduced in
any way for the training, development or operation of artificial intelligence
(AI) technologies, including generative AI technologies. The rights holders
expressly reserve this publication from the text and data mining exception
as per Article 4(3) of the Digital Single Market Directive (EU) 2019/790

A catalogue record for this book is available from the British Library

ISBN: HB: 978-1-0372-0075-5; TPB: 978-1-0372-0076-2;
eBook: 978-1-0372-0106-6

2 4 6 8 10 9 7 5 3 1

Interior design by Casey Hampton
Printed and bound in Great Britain by Clays Ltd, Elcograf S.p.A

To find out more about our authors and books visit www.bloomsbury.com
and sign up for our newsletters
For product-safety-related questions contact productsafety@bloomsbury.com

For Gary

See
You
on
the
Other
Side

1

STEPPING OUT OF the cab into the twilight, he felt a rush of nostalgia at the sight of the red-and-white neon sign hovering above West Broadway like an old movie title materializing on a dark screen. Like the start of a film set in New York, it signaled a certain promise—the promise of metropolitan pleasure, of social and gustatory and erotic adventures. The evening was freighted with possibility. The Odeon was one of the surviving landmarks of the protean city he'd inhabited for almost four decades, teeming with memories, layers of personal history, ghosts: prenightclub dinners with the boys punctuated by trips downstairs to the bathroom to snort cocaine, which made him feel as if he would live forever and the night would never end, bounding up the stairs afterward as if on springs to ogle the models and pretend not to notice the famous actors and painters at the adjoining tables; business dinners where he'd wooed authors he was hoping to sign, back when young novelists were the toast of the town, overnight celebrities who appeared in the gossip columns as well as the book pages; meetings to plot a hostile takeover of the publishing company that was his first employer and almost succeeding in buying it with borrowed money before the stock market crash of '87 had derailed that plan, the end of the overreach of his youth; recent lunches with Condé Nasters after their offices moved into the new World Trade Center that had risen ever so slowly from the ashes of the Twin Towers; date nights with his wife, Corrine, when they'd lived around the corner in an old-school loft with pressed-tin ceilings and warped plank floors over which they crept carefully on returning home so as not to trip and fall in their tipsiness and wake their kids; and lunches as a family, the kids venturing beyond grilled cheese to croque monsieurs. He hadn't been here in several years, and he found it reassuring that it endured, that the restaurant was waiting, unchanged, long after the monumental towers had fallen and the rented loft where his children grew up had been gutted and combined with the one above to make a deluxe duplex, although its survival also induced a nostalgia for all that had disappeared, for the declension of its bright, shining moment in the history of the city, just as its artful retro design conjured a lost city of Edward Hopperesque luncheonettes and cafeterias—like a layer of myth below the sedimentary strata of memory.

Russell's best friend, Washington Lee, had taken over the restaurant for the night to celebrate his thirty-fifth wedding anniversary—the least likely monogamist of his acquaintance somehow becoming over the years a model husband and father, as if to illustrate the fact that each marriage is a mystery, an iceberg of which only a fraction is visible from the outside, above the surface. His own wife took his arm now on the sidewalk, illuminated by the sinking sun of the magic hour, looking up at him and locking eyes, a ritual of affirmation, a mutual recognition of their union before they entered public space. They'd been together so long that it was sometimes hard to really see her, hard not to see instead the ghost of the girl she'd been when they first entered these doors, but tonight he scrutinized her closely, and he was happy with what he saw—to his eyes still a fine-looking woman after all these years, despite the lines etching her face. Yes, she'd had a brow lift seven or eight years ago, something to which he strenuously objected at the time but had come to approve of as the results were so pleasing. He'd been afraid she would look different, that he wouldn't recognize the face he loved, but in fact she looked more like herself, more like the girl he'd fallen in love with. *I don't recognize myself in the mir-*

ror, she'd said, arguing her case. It was a small victory against the relentless onslaught of age, which they were nevertheless losing every day. He knew he was thicker and softer in the middle, his forehead corrugated with age, creased from his nostrils to the ends of his lips, wattled in the chin. They'd both turned sixty a couple of years ago.

Their brief communion was punctuated by familiar voices, shrill soprano Nancy Tanner and her alto husband calling their names, greetings and questions from the scrum of familiars on the sidewalk outside the door, a scene that resembled the preludes to a thousand other gatherings, so familiar they could perform their roles by rote, and for a moment as they drifted toward the door all seemed reassuringly familiar, and then he remembered, feeling Corrine slowing as they approached the group, catching himself before he succumbed to the customary hugging and cheek kissing, refraining, or trying to refrain, since some of their friends hadn't gotten the memo, Nancy Tanner coming in close and nailing his cheek even as Russell extended an elbow toward her husband, trying out the new greeting in this time of incipient plague, Corrine holding back on the sidewalk in an attempt to circumvent the confusion. She waved to the group, waiting till they were sucked into the interior before taking Russell's arm and surrendering to the inevitable. She was very concerned about the virus that had infiltrated their city, convinced that it posed a serious threat, and as they gingerly navigated the room, they found others who shared her concern.

"I kind of can't believe we're here," said Dave Whitlock, an old colleague. Russell hadn't seen him in years, though neither acknowledged this fact. More than he himself, Russell thought, Whitlock looked his age, and then some, white-haired and wattled of chin.

Thinking of the old days, Russell said, "You mean, at the Odeon."

"No, I mean—did they even consider canceling this shindig?"

"And yet, you insisted on coming," his wife said—Russell could not for the life of him remember her name.

"Twenty confirmed guests canceled today," Corrine said. "I talked to Veronica a couple of hours ago."

"I wish we'd canceled," said Mrs. Whitlock.

"Russell wouldn't hear of it," Corrine said. "He thinks I'm an alarmist. But then, I've never yet been able to talk him out of attending a party. Why should an impending plague be a reason to stay home?"

"I don't know. This virus scare just seems a little overblown to me," Russell said.

"Russell's prefrontal cortex never fully developed," Corrine said. "He still has an adolescent sense of invulnerability."

"That's a little harsh. I prefer to think of myself as an optimist."

"You're an optimist, all right," she said, not unkindly. "I kept thinking you'd get more realistic with age."

"*Realism* is just another word for *resignation*."

"Russell was always famously Panglossian," Whitlock said.

In fact, Whitlock's version of Russell was at least twenty years out-of-date, but then, he didn't think his essential character had really changed. He didn't believe most other people really changed, over time, although it was a fundamental premise of literary fiction, self-help books, and Alcoholics Anonymous that they could. Does Mr. Darcy change during his pursuit of Elizabeth Bennet? Or does he merely polish his manners? Russell had taken some hits, suffered some serious disappointments. He had scars. He'd lost friends, loved ones, battles. He thought he had a healthy sense of realism, but he would never be a cynic. Had Washington changed? Perhaps. Mellowed, certainly. Age an agent of gradual change, for sure.

"I like to think I'm a little more nuanced than that," he said.

"You know his nickname, right?" Whitlock asked his wife. "Crash Calloway."

"Oh, God, yes, I haven't heard that one in years," Corrine said.

Mrs. Whitlock didn't get it. "Why 'Crash'?"

"A certain heedless enthusiasm," Corrine explained, "a lack

of guile and subtlety and more specifically a lack of acute spatial awareness. He tends to plunge forward, literally and figuratively, without anticipating obstacles, sometimes colliding with said obstacles."

"Are we talking about Biden," asked their host, joining the conversation. Stately, tall and lean, Washington had, it seemed to Russell, acquired a certain gravity of bearing in his later years.

"Yes, let's by all means talk about Biden," Russell said.

"Talk about pulling a Lazarus. Fucking guy was dead in the water before Tuesday. His old pasty white face looking more and more like that of a drowned man. Suddenly saved by the Black folks."

"Now maybe we won't have to feel the Bern," Whitlock said.

Since Super Tuesday, the relief among middle-aged, upper-middle-class liberal Manhattan Democrats, who formed a majority in the room, was palpable.

"Ah yes, Uncle Joe," Washington said. "I'm not sure I entirely understand the enthusiasm of African American voters in South Carolina and elsewhere for Uncle Joe. Didn't he once brag about working with segregationists, who opposed busing in the seventies and who helped craft the disastrous Clinton crime bill in '94 which helped put millions of Black men in jail. As what you people call a person of color, I'm not a fan."

"Understood," said Whitlock, "but if the goal is to defeat Trump, he may be our best hope." Russell was reminded anew of Whitlock's gift for dispensing conventional wisdom.

"No doubt that's what you said about Hillary in '16," Washington said. "That worked out well."

Washington loved being the contrarian, loved setting white people back on their heels.

"I'm pretty sure that's what we said about Walter Mondale back in '84 when we first started coming here," said Russell. "That he could beat Reagan."

"Oh, God, are we that old?" said Corrine. "Walter Mondale?"

"Yes, I'm afraid we are," Washington said. "We arrived in the city not long after Reagan arrived in D.C. Ah, yes, I remember having drinks here on election night in '84, talking with Paulina Porizkova at the bar."

"Remember the night you had to fend off Andy Warhol," Russell said to Washington. "In this very room."

"I think he mistook me for Basquiat," Washington said.

"You didn't have the hair."

"I had a lot more then."

Russell said, "I once shared a few lines with him down in the bathroom." Which was almost true. Russell had come out of a bathroom stall after snorting a few and found Basquiat standing at the sink, dipping a key into a paper packet, leaning backward so as to keep his dreads out of the equation. That was Russell's Basquiat story. Over time, he'd embellished the story slightly to the point that he almost believed he'd done coke with Basquiat. If he'd been smart, he would have bought a painting back then. Warhol and Basquiat both dead a few years later—'88, was it—hard to believe it was more than thirty years ago. A lot of Russell's memories of that period had this quality of being enhanced and burnished and supplemented by all that had been written subsequently about what was now enshrined in the collective consciousness as a golden age of New York. They had been there, lived through it, but the passage of time had dulled and smudged their recollections, and they were eager to fill the gaps with the testimony of other witnesses. Russell had reached a point where he'd forgotten far more than he remembered about those days.

The photographer Glenda Banes was indignant. "I mean, what the hell were they thinking," she asked, tucking her stringy hair back behind her ears. "If I get sick and die, I'm coming back to haunt their asses. If I get sick and live, I'll sue."

"Did you think about just canceling," Russell asked.

"Everyone knows I hate to miss a party," she said.

Glenda hadn't missed many parties as far as Russell could tell. He had, in fact, attended one for the opening of her retrospective at MoMA recently, where she'd worn a sleeveless dress that highlighted the pacemaker, like a small third breast, she'd had implanted at the top of her rib cage after triple bypass surgery. These days she was far too illustrious, and expensive, to take photos of authors who weren't Nobel laureates, though she'd once, decades ago, given Russell the rights to a photograph of Jeff Pierce that became the dust-jacket image on his posthumous novel.

She was with the restaurateur Julian Heath, who said, in a Cockney accent which had endured thirty-five years in New York, "I'd find this party slightly less offensive if they'd booked one of my restaurants. Business was down twenty percent over the weekend." Julian had, in the eighties and nineties, owned some of the hottest restaurants in New York, at one of which Russell had celebrated his fiftieth birthday, though only two of them were open now, and neither was nearly, in recent years, as hard to get into as they once were. Once upon a time Julian was the recipient of lavish gifts and sexual propositions from importunate diners, and it must have been hard for him to imagine, then, that it would ever be otherwise, to imagine that he was not the source of the heat but the recipient of its reflection. Russell noticed that Julian was walking with a cane—a rather elaborate one with a dark wood shaft and a silver elephant head for a handle—after breaking his hip in a recent fall.

Nancy Tanner appeared again, pulling her much-younger husband along with her. Nancy had a perpetually ageless, girlish look, aided and abetted by various nips and tucks over the years, though she was a good decade older than Brett, who worked in television. She'd met him in her incarnation as a Real Housewife of New York. Nancy was once known as a novelist, a progenitor of a genre of books about smart, horny young women prowling New York, but as the years passed, she had developed the persona of an ageless It Girl, which the reality show was eager to exploit. Nancy liked to pretend that the show was a big joke, a kind of ironic piece of performance art, and her friends largely did her the favor of pretending not to be embarrassed by it. Then again, most of them had, in one way or another, compromised the high artistic ideals of their youth.

"I can't believe all this doom and gloom," Nancy said. "Thank God there are still intrepid souls who want to have fun."

Corrine said, "I still don't know how it is that you and Russell aren't married."

"Oh, come on," Nancy said. "Everybody knows you two are the perfect couple."

"I thought they said we were the odd couple."

"You guys are like Bogie and Bacall."

Everybody mingled for another half hour, wandering among the tables and banquettes, miming kisses and hugs, negotiating different levels of anxiety about the virus. Some of the guests were congratulating themselves for having demonstrated their friendship by attending, and others wondering whether in doing so they'd made a mistake they would later regret. What should have been a festive occasion was a decidedly self-conscious one, haunted by the specter of the virus. A few were indignant that they had been invited to a possibly infectious party, although their presence seemed to belie their objections. Dinner was finally announced, and Russell and Corrine found their seats at the head table, where Russell sat between Veronica and her Harvard roommate, Christine Coles, whom Russell had seen infrequently over the years, and who had once inflamed lust in his breast, although she seemed to have aged considerably in the years since he'd last seen her, a fact that made him melancholy—a harsh marker of the passage of time. His female contemporaries, even those who'd once excited desire, were losing their power over him. Younger women were populating his fantasies. Although he was usually realistic enough to know he wasn't populating theirs.

Earlier he'd thought of the poem "A Litany in Time of Plague," and the lines *Beauty is but a flower / Which wrinkles will devour; / Brightness falls from the air,* lines which now, many years after he first studied the poem at Brown, seemed crushingly relevant.

Corrine was seated between Washington and Avery Finch, the writer, a lively seat by any measure. Avery was a professional stirrer of pots, a gadfly, an intellectual jester, a polemicist who delighted in puncturing political and racial orthodoxies.

Veronica looked at Russell and rolled her eyes. Leaning in, she said, "I don't know what Wash was thinking putting Avery at our table."

"Dinner and a show," Russell said.

"And you know how Wash loves a show," Veronica said.

As Russell took his seat, Christine said, "Didn't Harvey Weinstein try to crash Washington's fiftieth birthday?"

"I still can't believe he got convicted," Veronica said. "Not that I'm not glad."

"It was a political conviction," Avery said. "Weinstein may be a pig, he most assuredly is a pig, but the witness testimony was hardly credible. The verdict was emotionally satisfying, but it was legally dubious."

"The real heroines of the story were the girls who went back to Iowa and Kansas after refusing to sleep with him," Veronica said.

"Did you read the testimony about his genitals?"

"Please," Washington said. "We're about to eat."

"Do we get hand sanitizer between courses?" Christine asked.

Corrine said, "Can I just confirm that nobody's come from China recently."

"Or Italy," Veronica said. "They just locked down the whole freaking country."

"That should really work," Russell said. "The Italians are so excellent at following rules."

Two waiters circled the table, depositing frisée salads in front of the guests. "Love the frisée with lardons," Christine said. "Such a classic."

"What the fuck exactly is frisée," Avery asked. "It looks like what we used to call chicory when I was growing up down south."

"Same," Washington said. "*Frisée* is the French name, but the locavore-slash-farm-to-table restaurants are starting to go back to the American name. Sounds more rustic. Down-home—good. Fancy—bad."

"Washington could write a book on the semiotics of menus," Veronica said.

"Yes, our husbands are food fetishists," Corrine said, wearily.

"There are worse fetishes."

"Can somebody explain when and why kale became ubiquitous? And can we please make it go away?"

"Whatever happened to sun-dried tomatoes?" Veronica asked. "They were good. Back in 1987 they came on everything. Who decided they weren't cool? And who decided kale was?"

Washington said, "One of the things I like about this place—the menu hasn't changed since the Dinkins administration."

"French comfort food."

"Not that we ate much back then."

The conversation fragmented, with guests turning to their right or left. Veronica asked Russell about the kids and in turn heard about hers. He was fairly current on Mingus, her son, since he and his daughter, Storey Calloway, were dating—a fact that still amazed him, since they'd grown up together without ever seeming to take much interest in each other. He was also a little distracted, reviewing the toast he was about to make.

"Mingus doesn't tell me a thing," Veronica said.

"Storey tells me about his many accomplishments. I gather he had a story accepted by *n+1*. You must be very proud."

"Yes, actually. Definitely, but he needs to finish his book."

"I remember his hip-hop period. We heard him rap at Joe's Pub."

"His gangsta credentials were shaky at best."

"TriBeCa ain't the hood."

"Gangster rap is minstrel entertainment for white people," Avery piped up out of nowhere, having tuned in to their conversation. "It sells a caricature of the Black inner-city experience, a bogus glorification of so-called authenticity. Misogyny and Mammon worship and the glorification of the priapic male ego are the central themes of gangsta rap. People think it's crazy that Kanye West loves Trump, but it makes perfect sense, really; he's actually onto something in his own crazy bipolar fucked-up fashion—he sees the affinity between Trump's values and the values of rap. Do you all know that preelection, pre-2016, Trump is cited more often in rap songs than any other white person, there are over fifty references to him in songs by rappers like Jay-Z and DMX and Kanye. They share a value system. Trump may be a racist, he flat out is racist, but he's got more in common with 21 Savage and Lil Wayne than he does with George fucking Bush."

Russell was pretty sure none of the white people at the table were going to dispute this—certainly he wasn't, regardless of whether he believed it.

"I never did get Kanye's thing for Trump," Christine said.

"Now you know," Avery said, raising a champagne flute in her direction. "Same set of values. I'm just surprised Washington's good friend Jay-Z isn't here with us today."

"Good friend?" Washington asked.

"Could've sworn you two were big buds."

"Why, because you saw us talking once or twice at parties?" Avery rolled his eyes.

"Wash is more into jazz," Veronica said. "He's still mourning Miles Davis."

"Miles was the man," Christine proposed as Russell braced himself for the inevitable rebuttal. He'd read an essay of Avery's about Miles's electric phase.

"Oh, please," Avery said. "Miles was a sellout. He deserves the description that Nietzsche gave Wagner, 'the greatest example of self-violation in the history of art.' He was a genius, yeah, his early work is canonical, but then as the late sixties marched in, he wanted to stay relevant, wanted to sell more records, he starts flirting with rock and roll and electrifying his music. *Bitches Brew* is a corrupt sellout, a blatant grab for commercial and popular success."

"It worked," Washington said.

"You're reminding me," said Russell, "of the folkies who were pissed off when Dylan went electric."

"I leave that fight to the white folks."

The conversation again splintered into binary units. The frisée was consumed and cleared, wineglasses emptied and refilled with Sancerre and Brouilly. Russell stood up and belabored his wineglass with his fork, the din gradually subsiding.

"I'm delighted to be here to celebrate the union of my dear friends Veronica and Washington. There were times I, like a few of you, wasn't entirely certain that this day would come." Nervous titters bubbled up in the room. The ups and downs of their marriage were known among some in this crowd; they'd separated for a longish period more than a decade ago, after Veronica had discovered one of Washington's infidelities, an affair with Corrine's best friend, Casey Reynes. Glancing at Corrine, Russell could see that she was alarmed by his approach. "And yet, here we are: I can hardly think of a marriage that I find more inspiring than this one. Theirs is a great love story. They have weathered the storms and come out the other side stronger. They've abided and thrived and survived crises while raising two wonderful kids, forging two brilliant and challenging careers and creating a beautiful filigree of friends—of which we all feel lucky to be a part. I know I feel lucky to know them and to celebrate their enduring love. Please raise a glass to Veronica and Washington—and to their next thirty-five years." A rousing din arose from the company as Russell took his seat. He looked over at Corrine, who grimaced. He suddenly wondered if he'd bombed, although the applause seemed enthusiastic. Maybe he shouldn't have alluded to the hard times. But Veronica was smiling, squeezing his shoulder in approval. He wasn't particularly worried about Washington, who smiled inscrutably, nodding at Russell from across the table. It was hard as always to read his expression; he had a smile which seemed to be framed in quotation marks, ever verging on a smirk. Even after all these years he had the ability to make Russell feel that he wasn't entirely in on the joke. As the voices subsided and no one stood to follow Russell, Washington rose to his feet and waited, silently, not deigning to bang on his glass, as the room fell gradually silent.

"Thank you, Russell, for reminding me that age is taking its toll. And thank you all for being here to celebrate with us at the site of our very first date more than three decades ago. I'm kind of astonished to hear myself say those words, to hear that number. As I would have been astonished, thirty-five years ago, to imagine this moment. It is a tribute to Veronica, my wife, to her wisdom, patience and perseverance that we've made it this far—qualities few have accused me of having. Our first date took place in this very restaurant," Washington continued, "and in this town there aren't many institutions or marriages from that era still standing. Thirty-five years into it we have half a lifetime of memories, two beautiful kids, and we have you, our friends, who have enriched our lives immeasurably. To paraphrase John Donne: No marriage is an island. We are part of a community, an intricate and intimate network of familial and social connections. You are all part of our marriage. Thank you for coming."

"And risking our lives," Corrine muttered, sotto voce, as the room applauded.

Veronica leaned over and kissed Washington, to general applause, then stood up and waited for it to subside.

"Most of you know I'm not much for public speaking. Which is one reason I went into corporate law instead of emulating Perry Mason or Atticus Finch. Fortunately, my husband is more than willing and able to pick up the slack on these occasions. But it wouldn't be fair tonight of all nights not to add a few notes of appreciation for Washington. As some of you know, I faced a serious health challenge a few years ago," she said, referring to her breast cancer diagnosis and surgery. "I'm not sure that many husbands would have responded with the sympathy and compassion and patience that Washington showed. It was a dark and scary time for me and for my family, but Washington was beside me every step of the way. Not only was he my rock and my comfort in those days, but he was also that to Zora and Mingus. Please raise a glass to my beloved husband."

As the applause faded, Russell's phone chimed softly—an incoming text.

So great to see you yesterday, after so long. When can I see you again?

Russell lowered his phone and looked over at Corrine, who, if she had been watching him, might have seen a flush and a guilty look on his face. He was, at this moment, feeling a little hypocritical about having alluded to Washington's archival indiscretions in his toast.

2

THEY WERE SITTING at the table in the kitchen, their second full morning in the new apartment, hemmed in by boxes, reading the papers and getting ready to go to work, when Lisa Sherman called, Russell drinking a latte from his *New York Review of Books* mug with Joan Didion's image. In the last twenty years or so Didion had become whatever the literary equivalent of sanctified was—though she still appeared in the flesh, occasionally, at Manhattan literary events, looking almost ghostly, fragile and ethereal. Corrine had had to open three boxes before she found the coffee mugs, the packing paper still littering the floor.

Her phone rang. "Oh, hell," Corrine said, holding her phone so Russell could see the name on the screen. "It's just too early."

"It's always too early," Russell said.

She needed at least another cup of coffee before she dealt with Lisa. The clutter and chaos of the move were overwhelming her somewhat, not least since it had been preceded by her having to dismantle her mother's house and pack up her possessions after selling it this past month. It had been a thoroughly stressful couple of weeks. After a decade in a town house in Harlem they had decided to downsize and move back downtown. The kids were both settled in Brooklyn. They didn't really need all the bedrooms and bathrooms anymore, and West 126th Street had never been that convenient a location for either of them, although they'd watched the neighborhood gentrify around them, watched an efflorescence of the kind of amenities that people like them required—the opening of Whole Foods, new restaurants and boutiques. It hadn't been a bad place to raise their kids, although they had sometimes felt the tensions of integrating a historically Black neighborhood, of the residual poverty and the all-too-understandable resentment of their presence. Eleven years ago, they'd been priced out of TriBeCa and nearly left Manhattan altogether before buying, near the bottom of the last recession, the partially renovated, formerly majestic wreck of a brownstone for a relative song—a little over a million, most of which was mortgaged. They'd sold it last November for four times as much and purchased this two-bedroom penthouse in Greenwich Village. Corrine loved the new apartment, with its three terraces and gnarled greenery, like a little country cottage in the sky, but it had been a stressful month, winnowing the possessions, sifting through the memories, trying to tell herself that shedding possessions was liberating. But she'd had to fight back the intimations of mortality, the feeling that they were entering the final chapter of their lives, that this was the first step in an inexorable slide of diminution. It was possible that this would be their last home—a surmise that had only exacerbated the existential crisis that followed her mother's death last fall.

She thought that Russell had been less traumatized by the move—in fact he was exhilarated to be moving downtown again—to what he considered the dead center of Manhattan and hence of civilization in general, but he had been tormented sorting through his bookshelves, trying to edit the accumulation of a lifetime's bibliophilia, after adding thousands of volumes and dozens of feet of shelves during their long tenure in the town house. She'd come upon him in the library one evening, holding a book in either hand, an expression of anguish on his face, like that of a man who has been asked to choose between his children. When she mentioned this to him later, he said, "You ask yourself, Will I ever read *Anna Karenina* again? Is it possible it's been thirty-five or forty years since I last read it? And I was thinking, back then, time was limitless. The future was endless.

I want to believe I'll read it again, but it's nearly nine hundred damn pages." She had noticed last night that the novel was on his bedside table.

The phone chimed again.

She hesitated, decided to get it over with. "Good morning, Lisa."

Russell looked up, rolled his eyes.

"Hope I'm not waking you."

"I'm just headed out to the office, actually."

"So tell me about last night. Who was there? I'm kind of offended that I wasn't invited."

"Lisa, you barely know Washington and Veronica. This was an anniversary party for close friends."

"Like who?"

"Mostly publishing people. A few writers."

"That doesn't sound too exciting. Anyway, I have a small favor to ask."

Lisa often had a favor to ask, which inevitably had to do with dining—either the procurement of a chef, or a reservation. Lisa's world revolved around food, a fact which, among others, made Corrine dread these conversations. How they had become friends was still something of a mystery to her, though in fact they'd attended the same boarding school. Lisa was a couple of years behind her, and as far as Corrine remembered, they'd barely been acquainted, though Lisa seemed to have an entirely different recollection, telling anyone who would listen that they'd been great pals. Lisa had entered her life a little over a decade ago, when she bought a table at the Nourish New York benefit and made a hefty contribution contingent on the placement of a prominent chef at her table. She'd called Corrine directly, saying it had been too long since the happy times at Miss Porter's, mentioning a road trip to Groton, while Corrine struggled to place this alleged friend from her past. A call to her friend Casey Reynes had confirmed that Lisa was indeed more or less who she said she was, if not necessarily an intimate of theirs. Casey also mentioned that she'd inherited a significant Chicago meatpacking fortune not long after graduation. Corrine had convinced the chef, who was a great friend of the organization, to sit at her table, though afterward he'd implied that he'd taken a bullet for the team while chivalrously refusing to get into specifics. Corrine had stopped by the table that night, in part to see if she would recognize her long-lost friend, which she did not, and in part to thank her for her contribution. The following week Lisa had invited Corrine out to lunch, and while Corrine considered lunch a silly interruption of the day, she accepted, partly out of a sense of guilt at having no recollection of her former schoolmate and partly in the hope of inspiring future philanthropy.

Lisa had her own motives for lunch. It turned out that she'd become obsessed with Luke McGavock—the lover for whom Corrine had nearly left her own marriage—which their mutual friend Casey Reynes had indiscreetly confided to Lisa one night after too many cosmos at the Colony Club. Corrine was mortified, hoping that this chapter of her life was closed and sealed, but Lisa was desperate for any information that might give her an edge in pursuing Luke, and in the ensuing years, the knowledge that Corrine had succeeded where she'd failed, which might have made her resentful, had instead fueled in her a certain admiration for Corrine and a certain ongoing sense of competition which almost superseded her snobbery, her social circle being composed largely of those with multiple residences and large domestic staffs.

"What's the favor?" Corrine asked.

"Can I bring my son and his girlfriend tonight?"

"Lisa, I'm not really in charge of seating. Let me give you the number for the PR rep."

"Corrine, why would I talk to the PR rep when I know the mother of the chef."

"The mother of the chef isn't in charge of seating."

"Just tell them there will be four of us instead of two."

"Are you *definitely* coming?" Corrine asked, having had too much experience of Lisa not showing.

"Of course. Tell me who else is coming."

Russell looked up and shook his head censoriously. Even if he couldn't hear it, he could pretty much guess the other side of the conversation. He was not a fan of Lisa.

"Lisa, I'm not in possession of the guest list."

"I mean who's coming that we know. What about celebs?"

"It's really Storey's night, not ours."

"Is Eric Ripert coming?"

"I honestly don't know."

"I assume what's-his-name, Washington and his wife. Mr. Cool."

"Veronica, yes."

"I still can't believe Casey was fucking him all those years. Is Casey coming?"

"I think you just answered your own question." Though Casey was one of Corrine's oldest friends, she didn't get invited to events attended by Washington and Veronica. Not since their long-term affair had been discovered more than a decade before.

"Poor Casey. If only we could find her a man."

"Isn't she seeing that guy who works for Gagosian?"

"Oh, please. He's so bent he could blow himself without hunching over. And probably does."

Corrine tried not to picture this. She looked at her watch, glanced over at Russell and rolled her eyes. "Lisa, I really have to get going. If I make this call, you have to promise me that you're actually going to come."

"Of course I'll come. Why—are people canceling?"

"I'm just saying, you've been known to be a no-show."

"Are people canceling because of the virus?"

"I don't know, Lisa. I'm really not in charge."

"Who's canceled?"

"I have no idea. I'm just saying if I make the call for you, you have to come."

"When have I ever let you down?"

Corrine decided it was futile to enumerate the times Lisa had backed out of reservations and parties at the last minute. There were always several simultaneous events on her calendar. In her role as the director of Nourish New York, Corrine knew most of the restaurateurs in the city, and Lisa would sometimes call her when she was unable to bully her way into a hot restaurant. When Corrine refused, recently, to call one on her behalf, after she'd flaked on another reservation, Lisa had promised a two-thousand-dollar donation to Nourish New York. But it had taken two phone calls from Corrine's assistant to get her to make good on the promise.

"I've got to get to work, Lisa." She refrained from the temptation to point out that some people had actual jobs. "I'll see you tonight."

"Call and confirm after you talk to them."

"If you don't hear from me everything's fine."

She hung up. Lisa called back almost immediately. Corrine ignored the call.

"I can't believe you even take her calls," Russell said.

"She's not that bad," Corrine said, feeling suddenly defensive. "She's got a good heart."

"She has good *art*, you mean. At least that's what I've heard. Until the autopsy is performed no one will know whether she has a heart. But it seems doubtful."

"She gave me a nice donation recently."

"Wasn't that a bribe to get a reservation somewhere?"

Apparently, she'd told him about that one. She complained frequently about Lisa but somehow kept her close or, rather, failed to push her away. But then, her role as a fundraiser made it necessary to cultivate moneyed New Yorkers, and though she would disdain the label, Lisa was a socialite, part of the wealthy circle of New Yorkers based on the Upper East Side whose social life revolved around a series of charity galas, each of which competed for their attention and their donations. The galas provided a sphere of activity for heiresses and the wives of the titans of Wall Street, as well as a setting in which to show off their couture and their jewelry. It was an entire ecosystem with its satellite designers, jewelers, decorators, caterers and party planners. Lisa had never adopted a single charity as her own, as so many of her peers did, and Corrine kept hoping she would really commit herself to NNY one of these days.

Russell shrugged and returned to the papers. They took *The New York Times*, *The Wall Street Journal* and the *New York Post*, the latter as much for entertainment as news, for crime stories and gossip, though Russell kept threatening to cancel the subscription, saying that two Murdoch newspapers were one and a half too many. He liked the *Journal*'s business and cultural coverage, but the editorials drove him crazy—he would occasionally read passages out loud to her just to work himself up.

Inevitably, he was reading about the new virus.

"It's no coincidence that all the viruses originate around these live animal markets."

"Says the man who ate cod sperm."

"I can't believe you're still talking about that. That was, like, a decade ago."

"And yet I can't seem to forget it."

"So are we going to Storey's thing together?" he asked. "Or should we just meet there?"

"I can't help thinking it would be better if she postponed it at this point."

"It's a little late for that."

"I'm not dying to go out and rub shoulders with another hundred people tonight."

Corrine still found it hard to believe that her daughter was opening a restaurant. She was proud, but also slightly baffled. She'd presumably gotten her epicurean bent from her father, a serious foodie. As a child she'd had a period of near gluttony and gotten chunky, which had seriously distressed her mother. At breakfast she would ask about lunch and at lunch about dinner. She started joining Russell in the kitchen when he cooked—learning, assisting and tasting. She started baking at that point, making cakes and brownies and tarts for herself and anyone who would eat with her. Then, finally, thankfully, came the reaction, which Russell blamed on Corrine: In her high school years she slimmed down to the point that Russell wanted her to see a shrink for what he diagnosed as anorexia. Russell said Corrine's obsession with weight had given her an eating disorder, which was ridiculous. Though certainly Corrine sympathized with this phase much more than the previous one. Storey continued to bake, but now she gave away all of her production, as if she wanted others to eat for her. She had always been a very generous and giving soul, buying cards and presents for all occasions, decorating the house for holidays and, eventually, cooking the family meals. During her years at Brown and after, she remained admirably slim, while maintaining her interest in cooking and hospitality. Junior year she managed to get credit for a semester spent apprenticing at a bakery in Vienna.

Both Russell and Corrine were unhappy when she decided to drop out of Brown in favor of the Culinary Institute of America, though Corrine couldn't help thinking Russell could have been more forceful and sustained in his objections. She blamed the whole food thing on him. Storey argued that she had found her chosen profession and that a liberal arts degree would not be of any use to her, while her parents argued that she was a little young to be making irrevocable decisions about her future and that a liberal arts education was an end in itself. She countered that Steve Jobs and Mark Zuckerberg and Kanye West were all dropouts, to which Corrine said that Storey could neither code nor rap. After a year at the CIA she enlisted Corrine's help to get her a job with her friend Suzie Zhou in the kitchen at Chinois on the Lower East Side. She'd moved on after almost two years, with a glowing recommendation from the chef, to Lilia in Williamsburg to learn pasta. And the following year she'd done a stage at L'Arpège in Paris before deciding to open her own restaurant in Greenpoint. Corrine and Russell had put up some money, eventually, after trying to convince her to wait a few years, but Corrine was proud of the fact that Storey had raised the bulk from outside investors, despite not really understanding this career path her daughter had chosen. She knew it was superficial, but she thought it was a bit of a waste, a girl as beautiful as Storey hiding in the kitchen. It was a given, the starting point of any mention of Storey: her beauty. For better and for worse, she didn't seem to believe in it. In her own mind she was still the chubby sixth-grade schoolgirl with few friends.

Corrine trudged up University to Union Square and descended into the subway, slaloming through the labyrinth, squeezing in among weary commuters who gave a wide berth to a homeless man sprawled across the seats surrounded by shopping bags stuffed with detritus—lying in the middle of his own semicircular blast zone, the explosive in this case being olfactory. A rancid brew of sweat and shit and piss. She felt bad for this man, who must have once had hopes and dreams, family and love, but at the same time she looked forward to a life, someday, in which she would not have to ride the subway. Russell encouraged her to take a cab to the office, which she did on occasion, but it felt like an extravagance on a daily basis. She saw too much need, in her job, to be cavalier about small expenditures.

The news from the restaurants was ominous.
In her job at Nourish New York she was responsible for surplus food collections from restaurants all over the city, and she was hearing about canceled reservations and sparsely populated dining rooms. And chefs in turn were calling her to see if she had any knowledge of a possible shutdown by the city. On Monday morning she'd said it wasn't possible, but now, on Wednesday, it felt imminent. The Modern, Danny Meyer's restaurant in the Museum of Modern Art, had closed its doors Monday after a guest had tested positive for the virus. A few minutes after she arrived at the office, she got a call from Suzie Zhou.
"This is way fucked up, Corrine. We did thirty lousy covers last night and my staff's getting nervous. Half of them are afraid they're going to lose their jobs and the other half are afraid they're going to have to stay and get sick. I'm thinking about shutting down until we get a handle on this."
"I don't know what to tell you. It's a scary situation. Are we still doing a pickup this evening?"

"You might as well. God knows we'll have plenty of unsold food here. How's Storey holding up?"

"When we spoke on Saturday she was worried. I haven't reached her since." It was a constant source of annoyance to Corrine, how hard it was to reach her daughter on the phone. Except by text.

"Give her my love and tell her we're all rooting for her."

"Will we see you tonight?"

"I'm going to come by after service. I assume the party will be going late."

"Let's hope so for her sake."

Storey herself checked in just before noon.

"Speak of the devil. How are you, sweetie?"

"How do you think I am? I'm totally freaking out, Mom. We've had six cancellations just this morning."

"I was afraid of that."

"Empty tables are not a good look at an opening night."

"I picked up two people this morning if that helps."

"One of the cancellations was Chris Sedona."

"I don't know who that is."

"He's this amazing artist. He's, like, really famous."

"Have you thought about postponing?"

"Jesus, really, Mom? We're less than six hours away from opening the doors."

"I'm just wondering if it might not be better to wait till this thing blows over."

"Now you're making me even more anxious."

"I'm sorry. I just want everything to be perfect for you."

"That ship has sailed."

"It'll be great, I'm sure. Maybe Dad can come up with another author or two."

"I can't believe Jeremy isn't coming home for my big night."

"Well, honey, he's working. Michigan's not exactly next door."

"He's volunteering, ringing doorbells. He's not exactly a key figure on Bernie's staff."

"The primary's tomorrow, and he's invested a lot in this campaign. Isn't it possible that he's just as passionate about that as you are about your cooking?"

"He probably wouldn't come even if he were in town. He thinks fine dining is a bougie indulgence."

"He admires your work ethic and your dedication to your craft."

"Why did I think I could do this?"

"You can do it and you will. I'm sure tonight will be great. And maybe it will be better for being a little more intimate. You won't be overwhelmed. I mean, usually these things are chaotic and overcrowded and nobody ends up getting what they ordered."

"Shit, gotta go. I'll see you later if I don't jump in front of a cab first."

Corrine called Russell, who surprised her by picking up immediately.

"What's up?"

"Storey's in a panic. She's had six cancellations already this morning."

"Wimps."

"Honestly, Russell, if it weren't our daughter, I'd be sending my regrets. This thing is real. But I feel so bad for her."

"Didn't you imagine it would get easier when they attained the age of majority and moved out?"

"This isn't about us, Russell."

"Okay, I know."

"Do you think you could rustle up some fashionable folk? Maybe some young literary types?"

"I might be able to find one or two."

"God, please do."

She tried to imagine whom she might invite who wouldn't be insulted by being thought of at the last minute, and then she thought of that old hostess trick: the reminder email. To people who hadn't actually been invited yet. As if you'd already invited them once. But who hadn't she invited already? She'd invited a few friendly chefs, but maybe she could reach out a little wider. A couple years back she'd sent out a special chefs'-only invitation to the gala, offering free seats to twenty or so top toques in the city. She searched and eventually found it, erased the subject line and deleted the attachment and quickly rewrote the text.

Subject: Reminder—Tonight!
Hope you can join us for the opening of Storey's new restaurant....

She attached the invitation and clicked SEND. Those who hadn't already been invited might be free, given that it was Monday, when many restaurants were closed. It was worth a shot.

She had a sinking feeling—worry for her daughter and a larger, more general concern, a sense of impending doom. The move had unleashed morbid thoughts. Now that her own mother was gone, there was no buffer, no one between her and her own inevitable demise. And now here comes this virus, like the sinister embodiment of a thousand vague fears of a lifetime. The last epidemic had been selective, scything through a subset of the population, taking her friend Jeff along with some of the best and brightest and most colorful minds of her generation, but this one would be general.

Something wicked this way comes.... Unlike her husband, she always suspected that the worst was yet to come, and she feared she was about to be vindicated.

At ten-thirty she had a gala meeting—seven staff members in her office discussing the big fundraiser in May.

Earth, Wind & Fire—the current incarnation thereof—had been secured to play.

"Are there any of the original members?" asked Katie, the assistant director.

"I think the important thing is the original name," Corrine said.

"I heard them a few years ago at Alzheimer's and they were great," said Jane, the events coordinator.

"I sort of hate to say it, but they fit our demographic," Katie said, resignedly.

"Money usually comes with gray hair," Jane said. She'd

recently celebrated her thirtieth birthday and liked to remind the others of that fact.

"We've pulled in a lot of younger hedgies this year," Corrine said. "Not to mention all the young chefs working with us. Speaking of money, where do we stand with table subscriptions and ticket sales?"

Katie flipped a few of the pages in front of her. "We're up to two point two million. Our goal is three, but we've got two months to make it. And that's before auction items."

"Where's Carol? She has the auction stats."

"Out sick," Katie said.

"Ouch," Corrine said. "Speaking of which, is this virus worrying anyone?"

"Well, I'm just glad the gala is two months away," said Katie. "I think we'll all be fine by then."

"I hope so," Corrine said. "Meantime, sell those tables, sell those tickets." Of course, most of these otherwise very competent young employees and interns didn't know many people who could afford tables and tickets. Corrine made a note to try to talk Lisa into one of the fifty-thousand-dollar tables.

"Next up," Jane said, "presenters. We still need someone to present the award to Daniel Boulud."

"Ideally someone from the cultural world. A movie star would be nice. Someone who knows him. Call his office and see if he has any suggestions."

After a ten-minute call with the regional manager of a supermarket chain and a quick lunch of a hard-boiled egg Corrine went down to the warehouse, something she tried to do at least twice a week. They'd recently consolidated all food collections in a single space, restoring and refrigerating a nineteenth-century warehouse. Their offices would soon be moving there, too—something Corrine was slightly dreading, due to the commute to Bushwick. Today she just took an Uber, not having time for the subway. She noticed that her driver was wearing a mask, which made her self-conscious. Should she be wearing one, too?

They pulled up to the loading dock, where one of the trucks was pulling out, headed to one of their distribution points. Stepping into the cool vastness of the warehouse was always reassuring. Seeing, and smelling, rows upon rows of boxed fruits and vegetables, tended by men and women in green smocks, all of whom, eventually, greeted her in some fashion. She walked through the warehouse inspecting the produce, rescued from supermarkets and farmers' markets—the shiny eggplants, the squash, the carrots and several boxes of a white-and-purple tuber that she didn't recognize.

"What's this," she asked a nearby supervisor, who was hauling onions.

"That, actually, is a bit of a problem," he said. "Rutabagas. They've been sending them back. Nobody knows what to do with them. They're not part of the cuisine of the southern cultures we tend to deal with."

"Well, let's get our nutritionists on the case. Work up some recipes." Each giveaway station had a resident chef-nutritionist that worked up recipes for the food on offer. The recipes were handed out on laminated cards.

"We're on it."

She spent the next ten minutes examining the boxes, finding one very mushy cache of nearly rotten onions, which she set aside to be discarded.

"Where did these come from," she asked the supervisor. "Let's watch their stuff closely," she said, after he told her the source.

Normally she would have called Storey, or Jeremy, who lived nearby, before heading back to the office, to see if either was up for a visit or a coffee, but Corrine knew that Storey was at the restaurant, and frantic. Corrine was worried about tonight, worried that her only daughter was, through no fault of her own, about to preside over a debacle as she sought to launch her dream.

3

EVERY WEEKDAY MORNING Russell added ten minutes to his commute walking from the subway on Eighth Avenue to the Chelsea Market on Ninth, a vast edifice occupying an entire block, a former Nabisco factory where the Oreo cookie had been invented and produced which, by the time he arrived in the city, had been long abandoned, becoming a refuge for the homeless and the addicted, a shooting gallery which his then–best friend Jeff Pierce had occasionally visited to score heroin. Now the building housed tech and TV production companies above a ground-floor galleria—a redolent cave lined with bakeries, restaurants, specialty food shops and Russell's favorite coffee shop. Every morning he purchased a latte served up with a filigreed heart in the foam. It was an epicurean indulgence, a ritual that he wouldn't necessarily want to justify to his employees or his wife, a habit of more than a decade that had outlasted the very cute blond, pigtailed barista named Clarissa who'd initially inspired his patronage. He'd once asked her if she'd ever read the novel by Richardson, and she admitted that her father, an English prof, had named her after the heroine, but she'd been unable to get through the book. The current barista was a taciturn, intricately tatted young man with a meticulously groomed faux-hawk wearing a TUPAC DIED FOR YOUR SINS T-shirt. Russell was pretty sure Tupac had died for other reasons, but it was a catchy slogan for sure. He made a note to check if there was a good Tupac bio in print.

He walked down Ninth Avenue sipping his latte, past the hulking Apple Store, grazing the northeast corner of the Meatpacking District. Even after all these years Russell couldn't walk the cobbles of Gansevoort Street without the sense memory of the odor of rancid, decomposing flesh. Somehow his earliest memories of the area seemed more tangible than the current streetscape of chic little boutiques and restaurants—the hookers who cruised Washington Street after dark, one of them accosting him in his earliest days in the city, when he got lost over here trying to find a friend's loft. He had no idea, until his friend told him, as they snorted lines of coke from a Bowie CD, looking out over the desolate street, that the tall, sturdy streetwalkers were all men. And he remembered feeling suddenly, secretly embarrassed at his own fascination with the one who'd tried to talk him into a quick blow job in one of the abandoned warehouses. Long gone now—having migrated to prime-time TV with RuPaul.

He crossed over on 14th and a little before ten arrived at the nineteenth-century brick town house which housed his office. If anyone had asked him, he would have said his office hours were ten to six, though he couldn't remember ever making that official. It was more or less the industry norm; as if someone at some point decided that a leisurely start to the workday might take the sting out of the meager salaries. *You're unlikely to ever get rich but you can sleep in.*

Walking west along 14th was Jonathan Tashjian, Russell's publicity director, who'd been with him from the beginning. Bopping his head to whatever was playing in his AirPods. Russell had hired him just out of school—Yale and the Columbia Publishing Course. Despite his lack of experience Jonathan had a genuine love of literature and an easy familiarity with the Internet, as someone who'd grown up with it. Russell, who was something of a Luddite, recognized his weakness in this area, and Jonathan had proved to be one of Russell's most valuable employees, his lack of allegiance to the old rules mostly working to their advantage, building an excellent website and exploring unconventional marketing opportunities. But some aspects of the business had remained the same as they were when Russell had first arrived on the scene—like the author's tour. Jonathan had, in fact, often suggested that these tours were cost ineffective, between the travel and lodging costs for the authors, but Russell felt an obligation to support the independent booksellers who counted on author appearances, and like the other, larger publishers he continued to send his authors out on the road while Jonathan sent them out on Instagram.

Russell waited for him on the top step of the stoop, admiring his leather trench coat. Jonathan had a style and swagger unusual in the preppy world of publishing, dressing more like Julian Casablancas than like Maxwell Perkins. He cut a rakish figure.

"Nice coat."

"Thanks. God bless eBay."

"I hear it's quite the bazaar." Russell himself had never actually bought anything on eBay.

"I could show you sometime."

"My kids have already tried." He preferred to do his shopping in person.

"I'm not liking this virus news."

"I'm thinking if I ignore it, it will go away."

"Isn't that what you said about Trump?"

Russell held the door open. "So the universe owes me one."

Russell greeted Kristina, his assistant of three years, who contorted her face to indicate some combination of alarm and discombobulation. "You've got a visitor," she said, pointing to Russell's office. "Mr. Avery Finch."

"At this hour?" Russell was fairly certain he had never seen Avery in daylight. Russell thought of him as a permanent denizen of downtown bars and jazz clubs.

He found Avery sprawled on his couch, his dark, stubbled face glistening with sweat, wrapped up in a tweed overcoat and a billowing purple scarf.

"Twice in one week, Avery. To what do I owe the pleasure?"

Russell hung his own camel coat on the coat-tree by the door and took a seat at his desk.

"I hate to resort to clichés, but I was in the neighborhood. I was visiting a young lady in Chelsea in what I thought was her apartment. We decided to become better acquainted last night after a Hot Sardines show at Joe's Pub. She took me to a town house on 16th Street; she said she was staying there while her friend was out of town. I was rudely awakened this morning by an angry white man who claimed to be the actual owner of the apartment, who'd just flown into JFK from Boston. A very large, buff-looking white man. The young lady had disappeared in the night, along with my wallet. I assume he knew the fleet gazelle in some capacity, but he was too busy threatening to call the cops and I was too busy dressing to explore the connection."

Russell had to admit it was a good story. It may have even been true. Avery seldom disappointed in that regard.

"Sounds like you could use a little cash."

"If you could . . ."

"Hey, I'm just glad to know that someone of my generation is still picking up strange women in bars."

"I'm old school—an analog dater."

"You da man."

"As long as I'm here I thought I could pitch a book."

"What have you got?"

"I've been thinking about a biography of Sonny Rollins."

"What I could really use is a biography of Tupac." Russell thought he deserved to get some fun out of this.

"That'll be the day."

"You being such an adept of the genre."

"That boy kept it a little too real. Dancing with the devil. Playing with fuckin' Suge Knight. And it turned out to be very fucking real indeed."

"You remember what Vonnegut said."

"I remember what Vonnegut used to say. He'd say, 'Another, and make it a double.'"

"In *Mother Night* he said, 'We are what we pretend to be, so we must be careful what we pretend to be.'"

"I'm sure Tupac was thinking about that."

"By the way, aren't you writing a book for Washington?"

"I am prolific. Seriously, Sonny is one of the most important figures in the history of jazz. I have pretty much unlimited access to him and the archives. Not to mention impeccable cred."

"Write me a proposal," Russell said. He felt the chances were good that the famously self-declared prolific Avery would fail to produce a proposal. He'd signed a contract for a novel with Washington seven years ago. On the other hand, Avery on Sonny Rollins could be a very good book. "Meantime . . ." He took two fifties from his wallet and pushed them across the desk.

"Hey, I got an extra ticket for Robert Glasper at the Blue Note on Saturday if you're up for it."

"Sounds good. Lemme check with Corrine and I'll get back to you."

"Cool. Give her a big wet one for me."

After Avery left, Russell spent half an hour talking to his paper supplier about pricing. Such were the juxtapositions of his day.

"Actually, a biography of Sonny Rollins isn't such a bad idea if there isn't one already in the works," Jonathan said, when Russell mentioned it later.

"Maybe not, but we'd have to get in line between all the other projects Avery's sold all over town. I heard he was doing Amiri Baraka for Knopf."

Russell was finishing a sandwich at his desk when his phone dinged. He felt his face flush when he saw the sender's name.

What are you doing?
At the office.
Boring. Why don't you come out and play?
What did you have in mind?
A nice Negroni for starters. And then, who knows . . .

Russell was aware of himself grinning. It had been a very long time since he'd flirted via text or otherwise, and he had to admit it was exhilarating.

4

He'd run into Astrid last Saturday, the week before the Lees' anniversary party, at the Frick Collection. Russell was alone in the city, Corrine in Massachusetts, disassembling her childhood home—her late mother's house, on the heels of packing up the town house in Harlem for their move downtown. He loved being alone in the city on a Saturday, when he could savor his solitude on long walks, imagine for a spell that the metropolis existed solely for his benefit, for the fulfillment of his dreams and whims.

Taking a break from packing, he'd left home with only a vague itinerary, wandering his own neighborhood before forming a plan, taking the subway from 116th Street, getting off at Hunter College and walking over to the Frick Collection, a favorite refuge since he'd come to the city almost forty years before. On each visit he would single out one or two paintings to linger over; he had a particular affection for the eighteenth-century English portraitists, particularly Romney, with his deep sympathy for women. His favorite, which he saved till the end of each visit, was a small canvas in a hallway, *Lady Hamilton as "Nature."* He never ceased to be struck by her beauty, by her vivid pink cheeks and the lustrous and ample crown of auburn hair, by the sweet simplicity of her smile, directed at the viewer.

When he'd first seen the picture, in a slide in Art History class at Brown, he'd been stunned by Lady Hamilton's resemblance to Corrine Makepeace, a classmate whom he'd dreamed about, longed and lusted for. Years later, he was married to her, living a few blocks away from here, and she was at his side when he came upon this portrait on an autumn Sunday afternoon. It almost took his breath away, seeing the actual canvas, standing beside his wife, who seemed not to be aware of the resemblance.

A year earlier he might have pointed it out to her, but for some reason, he chose to keep it to himself, their marriage just old enough to have acquired shadows and secrets, perhaps because he was a little bit in love with a historical figure, and perhaps because he had learned since his first encounter with the painting—after years of imagining Lady Hamilton as a kind of ethereal patrician goddess—of her scandalous and adulterous history. The blacksmith's daughter who became the mistress of several London noblemen, one of whom introduced her to his friend Romney, who was looking for a model and a muse. She became a frequent sitter and the subject of many of his best-known portraits, making them both famous in London's most fashionable circles, until her lover, running low on funds, decided to marry an heiress and pass along his mistress to his uncle, Sir William Hamilton, the British envoy to Naples, who eventually married her, and subsequently turned a blind eye to her affair with Admiral Nelson, the most famous Briton of the day. The affair was the greatest scandal of the era; the newspapers relentlessly covered the ménage à trois, the comings and goings of the principals, the parties, Emma's wardrobe. Emma's fortunes declined after Nelson was killed at Trafalgar; she died in a shabby flat in Calais at the age of forty-nine, having fled her numerous creditors in England.

Last Saturday, standing in front of the painting, he became aware of the woman beside him, who, though she looked nothing like Lady Hamilton—a petite brunette with a shoulder-length blunt cut—was regarding it with studious intensity. She seemed vaguely familiar. Sensing his scrutiny, she turned toward him, and before he could look away he saw her face light up with recognition. "Russell!"

"Hello." He could feel his face burning, betraying his ignorance.

"You don't remember me."

"I do, I'm just . . ." It seemed rude to have forgotten this lovely person with the huge, saucer eyes.

"Astrid Kladstrup. I interviewed you about Jeff years ago. I edited that website. We had a very liquid lunch."

"Oh, God, yes." She'd been a college girl, interviewing him about Jeff Pierce, his long-lost best friend, whose fiction was then, after years of obscurity, enjoying a revival thanks to young enthusiasts like herself. They'd flirted pretty heavily; he seemed to remember that he'd heroically sent her on her way, resisting what seemed like a pretty direct invitation, though he couldn't remember all the details. There'd been quite a few drinks, a lot of innuendo. "That was, what, ten years ago?"

"Two thousand six," she said, apparently still young enough to remember years. Russell couldn't begin to peg past events to dates, except in the obvious cases: elections, anniversaries—and 9/11, of course. Two thousand one, always. So she would be in her early to midthirties; still petite and voluptuous, though she no longer looked like a comically overdeveloped child. She'd grown into the womanly figure.

"I read a story of yours in *n+1*," he said, pleased with himself for remembering. "It was very good."

"Coming from you that's quite a compliment."

"What are you doing these days," he asked.

"Actually," she said, "I'm kind of finishing a novel."

Normally, this declaration would have struck fear in his heart; as an editor and a publisher, Russell was bombarded with book proposals and manuscripts, by cabbies and bankers and accountants who insisted that the stories of their lives would make millions. In this case he found himself strangely serene, even intrigued. Her story had been good, as he recalled. "Define 'kind of finishing,'" he said.

"Sorry, that sounded really lame. What I meant to say is, I'm about three chapters away from the end of the second draft."

"Indeed," he said. "I'd ask you what it's about except I don't really believe it matters what novels are about. A good writer can make a ride in an elevator epic. It's all in the telling."

"I've been following your list—you've published some great stuff lately."

"We've been lucky the last couple of years." It was true, after nearly going bankrupt in '08, he'd been on a roll—in the space of sixteen months his authors had won a PEN/Faulkner Award and the Pulitzer. A moribund novel from his backlist had been made into a successful movie and sold more than half a million copies.

"I don't think you can attribute it all to luck."

He shrugged, accepting the implied compliment.

"Of course, I could take a tiny bit of credit myself," she said.

He cocked his head quizzically.

"I was the inspiration for Katie in *The Love Songs of Katie Bell*."

"Holy shit, that was you?" The novel, built around a middle-aged poet's pursuit of a beautiful Brooklyn party girl, had been a critical and commercial success for Russell. The poet is ultimately unable to pin down the object of his obsession, but the poems he writes about her finally give him the inspiration he's been lacking for years, and the published collection of those poems finally gives him a measure of literary recognition. The novel had been one of those rare crossover hits that had caught the attention of the lit blogs and the book clubs, in no small measure due to its beguiling heroine. More than one reviewer had compared her to Holly Golightly. She seemed to acquire greater density and luminosity with this revelation.

He studied her from this new perspective, superimposing the vivid literary portrait on the living woman.

"Strangely enough that's not the only novel I've appeared in. But I got tired of being a muse."

Russell surprised himself by saying, "Maybe I could look at your manuscript when it's finished."

They found themselves walking down 74th toward Madison. She stopped to pat a pair of King Charles spaniels that had puddled around her feet while their walker, a scruffy old dude in a Jets sweatshirt, checked his phone and a slender fawn-colored whippet trembled on its leash. The King Charles was the mascot of the Upper East Side, just as the French bulldog was the mascot of the Village. He liked that she liked dogs. He liked her energy, her self-assurance. He liked that they were walking together with no agenda and no looming obligations. It was the kind of Manhattan afternoon that seemed endless.

"Where are you headed?" he asked, after the dogs had been towed off toward the park.

"I don't know," she said.

"Shall we grab a late lunch? I suddenly realize I'm starving."

"That's a brilliant idea."

"Café Boulud's just up the street."

The lunch rush was over and the maître d' led them, without fuss, to a table next to the bar.

"So funny," she said, after they were seated, "running into you after all these years."

"The city's like that," he said. "Sooner or later, you run into everyone."

"It's true," she said.

"Where do you live?"

"Bushwick."

"Ah—the literary diaspora."

"Why a diaspora?"

"When I came to the city, writers and artists could afford the rents in the East Village and the Upper West Side and Chelsea. Of course, their apartments were likely to get broken into by junkies. And they often got mugged coming and going. But Manhattan was still the center, and everything was kind of walking distance from Washington Square Park. The bars, the clubs, the galleries. Now you all move to Brooklyn, but it's a sprawling borough. Not to mention Queens. There's no center. Greenpoint is a long way from Bed-Stuy and Red Hook. And Astoria's farther still."

"So you're saying I missed the golden age of Manhattan?"

"God, I hate when I hear myself sounding old."

Astrid suddenly turned around to face the hulking figure in a black suit sitting directly behind her at the bar. "That's the third time he's bumped into my chair." The man, who had the mien and the earpiece of a Secret Service agent, stared inscrutably into the distance.

Russell scanned the tables to see whose bodyguard this might be, spotting Bernie Melman, the corporate raider, sitting two tables over with his new wife. Back in the eighties, Melman had agreed to bankroll Russell's attempted leveraged buyout of the publishing firm from which he'd recently been fired. The transaction, derailed by the stock market crash of '87, was barely a hiccup for Melman, who'd gone on to make billions since, although rumors of his vast indebtedness had recently begun to surface. He'd just sold one of his planes, two of his houses and five of his Twomblys.

"Seriously, man," Russell said, feeling that he needed to make some kind of stand. "Could you just give us a little room?"

The maître d' rushed over. "Is there a problem here?"

"This man is practically sitting on top of my friend."

"Sir, perhaps you could move just a little," the maître d' said.

Looking over at Melman, Russell said, "Hey, Bernie, do you think your guy could give us a little space here?" Melman looked astonished to be addressed this way by a person he seemed not to recognize, but he eventually flicked his fingers in their direction, and the bodyguard, if that was indeed what he was, moved two seats away.

"That was very gallant of you," she said. "How exactly do you know his employer?"

"I once tried to get him to buy me a publishing house."

"It's emblematic of what's happening to Manhattan," Astrid said, sotto voce. "Rich people taking over."

And suddenly a memory that had been stirring broke the surface: his former assistant—he couldn't quite remember her name—another feisty brunette, who wore an EAT THE RICH button to work, way back in the eighties. Why couldn't he remember her name? But then, this happened to him more often than he cared to admit.

"Shall we order," he asked. He didn't want to leave this table, which seemed like the most pleasant real estate on earth at this moment.

"Why not?"

Russell flagged the waiter, asked for menus.

"Remember our last meal?" she asked.

"You were interviewing me about Jeff," he said, trying to keep things sensible. Jeff and he had been at Brown together, and later Russell had edited Jeff's first book, which was a great success; and the second, after Jeff died in the great epidemic that had devastated the city's creative community in the eighties, though Jeff, who was straight, didn't typify the victim profile, having presumably acquired the disease from a needle rather than from a penis. The novel he'd left behind was a roman à clef, the story of a love triangle among an artist, his best friend the gallerist, and the gallerist's wife.

"I think you owe me some of those royalties," she said. "When I published that interview with you, Jeff's book sales were practically nonexistent."

"It's true, you helped kick-start the whole revival." In the nineties Jeff's reputation had gradually faded, his annual book sales sinking into double digits; a decade ago, he'd been rediscovered by young readers like Astrid, who'd started a website devoted to Jeff Pierce.

The waiter handed them menus.

"Of course, the movie didn't hurt," she said. The 2010 film based on the posthumous novel, *Youth and Beauty*, had done well enough at the box office for an indie film, and pushed the book, which Russell had published, back onto the bestseller list.

He shook his head, admiring the taut skin of her cheeks.

"I still can't get over that your wife wrote the screenplay," she said. "I mean, given the circumstances. But maybe it's not weirder than you editing the book in the first place."

Russell shrugged. "It all happened a long time ago." Until

he was reminded like this, he could almost forget the actual circumstances, the story behind the novel, the putative love affair between his wife and his best friend. He could almost convince himself that it hadn't actually been consummated. Had Corrine really admitted it, or had they just talked around it? He couldn't remember at this point. In the book it had been an actual affair, all too explicitly portrayed, and it had nearly capsized their friendship. But at this point it was all mixed up with what Jeff had written, and the movie.

"You're still married, I guess."

He nodded. He was, though it had been a very near thing. They'd survived several crises over the years, the last almost fatal. Her affair with the rich guy had been a very near thing. "She's up in Massachusetts," he said. He didn't want to get into a big discussion about Corrine.

Her reaction to this information, the way she raised her eyebrows and pursed her lips, seemed like a provocation. It was hard to escape the impression that she was flirting with him, this ripe young woman who was a little more than half his age. What was supposed to be the formula for the second wife—half your age plus six? Some player pal of his told him that. Why six?

Melman and his wife stood up. The bodyguard with whom Astrid had clashed slid over to stand beside him. He glanced over at their table but showed no sign of recognition. It was as if they hadn't spent hours together going over the finances of Corbin, Dern, Russell's employer, planning a takeover, and indeed from this distance in time the whole episode seemed entirely unlikely. Legendarily short to begin with, Melman looked even smaller than the last time Russell had glimpsed him at the library benefit last fall, shrunken and stooped, and when he walked, he had the rickety gait of age, his balance failing, his skin hanging on his frame. It was kind of reassuring to know that in the end his billions were powerless against the ravages of age. Russell might have taken even more satisfaction in this realization if he were a little younger, a little further from the end himself.

"Good riddance," Astrid whispered. And Russell was glad

that she had no idea who he was, that his power had waned to that extent.

"Do you want to split some oysters?" Russell asked, studying his menu.

"Ah, so it's going to be that kind of date," she said.

"That was actually an entirely innocent proposal." This was true; he was so out of practice, so unaccustomed to the give-and-take of flirtation and seduction, that he hadn't even considered the erotic implications of suggesting oysters.

"If you say so."

They had parted, buzzed and aroused, on the sidewalk after a three-hour lunch. Her lips lingered on his and her tongue parted them as they kissed goodbye, but he had deflected her invitation to Brooklyn, tempted as he was, claiming another engagement.

Would it be weird to invite her to Storey's opening? he said to himself. Corrine said more bodies were needed. Would Corrine sense the chemistry between them? Or would it be a way to dispel the tension, to show himself to Astrid as a husband and father. He wasn't entirely certain what he wanted, even as he dialed her number.

"There you are," she said.

"Here I am indeed." It was the first time they'd spoken since parting on the sidewalk at Café Boulud ten days before.

"Whatcha doin'?"

"I was just looking at sales figures."

"That sounds boring."

"It's not all three-martini lunches with famous authors."

"Wow, that's such an archaic phrase. 'Three-martini lunches.' That's like something out of *Mad Men*, the lost world of men in hats and women in white gloves."

"I'm afraid I'm almost old enough to remember when it was a real thing."

"I'm sure publishing was more fun then. Now we have triple lattes at our desks."

"There was a certain glamour back then. When I first started working in publishing, I'd watch Norman Mailer or Gore Vidal sail past my desk at Corbin, Dern, and I'd think I was at the center of the world. A few days after I started working as Harold Stone's assistant, Lillian Hellman and Harold were headed out to lunch and she stopped at my desk and asked me for a light. She said to Harold, 'Wouldn't I love to play Mrs. Robinson to this one.'" All at once he worried that Hellman's name might be unknown to her.

"Hit on by Lillian Hellman. Wow. You should write a memoir."

"I've thought about it."

"*Really*. It would be amazing."

"I'm not so sure about that. I'm a behind-the-scenes kind of guy."

"You've observed literary history in the making. Not to mention the whole story of you and Jeff. I think it could be a really important book."

"That may be overstating the case. At any rate, I'm about to go into a sales meeting, but I called to ask a favor. If you're not busy tonight—"

"I could probably make myself available."

"My daughter, Storey, is opening a restaurant in Greenpoint. Tonight's the official first night and I was wondering if you wanted to come."

"Will you be there?"

"Yes, of course, although I'll be accompanied."

"You mean Corrine will be there."

"Well, yes."

"That's no fun."

"Sorry. But she is the mother of the chef."

"I suppose there's no way around that. May I bring some friends?" He liked the fact that she knew how to ask the question grammatically, *may* instead of *can*.

He wondered, briefly, after he hung up, whether he was pursuing a dangerous game under the false flag of helping his daughter. But Astrid was just the kind of guest that was needed tonight. Motives are usually mixed, after all. Life was more efficient that way, wasn't it? Two birds. He had no overt intention to cross the line, but it felt invigorating to have engaged the lusty attentions of a young woman half his age. And he felt entitled to his flirtation after Corrine's betrayal. Her brief liaison with his best friend he could rationalize with the knowledge that it had happened before they were married. It was something beyond infidelity, something more like incest. And yet, he understood it. He loved them both, and in the end, he had won the hand of the mutually beloved. He had prevailed and triumphed. That had made it entirely bearable—at least until Jeff had written a fictionalized version of their love triangle.

But the other thing, her big midlife affair—that had almost destroyed them. Some rich finance fucker. Luke. Luke something. Sometimes he wondered if his wealth was the big attraction; this might have been a solace, but in fact, he knew that Corrine was almost indifferent to material temptations. Which meant that the man had answered some other, more fundamental need that Russell had been unable to fill. He liked to think that they'd put it behind them, that he'd moved past it, but there was a scar, a dull ache deep in the heart, a dormant hurt that sometimes surfaced in response to some unexpected reminder, like an old bone fracture aching at the approach of a storm.

He, too, had broken his vows, on occasion, over the long arc of their marriage, but never for love. Random acts of lust. He could honestly say he'd never loved anyone but her. And as much as he tried to convince himself otherwise, he knew that wasn't true of Corrine. She hadn't betrayed him casually, for the sake of fleeting gratification. For better and for worse, she wasn't that kind of girl.

He felt like he could grant himself a little license in the matter of Astrid, that he was owed some slack, some karmic credit. For the moment it was an emotional adventure, and nothing more.

5

FROM HER OFFICE it was a short cab ride to the 34th Street ferry terminal and then a short hop across the river to Brooklyn. Corrine liked the idea of taking a boat to visit her kids. In all the years she'd lived in Manhattan she'd only recently become viscerally aware of living on an island, of being surrounded by water; the city having turned inward and landward long before she'd arrived, about five hundred years after the Dutch had sailed into New York Harbor, the priciest and busiest real estate being farthest from the rivers. She'd come to like the funky diesel-estuarial tang of the trip, the primordial-industrial reek of the river.

The sun was setting as she disembarked at Greenpoint, silhouetting the midtown skyline of Manhattan and casting a golden light on the Brooklyn waterfront, on the sleek new glassy high-rises and the stoic nineteenth-century warehouses, most of them repurposed as housing for app designers, podcast producers and famous artists she'd never heard of. At first she hadn't quite gotten it, but she'd come to like this neighborhood her daughter had chosen at the northernmost corner of Brooklyn. The site she'd found for her restaurant was a former dockworker's bar a few blocks from the river, which for some reason didn't show up on the Uber app. You had to walk a block north to get picked up, which worried Corrine, on behalf of her daughter's business, whereas Russell thought it would be a great selling point, a charming quirk that would add an aura of mystery and inaccessibility to the enterprise. New Yorkers liked a challenge, and more than almost anything else they liked imagining themselves as urban explorers, discovering corners of the urban grid unknown to the uninitiated. As for the name of the place, it was, in Corrine's opinion, similarly obscure: Condrieu, named after Storey and Russell's favorite white wine—from a little-known appellation in the Northern Rhône Valley of France. Russell had been delighted at the choice; it was he, after all, who'd introduced his daughter to the wine years ago. It was one of those father-daughter things, a shared enthusiasm that Corrine felt somehow excluded her. Not that she didn't like the wine—it was in her experience fragrantly floral. Obscurity aside, Corrine would have voted for a more easily pronounced name, but she held her tongue.

Outside the door a pair of smokers hunched and conspired, a white boy whose long dark hair had bright blue highlights and a young blond woman with an asymmetrical haircut, shaved on one side. They regarded her with mild curiosity before returning to their conversation. She couldn't help feeling, as the man turned away, that she used to command more attention as a younger woman.

Corrine got a faint whiff of woodsmoke and cooked meat from within. Storey had made a virtue of the very limited kitchen space—there was only room for four gas burners, but the original woodburning fireplace had become an essential tool, and a signature of her cooking. Last week had been a soft opening for friends and family, and the social media buzz had been strong, with a big emphasis on the spit-roasted meats and chicken. Pictures of the blazing fireplace crowded with cast-iron pots and sizzling poultry had proliferated on Instagram. The buzz had been great, even as the virus had moved in stealthily among them.

Corrine was distressed, when she entered, to find the place nearly empty. Six forty-five might be early, but the first seating was supposedly 6:00 p.m. She was greeted by Greta, the dreadlocked hostess, who looked almost anomalously glamorous tonight in a black sheath dress. Corrine had seen her only in casual attire, amid the chaos of preopening construction. "Hey, hey, Mrs. C. Welcome, welcome."

"Hi, Greta." They made almost simultaneous feints toward each other and backed off, just short of physical contact, remembering the new protocol.

"Oops, sorry."

"I know," Greta said. "It's weird. Makes my job kind of confusing."

They had hugged several times in recent months. Corrine liked her, thought she was very beautiful, and a great asset for Storey's team. Jeremy'd gone out with Greta a couple times, although he scoffed at the idea that these rendezvous at a Williamsburg bar had been dates. Apparently, *date* wasn't the right nomenclature. Apparently, it was a term associated with baby boomers, or the patriarchy. Or *whatever*. People didn't date anymore. They hooked up.

"So—the big night."

"Yeah, for sure."

"It's a little . . . empty."

"It's early," Greta said brightly. "Do you want to say hi to Storey?"

"Is it okay if I go back?"

Corrine walked to the end of the bar and cautiously pushed on the door to the kitchen, a claustrophobic, cluttered space which became even more crowded with her entry. Storey was leaning against the stove, between her sous-chef and her line cook, looking glum. Corrine couldn't help thinking that a tiny restaurant kitchen was the perfect incubator for a virus.

"Welcome to my funeral, Mom."

"It's early, sweetie."

"We had four more cancellations."

"Look," she said, pointing to the screen just across from Storey's station. "Here are three more." The screen showed the feeds from six cameras, covering the door and all the tables. Corrine thought it was a little Big Brother–like but it allowed Storey to monitor all of her customers.

Storey tended to pessimism, and it had always been Corrine's role to point out the bright side, the silver lining. But in this case she found it hard to do so.

"Is Dad with you?"

"He should be here any minute. Along with tout le monde." She realized as soon as she said it that this was a silly rhetorical flourish. "I'm going to stake out our table."

Greta seated a couple whom she recognized as friends of Storey's from college. The girl's name was Emily Barnes. The young man looked like a young version of Brian Ferry, dark and sulky, though he was in fact a friendly kid. Corrine groped for the name. Ryan, that was it. The Brian Ferry association was her mnemonic device. She tried hard to remember the names of her kids' friends.

"Hi there. So glad you could make it."

"Hey, Mrs. C," said Ryan, rising to his feet. Storey's cohort was stuck between titles and first names for the parents of friends.

"Please, sit. You're good friends to come out for her."

"We wouldn't miss it," said Emily, a Pre-Raphaelite redhead with translucent freckled skin.

"The place looks great," Ryan said.

"Doesn't it?" With its patched pressed-tin ceiling and its wide plank floors, its mismatched chairs and tables, it presented the cozy illusion of a venerable neighborhood establishment, although Corrine knew well how much work had gone into achieving the faux patina of graceful age—the space having been nearly gutted and redone to suggest its original incarnation as a hundred-year-old dockworkers' bar, a look that Russell described—although not in front of Storey—as "Brooklyn daguerreotype rustic." It was, according to Russell, a regional restaurant design aesthetic, originating in Williamsburg, that had developed over the last twenty years or so. Corrine did not consider restaurant design a subject for sustained study.

Russell arrived, wearing that eager expression with which he always greeted the start of the evening, ever hopeful about the prospect for discovery and adventure, doffing his camel-hair coat, looking very smart in his new Ralph Lauren navy jacket over navy turtleneck and jeans, an outfit which she helped him pick, which hewed closely to his preppy aesthetic while managing to look somewhat dashing, his salt-and-pepper hair fetchingly tousled. He could still stir her blood and her loins. She was proud of him, still thought him handsome, even as she just slightly resented the fact that he seemed to be aging more slowly than she was. Which was one of the reasons she'd had a brow lift.

Striding over to the table, he stopped to almost kiss Greta, raising his arms before dropping them and pulling back, looking from this distance like someone who has just realized he has mistaken a stranger for a friend. Instead of embracing they bumped elbows, exchanged a few words, Russell proceeding to the bar to chat with Alex, the manager and beverage director, with whom he had a sparring relationship, a kind of ongoing mock feud about the wine list. Alex, with his lavish beard and man bun—what Russell called the full Brooklyn. He called Russell "Pops."

"Hi, sweetie," he said, bending down to peck Corrine on the cheek before taking a seat beside her and surveying the room. "How's Storey holding up?"

"As you'd expect. Even at the best of times she's pretty high strung and self-critical."

"Can't argue with that. Should I go back and pay my fatherly respects or would that make her more nervous?"

"Go ahead. She was asking after you."

Two more couples were seated while Russell was in the kitchen, and then Washington appeared at the door, looking regal in a long black double-breasted coat, a black scarf billowing beneath his chin. He unwrapped himself slowly, with a sense of ceremony, unveiling his signature black Prada suit and crisp white shirt—somehow, he had the gift of appearing fresh and unwrinkled even at the end of a night out—bowing from the waist before handing off his outerwear to Greta. He had a keen sense of self-presentation, ever aware of the impression he was making, unlike his best friend, Corrine's husband, who moved headlong and heedlessly through space and gave the impression of being slightly windblown. Spotting Corrine, he bowed again, in her direction, before making his way to the table and delivering an air kiss.

"You're looking lovely tonight, O Mother of the Chef. Where's Crash?"

"He's in the kitchen trying to buck up his daughter. And Veronica?"

"I'm afraid she's feeling a little under the weather after our big night. She sends her love and regrets."

"That's a shame," said Corrine, who tried to mask her irritation, which deepened as she considered the circumstances. She and Russell had turned out for Veronica's big night, braving possible contagion, and now Veronica was bailing on Storey's—an occasion just as important to Russell and Corrine as their anniversary was to Veronica and Washington. And what were the chances that Veronica was playing it safe, that she was unwilling to risk possible exposure to the virus for the sake of her friends, the night after Corrine and Russell had done so for her.

Russell returned, slapping Washington on the back and asking after Veronica.

"She sends her love. Recuperating from last night. Touch of the Irish flu."

"Damn, that's a shame," Russell said. He didn't seem to be taking it amiss. "We'll miss her."

It irked her, too, that she'd refrained from inviting Casey Reynes—her best friend—because of Casey's affair years ago with Washington. If she'd known Veronica wasn't coming, she could have invited Casey. She certainly didn't think Washington would mind. The affair was over—at least she was pretty sure it was over—but she knew they remained fond of each other.

Alex appeared at the table, introducing himself to Washington as the beverage director. "Beverages are precisely what we need, my man," Washington said. "Make mine a Grey Goose martini with a twist."

"I'm sorry, sir, we actually don't stock vodka."

"You don't stock vodka?"

"We feel—"

"It's only the most popular spirit on the fucking planet."

"We just feel it lacks character, that it's a neutral spirit in the strictest sense of the word."

Russell said, "I've been telling you for years a martini is made with gin."

"Who's this *we*?"

"Well," Alex said, "I was speaking for the restaurant, but many of us in the artisanal cocktail community share that sentiment."

"I'm going to need to have a word with the proprietor. Who is my goddaughter, by the way. Meantime, give me a tequila on the rocks. Does tequila meet with the approval of the artisanal cocktail community?"

"We have some fine tequilas. I could recommend Tequila Fortaleza. We have the *blanco* and the *reposado*. The family has been making tequila for one hundred forty years. It's very much a handmade product, the agave cooked in brick ovens, fermented in wooden barrels and distilled in small copper pots. The *blanco* has notes of olive brine, roasted agave and fresh-mown hay. And the *reposado*—"

"I'll take the *blanco*," Washington said, blessedly sparing them a description of the *reposado*.

Corrine ordered a glass of Chardonnay, which pained both Russell and Alex equally.

"We don't actually have a Chardonnay by the glass, but I can bring you a Chenin Blanc from Anjou in the Loire Valley, which I think you'll like. Very mineral. It's got a nice orchard-fruit body with a touch of cardamom spice on the finish."

"What about the namesake wine? The Condrieu?"

"We have several fine examples by the bottle, but we haven't found one yet that fits our price profile for wines by the glass."

"Fine—I'll take the Chenin."

"And I'll have a Negroni," Russell said. "With Hendrick's gin."

Miraculously, they seemed to have Hendrick's gin, although possibly Russell already knew that.

"Busted by the cocktail police," Washington said as Alex returned to the bar.

"I'm surprised this is the first time," Russell said. "It's the whole speakeasy hipster cocktail movement. Vodka no bueno. Neutral spirit. No character."

"The spiritous equivalent of a dead white man? Yeah, yeah. I've heard that riff. But vodka has served me very well over the years. And given me a lot of character. Let's call it a persona. Consider how boring I might have been without vodka. The thousands of Absolut martinis."

"You're lucky he let you order tequila," Russell said. "I was afraid he was going to try to steer you to mezcal."

"And as an investor in this place you're okay with this?"

"Russell's been investing his energy in trying to influence the wine list."

"What's up with the wine list? No Chardonnay?"

"It's all-natural wines," Russell said. "No sulfur, biodynamic, harvested by virgins at the full moon. That kind of thing. I'm all for nature, but when my wine tastes like kombucha and smells like gym socks, that's where I draw the line."

By eight o'clock the tables were all full and there was a crowd milling around the bar. Several chefs, a reporter from the *Post* and a guy from LCD Soundsystem were among the throng. Bethany, the gorgeous perky publicist, had arrived, wearing a skintight sleeveless Balmain dress with a suggestive front zipper, accompanied by a small entourage of good-looking young women, and suddenly the place came alive. Corrine had wondered if a small restaurant in Brooklyn really needed a publicist, but her chef friends assured her it was necessary, and Bethany was allegedly the best. She'd come over to their table twice to introduce them to the LCD Soundsystem guy and a recent winner of the *Top Chef* TV series. Russell and Washington were impressed, men in their sixties regressing to their frat-boy selves. Neither one of them could quite hide his prurient interest in Bethany. Washington, as usual, was direct: "If you could just pay her to stand outside wearing that dress every night this place would be mobbed."

On the one hand Corrine was thrilled for Storey that her opening night had turned into a scene, and on the other she was nervous on behalf of everyone here. How would she feel, how would Storey feel, if some of these people ended up sick? The virus was out there, in the city, moving silently among unknowing hosts, exploiting the impulses and rituals of sociability and affection, passing from hand to hand and mouth to mouth. She could hardly imagine more fertile ground than the tight quarters of Condrieu. Their first courses arrived, with apologies from the waitress, some forty minutes after they'd been ordered. "We got kind of slammed," she explained. Washington and Russell scrutinized the plates with a lustful intensity before diving in.

"The barley risotto's great."

"What's the stock?"

"Believe it or not, veggie."

"Pretty intense."

"Try the *gnudi*."

Sensing a slight collective ripple of perturbation moving through the crowd, she turned to the door and spotted Carlo Russi, the disgraced chef, one of the earliest casualties of the Me Too movement. Russi had disappeared from Manhattan after being the recipient of a cascade of sexual harassment allegations, his restaurant empire more or less collapsing with the closure or sale of its outposts. Carlo was an old friend of Russell's, who hadn't heard from or seen him in more than two years, the rumor being that he'd retreated to Vermont after narrowly dodging a criminal investigation and settling a civil suit. Corrine could see him standing near the door, looking uncharacteristically awkward, this alpha dog who'd once had his own TV show and hung out with sports and movie stars. He'd been a commanding figure, bearish, fat and hairy, Falstaffian in stature and manner, but he'd lost a great deal of weight and now looked as if he would rather blend in than stand out, or so it seemed to Corrine from this distance. What the hell was he doing here? He spotted them, his face lighting up, and made his way over, nodding to some of the diners along the way, pulling up alongside their table.

"Ladies and gentlemen," he said. "Good to see you all."

"Long time, no see," Russell said. He only resorted to cliché when he was truly flustered.

"Yo, my man Carlo. Looking good." Of the two Washington had better self-command. "How've you been?"

"Not too bad. Been laying low. Going to school up in Burlington, filling in some of the holes in my education. Philosophy, religion. Getting a lot of reading done. Thanks for the books, by the way."

"Good to see you," Russell said. And then, with more conviction: "I hardly recognized you. You look like you dropped forty pounds."

"Almost fifty," he said.

Corrine felt the eyes of the room upon them. What the hell was he doing here? "Maybe your next book should be about weight loss," she said, when the silence was becoming awkward. "You look great," she added, not entirely sincerely. Corrine never thought in a million years that she'd ever disapprove of weight loss, but in this case it seemed a sign of diminishment and defeat. His skin seemed to hang from him.

"I'm not sure I'd recommend the circumstances that led to my shrinkage to the general public. Though *The Humiliation and Repentance Diet* does have a certain ring. But thank you. And thank you also for your kind invitation. I don't get a lot of those these days."

Corrine was afraid that her confusion was evident, as was Russell's expression of surprise. Why was he thanking her? It would be rude to deny she'd invited him, but she didn't want to be blamed for his appearance. But it suddenly occurred to her that perhaps she had invited him, that he must have been on the address line of that email blast to chefs she sent out in haste this afternoon. The previous invitation, the one that she'd doctored, must have predated Carlo's fall from grace. And he had considered it a genuine, current invitation, one of very few that he must receive these days.

A young woman in a floral-print jacket with a look of fierce purpose on her face was projecting herself in their direction, her eyes fixed on Carlo. Russell recognized her as one of Washington's colleagues, a senior editor at Random House. "As a rape survivor, I'm not comfortable with you being here," she said.

"I'm sorry you feel that way," Carlo said.

"I do." Now that she'd arrived and delivered her message, she seemed to lose some of her conviction. "I don't understand why you're here."

"I'm just here to celebrate the opening of a friend's restaurant. I certainly don't wish to make you uncomfortable."

Those in the immediate vicinity had gone silent. His accuser seemed to be losing even more of her conviction in the face of his meek response.

"Well, I don't think you should be here," she said, before turning and retreating.

"Jesus," Russell said.

Carlo shrugged. "So much for blending in."

"Not something you've ever been known for," Russell said.

"It's a skill I'm trying to learn later in life," Carlo said. "Sorry you had to be part of that."

Corrine couldn't imagine how to fill the awkward pause that followed. Should they invite him to sit down? She felt as if she, as the instigator of this situation, shouldn't exacerbate it by inviting him to stay, though it seemed the decent thing to do. Russell, with his good heart and his good manners, jumped into the breach.

"Would you care to join us?" he said.

"Thanks, man. I appreciate it. But I think I'll just slip away, if that's possible, before I draw any more attention."

Before Carlo could make his escape, he was accosted by the

reporter from the *Post*, who'd come up to the table and was blocking his route.

"Carlo, Jim Riley, *New York Post*. I wonder if I could ask you why you're here."

"Just paying my respects," Carlo said, lowering his head and ducking around the reporter.

"Were you invited," he asked, putting his hand on Carlo's shoulder.

"Fuck off," Carlo said, slapping his hand away and scrambling toward the door, his exit precipitating another diminution of the din, silence falling in his wake, as he opened the door and collided with an incoming group before finally making his escape.

One of the new arrivals said, "Was that Carlo Russi?"

"Isn't he in jail?"

"You're thinking of Harvey Weinstein."

The *Post* reporter turned back to the table. "You're the parents of the chef, right?"

They nodded, sheepishly, in unison.

"Was Carlo Russi officially invited tonight?"

"I honestly don't know," Russell said. "We weren't in charge of the guest list. You'd have to ask Bethany. She handles the publicity and the guest list."

"But you know him? I mean, you're friends?"

"I've known Carlo for many years," Russell said, "and I've eaten at all of his restaurants." She was glad Russell wasn't pulling a Saint Peter, denying his old friend.

"Did you ever witness any of the kind of abusive behavior he was charged with?"

"Please, we're here to celebrate the opening of our daughter's restaurant."

His eyes lit up, sensing a new line of attack. "Was Carlo friends with your daughter?"

"I don't believe she ever met the man," Russell said. "In fact, I'm sure she didn't."

"Did she ever talk about workplace harassment at any of the places she worked at?"

"Not that I can recall," Russell said, though of course this wasn't true. They'd heard quite a bit on that subject from Storey.

"I mean, she's a very beautiful young lady, if you don't mind my saying so. It seems like she must have run into some of these problems along the way. Seems highly unlikely that she wouldn't have."

"She's a strong person," Corrine said. "And we're very proud of her. And now if you'll excuse us, we'd love to enjoy her food."

When the reporter lurched off, Russell said, "What the hell did Carlo mean when he said you invited him?"

"It was an accident. When we thought we needed more bodies for tonight I repurposed an old email invitation to a bunch of chefs. His name must have been on it."

"Good luck explaining that one to your daughter."

"Oh, hell." When exactly was it that she'd become afraid of her daughter's censure?

"Because I have a feeling Carlo is going to feature prominently in the *Post* story."

"You're the one," Washington said, "who would have been in the shit if he'd accepted your offer to sit down."

"Thankfully, he was tactful enough to refuse. Actually, if you'll excuse me, I need to greet some new arrivals." Was he blushing? What was that expression on his face—was it guilt?

"Who are they?" Corrine asked Washington about the three young women Russell was ushering into the room.

"Young Brooklyn litterateurs?"

"The short brunette with the eyeliner is definitely flirting with him."

"Not to undersell your husband's charm and good looks, but I'd say she undoubtedly has a novel she's eager to publish. I have some experience with these kinds of situations."

"She's definitely working it. He doesn't seem to know the other two. I find it interesting that he's taking them over to Greta rather than bringing them here to introduce to us."

"I suspect in that regard he's doing us a favor."

"Are you seriously professing a lack of interest in three cute young things?"

"Corrine, I'm an old married man, just trying to enjoy a nice dinner with his friends."

"Seemed like you were enjoying Bethany's dress a few minutes ago."

"I'm a dedicated follower of fashion."

"How's Mingus?" she asked.

"I was hoping you could tell me. He and Storey seem practically to be living together."

"She's been working so hard these last few weeks I'm not sure they've been seeing each other that much. I know she's eager tonight to have him here for her big debut."

"Punctuality was never a signal virtue with Mingus."

"Wonder where he got that from?"

"Does it worry you, this relationship?" Washington asked. "I mean, what happens if and when it goes south? Isn't that going to be awkward for all of us?"

"I've tried not to think about that."

"And of course there's the X factor."

"What X factor?"

"Relationships are hard. Interracial relationships are even harder."

"I don't know. I like to think their generation is free of those kinds of hang-ups."

The look he directed at her seemed to compound amusement and pity. "Wouldn't it be pretty to think so?"

He always had a way of making her feel like a clueless white person.

"I guess you're right, of course."

"Ya think so?"

"Well, you and Veronica have done pretty well in the long run," she countered.

"To you it must be a miracle wrapped in a mystery."

Russell returned to the table, not a moment too soon, wearing the expression of a man who wished it to be known that he'd taken care of some tedious but necessary business.

"Are you going to tell us about your girlfriends?"

"I only know the one—the young novelist. She used to run a fan website dedicated to Jeff's work, which is how I met her. I'm surprised she never got around to interviewing you."

Was that a dig?

"When you called and raised the alarm about cancellations tonight, I called her and she brought a couple of friends."

"Not sure if you're aware of the fact that she has a crush on you, but her body language is easy to interpret."

"Given the choice between being published by me and sleeping with me, I'm pretty sure she'd choose the former."

She refrained from voicing her suspicion that the young novelist might be interested in both. She could detect a certain unease in his manner, an undercurrent of guilt, whether over the girl's perceived intentions or his own desires. Russell was fairly transparent, which was why she didn't think she needed to worry too much about it.

"Do you ever just suddenly feel old?" Washington asked. "I mean, seriously, sometimes don't you just say, 'Fuck, I'm old.' Like tonight, when some punk ass kid tells you that vodka's no longer cool. You wake up in the morning, you're hungover for the ten thousandth time and your joints are stiff and your back hurts and it's been years since you woke up with a hard-on."

Russell didn't feel that way, she knew. It hadn't happened to him yet. Well, the hard-on maybe. But his outlook was still improbably youthful.

"Sometimes," he said, to be agreeable.

"No, you don't," Washington said. "You still think you're going to live forever."

After they'd finished their mains, it became clear that they would best serve the cause by yielding their table. They said goodbye to Storey, who was harried and sweaty, but happy. The night was a success, qualified only by Mingus's continued absence, and his failure to check in.

"I mean, seriously, he has something more pressing than his girlfriend's opening?" she said.

He arrived just as they were leaving.

"Best get your ass into the kitchen," his father said. "Your extreme tardiness has not gone unnoticed."

"I had a thing at Joe's Pub," he said.

"Tell it to your girlfriend."

Mingus was buzzed, hazy of demeanor. Washington seemed genuinely annoyed at him.

All at once Corrine had a sense of foreboding; she was worried for her daughter. Suddenly it all seemed so obvious—the inevitability of an unhappy ending with Mingus.

6

THE VOICE OF Lil Nas X—his ringtone—woke Mingus from his nap. He had planned only a brief catnap, but instead he emerged from a deep sleep after an hour and a half on his couch, his cheek indented by the seam of the sofa cushion. He'd been more or less blocked all day on the article he was writing about Sonny Mehta, the legendary publisher who'd passed away recently who had once been kind enough to read and edit an autobiographical piece Mingus had written in his sophomore year at Yale. Mingus's dad had been a friend and colleague of the great man, and Mingus had grown up seeing him occasionally at cocktail parties for authors, and precociously engaging him about books and authors, which is what emboldened him to send the piece to Mehta without his father's knowledge. Not only had Mehta encouraged Mingus, but he had forwarded the piece to *The New Yorker*, where it was eventually published—a ruefully humorous essay about being a mixed-race kid from New York navigating minor and not-so-minor indignities in the Ivy League—and had drawn a fair amount of attention to the young author, so much so that he had acquired an agent and a book contract, which turned out to be a very mixed blessing indeed, since he had yet to complete the book after seven years, gradually evolving from a young prodigy to a delinquent author. What had initially filled him with a sense of pride and accomplishment was becoming a major drag on his spirit. He had of course put the book aside many times, occasionally trying on other occupations and identities. He'd become a bit of an itinerant journalist after he'd run through the advance, writing pieces about music and food, doing book reviews, but the book was always waiting for him, nagging at him. His early literary celebrity had paradoxically made it possible to dodge the book with periodic writing assignments. Now that Storey was opening a restaurant, he felt the pressure even more acutely. He was definitely not a macho douche, but at the same time he didn't want to be a plus-one. He was happy for her, and proud, but he also felt a little as if he was being left behind. It was time for him to get off his ass and finish the damn thing. It was already dark outside. In the meantime, Jackson was on the phone.

"Hey, man, I got you those tickets you wanted for Joe's Pub for tonight's show."

Jackson was his former roommate and best friend, an aspiring theater director who currently worked at the Public. He'd just started as an intern there when an unlikely play which was a hip-hop version of Alexander Hamilton's life got workshopped. Mingus thought it sounded a little nuts, but Jackson had been smart enough to enthusiastically take up the cause and his star was now ascendant.

"Oh, hell, is that tonight?"

"Yeah, man. Although I still don't understand your yen for country music."

"It's Americana, dude." In fact, Mingus enjoyed the fact that he was, in his circle, unique in his appreciation for country music. He'd started off with Hank Williams and eventually reached the present. He wore it as a badge of honor, a way of saying— *You think you know who I am? Think again.* People just fucking assumed he was into Kanye and Lamar. As for Jackson, he was a heterosexual theater buff, which was also somewhat anomalous, as Mingus occasionally liked to point out to his friend.

"You don't drive pickup trucks," Jackson said, "you sure as hell don't go to church, and you don't line dance. What's the appeal?"

"I don't like gefilte fish either, but I like Isaac Bashevis Singer's stories. Plus, Carly Pearce is fucking hot."

"I don't even know who that is."

"She's on the bill tonight. Come with me. You won't be disappointed."

"I don't know, man. There's a party in Fort Greene...."

"Oh, shit, I just remembered it's Storey's opening."

"I'm sure she'll understand that you have a crush on a hot country singer who's playing tonight."

"What time does the show start?"

"The first set's at seven. Plenty of time for you to ogle that chick and then go to Storey's opening. We can go to the party after."

"That sounds doable." The Public was a short walk away. He'd catch the first half of the show and then Uber to Greenpoint.

"Meet you out front at seven."

It was just past six. Mingus showered and got dressed, pulling on a pair of black jeans and a black embroidered western shirt. He thought about calling Storey, but he figured she would be neck-deep at this point. Better to just show up and surprise her.

"Jesus, *Grandpa waving from the balcony*?" Jackson muttered in the middle of "It Won't Always Be Like This."

"I grant you it's a little far out on the cornpone spectrum."

"A little?" But Jackson warmed up as the set went forward.

"Now that's poetry," Mingus said, after she sang, "We're living on a fault line and the fault is always mine." He appreciated the genre of the country music breakup song; in fact, he was planning to write a piece about it.

Jackson was probably putting up with this for the visuals—she was really radiant up there, in a flowy white dress, and her flowing auburn locks. And she was alluringly close, in the 180-seat venue.

"Too bad she's married to the headliner," Jackson said, referring to country singer Michael Ray, whom she'd recently wed.

"We may need to kill him," Mingus said.

"Well, we can definitely skip his set," Jackson shouted in his ear. "Let's get a drink at KGB."

"I don't know, I should probably get to Storey's opening," Mingus said when they were out on the sidewalk.

"One drink," Jackson said, handing him a joint. "We're almost there."

It was barely eight-thirty; he figured he had time for one. They walked down to 4th Street, sharing the joint along the way. The phrase *positively 4th Street* sprung to mind. He liked the fact that he was walking these streets that Dylan and Ginsberg and Kerouac had haunted. And Debbie Harry and Tom Verlaine.

He felt reassured when the bartender greeted him warmly and told him his drink was on the house. He liked the feeling of being a regular. His dad and Russell used to hang out here, though he didn't worry about running into them now—they both liked to go home after dinner these days. Get buzzed on expensive wine over dinner, then crash on their memory foam mattresses. Mingus had taken the reins. KGB hosted readings and had a literary vibe. Mingus himself had read here a few years back to a warm reception. He felt the warm glow of the Blanton's suffusing his body as he settled back in his chair. It was early yet; he didn't recognize anyone among the few patrons.

"I've always thought it was strange," Jackson said, "that you've known Storey pretty much all your life, and you at some point became romantic. How does that happen?"

Mingus was about to try to explain when Jackson said, "Hold on, it's Baron. Give me fifty bucks. I want to score some blow. We'll definitely need some for later."

Mingus opened his Berluti Scritto wallet, a gift from his dad, as was much of the contents of the wallet, and forked over the fifty. Jackson was always short of funds, but he was good company, and he tended to take the role of catalyst, leading the way to various urban adventures. He went over to where the dealer was ensconced in the corner and returned a few minutes later.

"All good?"

"All good. So you were about to regale me with your love story."

"I never told you this?"

"Not that I remember. Not really."

"Well, it's hard to pinpoint when it started. As Storey hit adolescence I couldn't help noticing that she was turning into a babe, so I guess you could say I had a little crush on her. But I didn't dare act on it. The winter after I graduated from Yale my parents took us to Saint Barth's. The Calloways came with us. They've been around for as long as I can remember, Thanksgivings, sometimes Christmas. We rented adjacent villas on Gouverneur's Beach. So we used to have dinner together every night, at one of the houses or at Maya's, the restaurant near town. And we started exchanging looks. And I thought, Hey, maybe she likes me, too. Then we started sitting together. It just sort of happened. And I started getting signals. So one night we agreed to meet after dinner and take a walk on the beach. I think we snuck out of our respective houses. We walked and we talked and it was just kind of magical. One thing led to another. We held hands and later we sat on the beach and started to kiss. We made out for like an hour. We did the same thing the next night except this time I brought a blanket with me. And we made good use of it."

"And this was, what, five years ago?"

"Yeah. We tried to keep it under wraps for about a year, but I don't think we were fooling anybody."

"Secrecy is definitely an aphrodisiac."

"Indeed," Mingus said, with a slight pang of nostalgia.

"So at this point the parents obviously approve," Jackson said.

"Yeah, but sometimes I wish they didn't."

"No Montague and Capulet drama for you two."

"Man, I better get the hell over to Greenpoint."

"You want to sample the coke first?"

"Fuck yeah."

Much as he knew he should get moving, Mingus found it very hard to turn down the offer of cocaine. It had been calling to him ever since Jackson made the score. Whispering from Jackson's pocket. It would definitely perk him up for the trip.

Jackson slipped him the sachet and he went to the bathroom, carefully unfolding the packet and slipping his key into the powdery pile. He did a quick couple of bumps and then, realizing it would be his last for a while, he did two more.

When he got back to the table he felt a little jumpy; another drink seemed in order, to calm himself down. Jackson took the coke to the bathroom to check it out.

The next time he looked at his watch it was almost ten and he realized he had to get out of there. "You want to join me?" Mingus asked.

"Not feeling very hungry, dude. Let's just hook up later. There's the party plus I want to check out this *amaro* bar in Williamsburg. Luis is bartending."

Mingus was suddenly very anxious. He was always running late. Half his life he'd struggled with this feeling of trying to catch up, of having to apologize for disappointing his friends and family. And he couldn't figure out why he kept doing it. It was like his book. He couldn't quite understand how seven years had come and gone, and he couldn't help feeling guilty about it. Sometimes he felt as if he were encased in a membrane that separated him from the common tasks of life, and from others, especially when he was high or wired in the company of those who weren't.

He would arrive toward the end of Storey's shift, he figured, take her home and have a not-too-ridiculously-late night. She would probably be exhausted. He decided he was going to finish the piece about Sonny Mehta tomorrow and then dive back into the book.

7

"Hey, baby, congratulations."

"Nice of you to stop by."

"Fashionably late." He kissed her—tasting of weed and coke. His presence made the kitchen feel very crowded, but in a good way. He carried an electrical charge that made her surroundings seem more vivid, throwing everything into high relief. She couldn't help feeling a little proud and possessive in front of her small kitchen brigade—Erica, the kitchen manager, and Emilio and Felix, her line cooks. It was strange, the fact that she'd known him all her life, that he'd always been there, and yet he'd become irresistible to her.

"I figured you'd be crazy busy."

"It started slowly. I was really nervous."

He leaned forward slightly, reading the index card that was taped against the backsplash: *It's not rocket science, it's only food. But it fucking matters.*

"I like that," he said.

"It was something Suzie Zhou used to say."

"Cool."

"Words to cook by."

"Why don't you come out and greet your adoring public."

"Let me just tie up a couple loose ends. I'll see you in a minute." She lifted herself on her toes and kissed him again, conscious of the fact that her success, if that's what it was, was more palpable now that he was here to witness and verify it. She knew that wasn't very feminist of her, but it was true. She left Erica in charge, doling out a few instructions, and walked out into the dining room, eliciting a smattering of applause and cheers from the crowd, mostly friends now.

Bethany appeared beside her and walked her around the room, introducing her to the people she didn't know, a hot vegan chef and an actress from a new Hulu series, and then Mingus commandeered her and sat her down at a table with friends. It was exhilarating but also exhausting. She was not entirely comfortable with this level of attention, with accepting the compliments and having to respond to them. Her mind was still in the kitchen, thinking about some of the glitches, about the big backup of orders midservice, about whether Felix was going to work out. It all felt a little unreal. But she realized that she was lucky, that she should be grateful for all the support and all the love in the room, and so she hung in there, trying to engage, trying to keep up with the conversation, accepting compliments about her corn fritters and eggplant caviar, staying at the table far longer than she wanted as Mingus regaled the company with tales of dining adventures from his trip to Spain this past summer, turbot fresh out of the sea that morning grilled over wood at Elkano down the coast from San Sebastiàn—"The boats go out before dawn and they come back with these turbot that they grill over a wood fire in front of the restaurant"—and of trompe l'oeil dishes at Disfrutar in Barcelona: "There was this amazing dish of corn and foie gras, with a crispy, thin corn-chip base with foie gras in the middle and then this sphericalized corn on top—this brilliant reconstituted corn, it's like a liquid aspic—that looks exactly like regular kernels on a cob but with like ten times the intensity of corn flavor. And corn, of course, is exactly what the goose eats in order to create the foie gras, so it has this conceptual thing going on. These guys trained at El Bulli, which was the birthplace of molecular gastronomy, and they're taking it to a whole new level."

It was all very impressive sounding and Storey couldn't help thinking that it was putting her own modest cuisine in the shade.

What he was talking about was kind of the polar opposite of what she was doing, which was based on great ingredients and a minimum of trickery. Wasn't this her opening? How had it become about Mingus's travels? But then again, she really didn't crave the spotlight the way that he did. She just wanted to cook. So it was okay.

Eventually, thankfully, the tables emptied. In the excitement of the moment, and burnt out as she was, Storey totally forgot to not hug and kiss her departing friends as recommended by health authorities. Mingus wanted to go to an *amaro* bar in Williamsburg, but she was exhausted.

"You can go if you want," she said.

"It's a supercool place. My friend Luis is bartending tonight."

"I want to close up here and go home. I'm fried. You go."

"Maybe I'll just get a nightcap."

"Fine."

"Will you be mad at me if I go?"

"No. Go ahead." Why didn't she just ask him to come home with her, she wondered. She would love to have him take her back to her apartment and snuggle, maybe make love. As well as the night had turned out in the end, she was feeling a little fragile and hollowed out. "Will I see you later?"

"Sure, if you're sure I won't be bothering you."

"You never bother me."

"Okay, babe. Thanks. And congrats." He picked her up in his arms and kissed her, then swept out the door.

Normally, in her years of working in kitchens, the night was just beginning at this hour when the civilians went home, and she was eager to go out, slam drinks and decompress with her colleagues, her tribe. It was a ritual of survival—of having made it through another shift, of having survived the pressure, the burns and cuts and the heat and the yelling and the jostling for space and the groping of the line cook. Rare was the night when she went directly home from her shift. She would be all cranked up, on adrenaline and sometimes Adderall, the synthetic fuel of professional kitchens everywhere, and not infrequently, they would counterintuitively further fuel themselves after work with coke. Storey could hold her own; it was a point of pride with her, though her weight hovered between a hundred and one ten, that she could drink with the boys. And they were always surprised that she drank whiskey. Bourbon, specifically. It was her signature, her way of saying—*Don't assume I'm some chick who drinks fucking cosmos.* You didn't want to be femme in the kitchen. And you don't want to be the first one to call it quits after work. When others were relaxing and playing, eating and being served, you were working your ass off, and when the last customer finally left, it was the beginning of your night. Psychologically it made perfect sense, getting all fucked up, trashing yourself, even if you were exhausted, especially if you were exhausted, even if it didn't necessarily make it easier to wake up the next day and do it again, hence the midday breakfast of cold brew and Advil and Adderall.

"You deserve something special," Alex said, handing her a glass. "This is a Weller twelve-year-old. It's like an affordable version of Pappy Van Winkle. They use the same wheated mash bill as Pappy, it's basically the same wheat-heavy recipe, but it's aged a little differently. Killer stuff."

"I have no idea what you just said." She took a sip. "But I love it. Pour yourself one."

"I'm thinking about a Sazerac for my first drink of the night."

She went back to the kitchen where she found Erica and Emilio cleaning up. "Come have a drink," she said. "You've earned it."

And as the whiskey kindled a sense of well-being which spread through her body, she caught her second wind, and eventually she began to regret that she hadn't gone out with Mingus, although, really, she wanted to share this moment with her colleagues, with Alex and Erica and Emilio; they'd been through a battle together, and it was time to savor their victory. They sat together at the bar till two-forty, at which point Storey was eager to join Mingus, but she didn't know the name of the bar, and her call went straight to voicemail. She was pretty buzzed and happy, so much so that the end of the night was a bit of a blur, in fact she couldn't remember the Uber ride at all, but she remembered calling Mingus again from her apartment, before she passed out, horny and eager to see him, getting voicemail.

She awoke, dry of mouth and aching of head, a little before noon, her phone loaded with texts and voicemails which she wasn't ready to face right away. There was no sign of Mingus, nor of her roommate, Kiki. She tried to remember the latter part of the night. She groped her way to the kitchen and decided nothing had really gone wrong, at least nothing that she could remember, except it had been weird that Carlo Russi showed up, a man she once revered who was now anathema. On the other hand, her boyfriend was MIA. She hated being clingy, but she couldn't help worrying, couldn't help wondering what he'd gotten up to last night.

She picked up her phone, poured some cold brew she'd made yesterday into a glass with some milk, downed three Advil. She felt a sense of dread, an intimation of some forgotten failure or transgression. She couldn't pinpoint the source of her concern— the opening had been, all in all, a success. Nothing bad scrolling through her texts, none of which were from Mingus. Many congratulatory messages, including from her mother and father and several chefs.

Now she was mad. He'd come late and left her behind. On possibly the most important night of her life, so far.

She was trying to decide whether to call him when he beat her to the punch.

"Hey, babe." His voice scratchy and crowlike.

"Nice of you to check in," she said, unable to keep the resentment out of her voice.

"I just woke up. I figured you needed a good sleep last night, so I went back to my place."

"A text would have been nice." God, she hated hearing herself whine.

"I would have texted, but to tell you the truth I passed out on the couch. I'm sorry, babe. Let's have lunch. I need some grease to soak up the alcohol. What say we meet at Kellogg's in an hour."

"I've got to be back at the restaurant by three." It was twelve thirty-seven.

"I'll get showered and dressed and see you there."

"Okay."

Now she was going to be rushed, she realized. Not to mention that she was not in the least interested in eating. She should call him back and cancel. Instead, she turned on the shower and swallowed an Adderall.

8

The aromas of dark roast coffee and bacon infused the kitchen like a spritz of morning perfume. The front page of the *New York Post* showed the Wall Street Bull statue wearing a blue surgical mask. MARKET DROPS 2000 POINTS.

"If I had to go out again tonight," Corrine said, "I think I'd kill myself."

"I have my wine club tonight," Russell said, reading *The New York Times* on his phone. The *Times* had not been delivered this morning, for some reason. He preferred the real thing, the hard copy.

"You're kidding."

"I don't kid about wine."

"Have you heard about the coronavirus?"

"This is a very small gathering, unlike the ones we've attended the last two nights. And I have a strong suspicion that the virus may be killed by expensive, aged Burgundy."

"The last two nights were milestone events that we couldn't in good conscience avoid," Corrine said. "This thing you're going to tonight is entirely optional. And frivolous."

She was wearing that nubbly brown cardigan that he hated.

"I would hardly call it frivolous," he said. "Kip Taylor is opening a '71 La Tâche."

"I'm *serious*."

"So am I."

"Come on," she said. "I really think you're being cavalier about what's happening. Wall Street's taking it seriously."

"There are just eight of us. Private room at Per Se."

"That's seven people more than you should be seeing tonight. All it takes is one."

Russell knew that she was correct to be concerned, even as he found it hard to believe that the threat applied to him personally, or perhaps it was more that, in weighing a vague risk against the very tangible pleasure he anticipated tonight, he couldn't help but come down in favor of the latter. He'd always believed in his luck, and on balance that belief had served him well. He would never have started his own business without that belief, never have published some of the long shots he bought that subsequently paid off in prestige or profit or both—books that the big publishers had passed on.

The papers this morning were full of ominous warnings about the virus, more than a thousand cases confirmed in the United States. Schools suspending classes. Italy shut down. A man wearing a mask and gloves who had tested positive for coronavirus boarded a flight from JFK to West Palm Beach, potentially exposing both airports and an entire plane to the virus. Still, it all seemed pretty remote, compared with the very palpable gratification in store for him tonight. Russell had, a few years ago, been initiated into a group of wine collectors and connoisseurs, all of whom were wealthy, who owned and liberally opened bottles that he could never dream of otherwise tasting—thanks to his friend and business partner Kip Taylor. They'd been acquainted at Brown and later reconnected in New York, after an encounter at an uptown dinner party, when they discovered that Kip had a son the same age as their twins. Like Russell, Kip had been an English major, but after a year in Paris attempting to write the Great American Novel, he'd entered the training program at First Boston and had later started a private equity firm while maintaining his subscriptions to *The New York Review of Books* and *The Paris Review*. Kip's son hit it off with Jeremy, and Russell shared Kip's passion for fly-fishing and for wine. It had been on a fishing trip to Wyoming, on the North Platte River, that their business partnership had been conceived.

Russell was chafing in his old job, working as an editor for a once-august publisher that had been subsumed into a sprawling empire owned by a French conglomerate. He'd been increasingly unhappy since the change in ownership, and after the events of September 11 he felt an urgent need to seize his destiny while there was still time, to help carry the American literary tradition into the new century. This was his patriotic vision—his version of enlisting in the armed forces. Eventually a small but venerable publisher, McCane, Slade, had come up for sale, and Kip pounced, bargaining hard with the outmatched heirs and giving Russell 20 percent of the company, with additional equity contingent on performance.

The company had nearly capsized in the wake of the financial collapse of 2008, and Kip, with his own liquidity problems, was reluctant to inject additional capital. It had been Corrine who had improbably come up with the cash to save McCane, Slade, selling a painting that had been given to her by an admirer in the eighties and had appreciated wildly in value since. But Kip, who had survived his own crisis and made many more millions in the years since, felt bad about abandoning Russell in his hour of need and had been making up for it ever after, taking Russell on fishing trips and eventually recruiting him into the wine group, a confederation of deep-pocketed finance and real estate guys who competed to bring rare and expensive bottles to their monthly gatherings. Russell would never have been able to play in this sandbox if Kip didn't quietly subsidize him, bringing bottles for both of them, sometimes having the wine dropped off at Russell's home a few days before the dinners. Whether or not the others were aware of this arrangement, Russell liked to believe that he was an asset to the group, welcomed as a breath of fresh air, an emissary from the world of arts and letters.

Russell liked to say—though not in front of this group—that there were two teams, the team of art and love and the team of power and money, and his wine club gave him a little entrée and insight into the other side. Actually there were two other members of the group who came from outside the world of finance—a chef with an empire of thirty-eight restaurants around the world who'd amassed a superb wine cellar over the years and a concert promoter who owned and operated the largest booking agency in the world. Corrine thought it was all a little silly, and extravagant; if she only knew the price of the bottles that were opened and consumed, she'd be appalled, as he sometimes was. His son would see further evidence of the need for revolution, or at least an immediate transition to socialism.

Thinking of their son, he said, "The Michigan primary's today."

"Oh, God. I hardly know what to hope for," Corrine said.

Democrats both, neither of them wanted Bernie to win, believing him to be unlikely to defeat Trump—not that that was their only concern—on the other hand, their son was a passionate believer, and a low-level campaign staffer. He'd been bitterly discouraged, even disillusioned, by Bernie's defeat four years earlier. He'd dropped out of Brown to work on the campaign, deeply disappointing his parents, and had yet to finish college. It had been a double blow, coinciding with his sister's almost simultaneous withdrawal from school, but at least she'd dropped out in the service of a specific vocational path. The subject of their only son was one around which they trod lightly. It was as if they were both holding their breath, hoping that he would find his course in life, hoping that what was coming to seem like the inevitable defeat of his political standard bearer wouldn't derail him further.

"I think he comes back tomorrow," she said. She'd spoken to him recently. It had been almost a week since Russell had connected with his son, though he'd left several messages. Like all kids his age, he seemed to have something against actual voice contact.

Walking from the subway to the office, Russell dialed and miraculously connected with Jeremy.

"How's it going? Just wanted to wish you luck."

"I don't think you really mean that."

"I think Bernie's a great man, and he's created a powerful movement. Are you optimistic?"

"The polls don't look good, but of course we're hopeful."

"When are you coming back?"

"Tomorrow, actually."

"Let's have lunch." Russell clicked on his calendar. "How about Thursday?"

"Okay, I guess."

Russell tried to think of a venue that might tempt him or, at least, not offend him. Should he offer to go to Brooklyn? But he had a three o'clock meeting.

"How about Balthazar, one o'clock." Russell hoped the place might have fond associations for Jeremy; they'd sometimes had family brunches there when they lived in TriBeCa.

"Fine, whatever."

Russell nudged the conversation forward for a few more minutes before signing off. Why was it so hard to talk to him sometimes? Why did it feel like he was always impatient with his parents? Why had he rejected the father-son rituals—skiing, tennis, fly-fishing? These were passions he'd dreamed of passing along to his son. Did Jeremy really think they were bourgeois pastimes? At least he'd inherited Russell's love of reading. He was better read in history, philosophy and English literature than most grad students. But what the hell was he going to do with his life? Before he'd thrown himself into the Sanders campaign, he'd been a barista at a coffee shop in Williamsburg. Being a member of the proletariat seemed to be an important part of his identity, although he was not so ideologically pure as to reject being substantially subsidized by his bourgeois parents.

Russell glanced across his desk at the framed picture of Bernie standing stiffly beside a grinning Jeremy—a souvenir of the last campaign—juxtaposed with another from 2016 of Russell and Corrine with Hillary Clinton, Russell leaning awkwardly, shrinking in Hillary's direction, taken at a fundraiser in the Hamptons. One of several in his desktop gallery: Jeff Pierce slouched against the door of his East Village apartment; a photo of bearded, brooding John Berryman; a signed publicity still of Jack Nicholson from *The Shining*—*To Russ, who gives good book*— a photo of a slouchy, bescarfed *Exile on Main St.*-era Keith Richards, just because; a photo of Russell and Jack Carson, his southern writer, on a center-console boat in Montauk, holding a large striped bass, not long after the publication of Jack's book of short stories, not long before he'd died in a Lamborghini on the West Side Highway, wired out of his gourd; a photo of Storey in chef's whites with Chef Alain Passard in Paris. Storey had given Russell the photo with the specific instruction that it join the collection on his desk, whereas Jeremy was slightly embarrassed when he saw his four-year-old photo with Bernie here a few months ago.

Russell logged in to his email and spent the next half hour dealing with the most pressing work matters while skipping lightly over the dozen or so alarmist and importunate emails from various factions of the Democratic Party: *Barack Obama is asking (final plea). Friend, they voted to confirm Kavanaugh. Now we can replace them. Thousands have already signed up to fight hate. Emily's List. We need to hit this goal by midnight. Joe Biden OVERWHELMED. All hope is lost! Mitch McConnell STOMPED. Amy McGrath just shot ahead. Barack Obama just BLEW US AWAY. I am asking you one last time before tomorrow's deadline. Republicans are coming for us in Iowa.*

He took a call from Kurt Winfield, the author of an excellent Jefferson biography that Russell was publishing next month. Although Kurt had been working on the book for years, his opus could be imagined as a riposte to the Ron Chernow biography of Hamilton and the wildly popular hip-hop musical partly inspired by it. Russell personally believed that the play was unfair to Jefferson. In his view, Jefferson, for all his Virginia aristocratic background and his slave ownership—inherited, it should be noted—had better credentials as an icon of democracy and personal liberty. Hamilton was an elitist at heart, the voice of big government and finance. Were he to be reincarnated now, he would have been a dyed-in-the-wool Republican.

Normally a biography like this one wouldn't warrant a national tour. But Kurt's previous book, a bio of George Washington published almost a decade before, had been a national bestseller, lingering in the middle of *The New York Times* list for months. And of course, the Hamilton connection was bound to stir up press interest—in fact, Russell and Jonathan had already planted that storyline with a number of journalists. Kurt was excited. An academic who'd been cloistered with his research for years, he was eager to thrust himself once again into the wider world. He'd been eagerly involved in all the aspects of publishing his book, from the jacket design to the marketing campaign. Kurt was a nerd, a serious scholar with halitosis and a closet full of ugly cardigans, but he was not diffident or aloof when it came to self-promotion. He loved being interviewed, especially on TV, and he seemed to be an expert on the proclivities of various talk-show hosts and their ratings.

"Any luck getting me on *Morning Joe*," he asked.

"Jonathan's working on it. I think we've got a very good shot. We'll talk next week."

"Joe Scarborough has a thing for presidential history. He's got Michael Beschloss on the show all the time."

"We're on the case, Kurt."

"What's he like off-screen? I've heard he's a decent guy."

"Who, Beschloss?"

"No—Scarborough."

"I've never actually met him," Russell admitted.

"Really?" With this one word he managed to convey disillusionment, sadness, a sense that perhaps he'd picked the wrong publisher. Didn't all these New York media types hobnob at Michael's, or over cocktails in Gay Talese's town house? Wasn't Russell a member of the club? Over the years Russell had noticed a tendency on the part of many of his heartland authors to imagine him as their vicarious representative to the New York intelligentsia—a society they conceived of as fraternal, homogeneous and all-powerful in shaping the cultural landscape—and to admire, envy and resent his membership in this imagined fraternity. The fact that there was a glimmer of truth in this notion didn't mean he could call up the editor of the *Times Book Review* and dictate favorable coverage, as some seemed to imagine. But sometimes he wished it were more true, and it had been, certainly, when he first arrived in New York, when it seemed that all the writers and editors and journalists could be found rubbing elbows at Elaine's, the long-shuttered Upper East Side watering hole, or at the raucous parties at George Plimpton's town house, which also housed the offices of *The Paris Review*. Russell had done it, certainly.

"We've got some great prospects; let's get on a conference call with Jonathan, since he's the one directing this campaign. Let me get this call and we'll talk next week," he said, switching over to the call from Jean-Claude Brouilly, the chef who was one of his wine club brethren.

"Russell, *ça va*, how are you?"

"I'm good. Looking forward to tonight."

"So you are definitely still going?"

"Definitely. And you?"

"Honestly there's no way. Business is falling apart, reservations are being canceled, my staff is freaking out, and it does not look good for me to be drinking expensive wine at the most expensive restaurant in New York. I cannot see myself on Page Six. I mean, I'm afraid I will see myself on Page Six. Not just that. I'm not really worried for myself, but, you know, it's a question of appearances."

"I get it."

"So will you tell the guys? Tell them I'm sorry. I'll be there next month with a great bottle of DRC after this shit is over."

"I'll tell them."

He was sort of flattered that Jean-Claude had chosen to call him as opposed to one of the others. They were both relative outliers in the group—probably the only two who didn't own a Bloomberg terminal.

At six-thirty, he sent his last email and headed out to dinner, grabbing his old Ghurka leather satchel with the two bottles of wine that Kip had sent over a few days ago, which he'd been careful to keep upright all day to let the sediment settle, donning his coat and scarf and bidding farewell to the few young staffers who were still toiling in the office, descending to the sidewalk and heading east on 14th Street.

It was a warm evening, which seemed to promise an early spring, the last light of the day blending with the illumination from the familiar storefronts, the bars and restaurants and nail salons welcoming, beckoning the pedestrians with signage and light, framed menus and reviews and promises of discounts and ladies' nights. Russell loved this, the transitional hour between day and night, work and play, office workers flooding the streets and pouring into the subways, being replaced with early diners and drinkers. Changing shifts, from labor to leisure. At times he imagined Manhattan as a hydraulic system in constant flow toward a never-achieved equilibrium.

He descended into the subway at Eighth Avenue, jamming himself into a packed A train, so closely pressed by fellow passengers that there was no need to hang on to the overhead railing, clutching the precious satchel to his chest, inhaling the strawberry cologne of the young woman in the puffy pink parka pressed up against him, shifting his weight and his position as the door opened at Penn Station and again at the Port Authority, passengers swimming to the doors and exiting, their replacements squeezing past them and establishing their space, pressing forward against the amoebic mass of remaining riders. He was pretty sure he was the only member of tonight's wine group that was arriving by subway, a fact which he would perhaps brag about if the atmosphere became too precious and rarefied.

He was greeted at the door of Per Se by a pigtailed young woman in a somber three-piece suit and told he was the first to arrive. He handed over his coat and scarf and followed her through the restaurant, into the churchlike hush of the main dining room, where two Asian couples were seated, to the private dining room. In his limited experience, this was a destination for wealthy foreigners more than it was a New York scene, but his wealthy wine friends loved this room, a separate cocoon with sweeping views of Central Park and the East Side skyline, the thicket of shiny new sliver towers piercing the sky along Central Park South, Columbus peering down from his pedestal in the center of the traffic circle. As the first arrival Russell was entitled to the prime seat across from the window.

"Ça va?" asked Michel, the compact balding sommelier, bedizened with a silver cup on a chain around his neck.

"Ça va," he said, handing the wine bag over. "How's tricks?"

Michel gestured to the nearly empty dining room. "Not good. Damn virus. People canceling reservations."

Russell had forgotten about the virus, but indeed, that would explain the nearly empty room.

Dale Cornell shuffled in, a shambling giant of a man in an ill-fitting navy blazer worn over a New York Yankees T-shirt and baggy jeans, followed by Tony Provenza, his sartorial foil, who wore a mint-green Isaia jacket over a pair of tight pink trousers. Taking in the outfit, Dale said, "Looks like Tony's just come back from Palm Beach."

"Palm Beach is a bore," Tony said, missing the joke. "You wouldn't catch me dead there. And if I *were* dead, none of the other stiffs would notice."

"You'd never get in," said Kip Taylor, from the doorway. "We stop Italians at the bridges."

"That's one of the reasons there's nothing decent to eat."

"We've got Daniel Boulud," Kip said as Bobby Cohen arrived with his wine tote, walking in with Rufus, the limping concert promoter.

"Everyplace in the world has Daniel Boulud," said Cohen, ostentatiously plunking a bottle of 1971 Richebourg on the table.

"I once brought a bottle of that backstage to a Van Halen

concert," Rufus said, indicating the Richebourg. "Eddie chugged the whole thing in like two minutes."

"Rock and roll, baby," said Tony.

"Have you checked your email?" Bobby said. "It seems that Perlmutter has bailed on us at the last minute. He has fled to his oceanfront manse in Southampton, blaming his wife for her abundance of caution."

"Jean-Claude also bailed," Russell said. "He's got an empire to crisis manage."

"What, all because of the stupid virus?" Tony asked.

"Stupid but deadly," Dale said. He barely suffered Provenza. Dale was old school. He'd been a partner at Bain Capital, known to the nonfinance world as Mitt Romney's private equity firm. Dale, who was actually the only other Democrat in the group, had retired a few years ago and now devoted himself quietly and strenuously to giving away much of his money through his family foundation. He did his best to disguise his wealth, and his accomplishments, if not necessarily his intelligence.

"You know this thing is biowarfare," Tony said. "Manufactured by the Iranians and the Chinese to be used against us, except unluckily for them it escaped the lab prematurely. Think about it. The second-highest rate of infection is in Iran, it's absolutely rampant there; Iranian scientists unwittingly carried it back from the lab in Wuhan."

"I wouldn't know how to interpret the news if not for Tony's analysis," Dale said.

"It's true. Mark my words. You'll be hearing about it."

"Rufus may need us to pay for dinner tonight," Dale said. "I don't expect people are going to be flocking to concerts anytime soon?"

"I've got a few bucks tucked away," said Rufus, who looked like a skinnier version of Benjamin Franklin, or maybe Leon Russell—long wispy white hair and granny specs. "I mean, how long can this thing last?"

"Bobby must be a happy boy today," Dale said. "Make a lot of money yesterday, Bobby?"

"I did pretty well," he said, smugly.

"Even a broken clock's right twice a day."

Russell didn't always follow these conversations, but he'd learned over the years that Bobby—who, after twenty years at a very successful hedge fund, had retired and now played the market for himself—was a bear, inevitably betting against the market, in keeping with a temperament that tilted very pessimistic. In Russell's experience, Bobby's pessimism was only exacerbated by the fact that in recent years the market had been on a nearly unbroken bull run. Short sellers were on the wrong side for years. The fact that the Dow Jones had lost two thousand yesterday and another fourteen hundred today was good news for a short seller.

"Bobby should definitely pay for dinner," Tony said.

"Absofuckinglutely."

"Did anyone tell Michel we're only six now?" Russell asked. "Chef Michael is bailing for obvious reasons."

"I can't believe Perlmutter wimped out on us."

Provenza said, "If I could hole up in Southampton with Perlmutter's wife you wouldn't see me here." Perlmutter's third and latest wife was a former Victoria's Secret model, much admired by the members of the wine club, subject of greedy speculation about which particular body part each of them would sacrifice to sleep with her.

"No Perlmutter, more La Tâche for us."

"Did he send his wine ahead?"

"We'll have to drink it."

"It would be rude not to."

The six-course dinner started with a dollop of smoked salmon in a tiny sugar cone and a bottle of 1964 Dom Perignon, decapitated by Tony with a short saber designed specifically for the purpose, which he carried in his Louis Vuitton briefcase. There was no drumroll, although Dale rolled his eyes. Tony held the bottle aloft in his left hand and lopped the top off with his right, the cork and the top of the neck shooting across the room and narrowly missing Dale's head.

Michel took the bottle and poured it around the table. "This is a perfect example of this wine," Tony said. "And I have twenty-eight more bottles of it in my cellar. I probably have more than they have at Dom Perignon."

"We're all very happy for you," Dale said.

To Russell it tasted like . . . old champagne. The effervescence had dissipated over the years; the few surviving bubbles ascending lazily from the bottom of the glass, escaping anticlimactically into the atmosphere after more than fifty years of captivity. He didn't really get the old champagne thing. Of course, he realized that most sensible citizens of the planet wouldn't get any of this—the old Burgundy, the black truffles, the wanton extravagance. It was excessive, extravagant, over the top. But he kind of loved being part of it.

The meal progressed to the oysters and caviar appetizer as Michel poured the next wine, a 1996 Montrachet, and the talk turned toward some Wall Street tycoon who apparently owned cases and cases of this rare beverage, and much else of the world's bounty besides: houses, yachts, Jeff Koons sculptures, an NBA basketball team. "He's got three G550s," Tony said, with an air of reverence, "one for him, one for his wife, and one for his girlfriend."

"The guy must really love Mercedes," Russell remarked.

His remark seemed to baffle the company, till Kip said, "You're thinking of the Mercedes G550 wagon. The G550 is the jet. Gulfstream 550."

Oh, Jesus, he thought, reminded not for the first time that he was operating way outside his usual field of reference. He didn't know anyone who had a single private jet, let alone three. He'd ridden in a chartered one with Kip a few times, on bonefishing expeditions to the Bahamas, although, when Washington interrogated him about it, he'd been unable to say just what kind of plane it was.

"I want to hear about Kip's love life," Bobby said.

"What's love got to do with it?" Tony said. "You mean his sex life."

Since he'd separated from his wife, Kip had been on a dating marathon, and the others, married men all, were mesmerized by his stories.

The boys moved on to the subject of the bloodbath in the financial markets. Russell was not an active investor; his 401(k) was managed by Fidelity. He was aware that he'd lost a lot on paper in the last two days, but over the years he'd done pretty well by not paying close attention to the fluctuations in the market. He wondered if this was different.

"How serious is this," he asked, throwing the question out to the table.

"Could be very serious," Kip said. "Think about the implications for global supply chains, the airlines, hospitality."

"We're in for a very rough ride," Bobby said. "I think the market's nowhere near its bottom."

"*He said with glee.*"

"Seriously," Tony said. "How much money did you make yesterday on your shorts?"

"A gentleman doesn't tell," Bobby said.

"And I repeat, how much?"

"I don't think anyone knows what's next," Dale said. He was the richest, probably the smartest guy in the room. And the least likely to pontificate. "Except a whole lot of uncertainty."

"Our president seems to think it's nothing," Russell said.

"That's good enough for me," Kip said, rolling his eyes.

"Say what you want," Bobby said, "he's been damn good on the economy."

"He inherited a good economy," Russell said, "which has continued to improve. Not nearly at the rate he claimed it would."

"Oh, please," Tony said. "Barack Obama was demonstrably the worst president in history."

Even as he knew he was being baited, the token liberal in the group, he could hardly believe his ears, hardly believe that someone could say this with a straight face, with Donald Trump in office.

"Are you fucking kidding me," Russell said. "Donald Trump wakes up every day and wins that title again before breakfast."

"Please, tell me one thing Obama accomplished, and don't say Obamacare because it's a disaster."

"You think it's a disaster that twenty million more Americans got insured?"

"The system's collapsing under its own bloated weight."

"It's wobbling a little because of Trump's assaults on its underpinnings. But after three whole years he hasn't proposed any alternative. Nor have any of the Republicans in Congress. Nada."

"Obama basically did fuck all," Tony said.

"He would have done a lot more without unrelenting obstructionism from the Republican Congress."

"It's called checks and balances."

"It's also called racism," Russell said.

As soon as he heard the words come out of his mouth Russell wished he could retract them. There were at least seven steps missing in the argument before that statement would have followed logically, and in the heat of the moment he'd jumped way ahead of himself. But Tony's statement that Obama was the worst president in history had inflamed him. Now he was a little embarrassed, not because he didn't believe that a great deal of the opposition to Obama was based in racism, as the last few years had so richly demonstrated, as that he hadn't really built up to his assertion, which seemed, without context, hyperbolic. And he was a little irritated, too, that no one had jumped in to help him out—the rest of the crew being politically pragmatic, if not liberal, and generally disdainful of the current occupant of the White House. At least, he thought they were.

In the end, by Dale's calculation, corks were pulled on some forty thousand dollars' worth of wine, a fact which amazed none of the drinkers at the table except for Russell. Dale added up the damage after every meal—donating the amount to one of his charities the next day. Russell's theory was that he announced the total in order to encourage others to follow his lead, but if anyone else in the group had been so inspired, they hadn't said so.

9

THE PHONE CHIMED once at ten-thirty and again at eleven. In between he was having colorful anime dreams. He heard it and wondered why he hadn't turned DO NOT DISTURB on last night before rolling over and drifting back to sleep, noticing Tali in bed beside him, slowly remembering the latter part of the night, Tali in full costume and makeup as Mikasa, her anime persona, squeaking in her Japanese accent, pleading not to be ravished. The third time the phone rang, he looked at the screen and decided to answer, seeing that it was his dad. Why did he always call in the morning, inevitably waking him up? Checking up on him.

"What's up?" he said, trying to sound as if he hadn't been sleeping moments before.

"Hey, it's Dad." As if he was unaware his name appeared on Jeremy's screen.

"Yes, I know, Dad."

"Just wanted to confirm we're on for lunch." Jeremy had to give him credit for not asking, as he inevitably used to, if he'd woken him up.

Lunch? "Um, yeah. Right. Is that today?"

"One o'clock, Balthazar? Does that still work?"

"Yeah, Balthazar. One o'clock." Buying time. He vaguely remembered agreeing to lunch when it had still been several days safely in the future, when he was in another time zone. It wasn't that he minded the idea of having lunch with his dad, but he wasn't really psyched about getting ready, mentally and physically, and making the trip into Manhattan on less than two hours' notice. He sometimes went weeks without going into Manhattan—it was sort of a point of pride. Manhattan was the land of offices and steak houses.

"Okay, great. See you in a couple of hours."

He nudged Tali, who was splayed on her back, half exposed, her faintly veined left breast pancaked across her ribs, makeup smeared on her face, her silver-pink hair fanned across the pillow. In the light of day she looked all too much like a real girl.

He was going to tell her to get up, but when he came back from the bathroom from taking a leak he still had a hard-on and she was still lying there so he climbed back into bed and curled up against her, stroking her right breast until she started to moan, turning and presenting her backside to him and he slipped it in, lazily sliding in and out, almost losing his hard-on in the middle until she squealed in a high-pitched voice, "You too big for Mikasa," and then getting it back as he built toward his climax and came in a series of spasms.

"That was nice," she said, in her normal voice.

"It was. I can reminisce about it while I'm having lunch with my dad."

"You're having lunch with him today? I thought we were going to spend the day together. I haven't seen you in weeks."

"I forgot. He caught me at a distracted moment a couple days ago."

"Maybe you could bring me with you."

"I haven't seen him in ages. I think he really needs to do the father-son thing."

"Am I ever going to meet your parents?"

It wasn't something that Jeremy had remotely considered. He didn't think of them as being at that stage of whatever this was. They'd been seeing each other, on and off, for a few months. Jeremy was a little ashamed of this side of his life. He was pretty sure that his parents wouldn't get her—a bisexual whose life revolved around cosplay, who made a living, such as it was, selling photos of herself as a mermaid and a fairy and a Japanese anime character to freaks she met online. Jeremy, too, had met her online, on Bumble, as her anime character Mikasa. Jeremy had a thing for Japanese anime—he'd grown up with that whole imaginary universe of Pokémon and Dragon Ball Z and Mario— and for the anime girls with their huge saucer eyes and tiny noses and mouths, and while her representation could hardly reproduce, in their extreme stylization, those features, he'd been willing to suspend disbelief that first night she came over. In fact, he'd been really turned on. More than he cared to admit. She had several online profiles catering to niche tastes, and he had only found out about the other stuff after he'd slept with her as Mikasa, her anime incarnation. The fairy thing, the pointed ears, the flowers in her hair, the idea of a twee magical woodland sprite, didn't really do anything for him. Let alone the mermaid tail. Even in her Tali persona he couldn't imagine introducing her to his parents. It was just, what would be the point? It would be like introducing people who had no common language. And by the way, Mom, Dad, call her *them* and *they*. Nope. He didn't think so. Even he had a hard time with that one.

"Why would you want to meet my parents?"

He instantly regretted the question, worried that he might provoke some intimate declaration, but she only said, "I don't know. I'm just curious."

He felt a sudden unexpected instinct to protect his parents, to shelter them from certain aspects of contemporary reality and of his own life. They were really kind of clueless in a somewhat-endearing way.

"Who's that?" she asked, pointing to a poster across from the bed as he pulled on his jeans.

"Che Guevara." He wondered if he needed to annotate. But whether she knew, or was now too intimidated to ask, she merely nodded.

She seemed reluctant to leave, whereas he was eager to get her out the door. He really didn't want her staying alone in the apartment; he couldn't say why exactly, but he didn't want her going through his stuff, trying to learn about him. Their relationship, such as it was, was based on role play and artifice, and it seemed awkward to have her here in the daylight, among his possessions, interpreting his books and posters and knickknacks, his Biggie Smalls poster, with its printed quotation: STAY FAR FROM TIMID / ONLY MAKE MOVES / WHEN YOUR HEART'S IN IT / AND LIVE THE PHRASE / SKY'S THE LIMIT, which suddenly seemed like the artifact of a younger self, a younger, more naïve Jeremy Calloway, which in fact it was. Did she even know who Biggie was? And his bookshelf; she would probably get his *Lord of the Rings* trilogy, but what would she make of the other titles, Jon Lee Anderson's fat biography of Che, Orwell's *Homage to Catalonia* and *Down and Out in Paris and London*, Jack London's *The People of the Abyss*, Frantz Fanon's *The Wretched of the Earth*, Kierkegaard's *Fear and Trembling*.

He waited while she showered and dressed. In street clothes, without makeup, she was, it had to be said, a fairly ordinary-looking girl, except for her silver-and-pink hair, which hardly stood out on the streets of East Williamsburg. He thought about stopping at Champs Diner, DEATH BEFORE DECAF, for a coffee, but he was already running late. They walked in silence to the subway.

"There's a thing tonight at Bembe," she said. "I'm going to be there after ten."

"Text me," he said. He kissed her at the subway entrance.

He took the L to Union Square and the 6 down to Prince Street.

There was no line outside Balthazar, which was unusual in his experience. He used to come here with his parents as a kid. Inside, it was as quiet as he'd ever seen it. A very hot Asian hostess who reminded him a little of Akame from *Akame ga Kill!* took him to his dad, who was waiting in one of the booths. Jeremy could just tell how pleased his dad was to score a booth. It was one of those things that mattered to him, that he was a guy who could get a booth at Balthazar.

"Hey, Dad, sorry I'm late."

His dad extended his hand. "Good to see you, son." His hair had gotten grayer, more salt than pepper now, though he still had plenty of it, and wore it long in the style that had been prevalent when he was still in school, the rock-and-roll era, Beatles and Stones, the style he'd worn it all of Jeremy's life. Was that his era? His dad sometimes liked to say he was an old hippie, though he was actually about half a generation too young for Woodstock and Kent State and all that. He suddenly wondered whether his dad had ever done acid, or mushrooms.

"How's Mom?"

"She's good. Doing God's work. Feeding the hungry. How goes the campaign?"

"I don't think I have to tell you it's pretty much over. Michigan was a death blow, in my opinion."

"So it would seem. Are you going to quit?"

"I'll probably soldier on for a while. But it's hard not to be really discouraged. It really pisses me off to hear the libs say, Yeah, Bernie tried twice and he failed twice. And it pisses me off to hear them say that Biden has a better shot at beating Trump. That's what you all said about Hillary, and look where that got us. Because they've bought into that propaganda. The left has little to no grassroots, we have almost no unions left, we have jack shit, we've been dormant for decades, and Bernie comes out of nowhere, and even with the establishment Dems and corporate media attacking him left and right, he did as well as he did. He made these bastards sweat and they even had to drop candidates to support Biden and keep Warren in the race to defeat him. Bernie has shown that the left has the potential to be very strong. We might have thought that it would have taken decades to grow this much. Eugene Debs would be proud. Now we just need to grow from the bottom up and keep going."

"Will you vote for Biden?"

"I may, I don't know, but a lot of Bernie supporters won't. There's a feeling of betrayal. The DNC is the enemy. They use their resources to keep the party dead in the center. They won't commit to Medicare for All or the Green New Deal. There was less evidence of actual betrayal this time around than with Hillary, but it's still biased. Hillary and Biden had plants in the Bernie campaign. The progressives are taken for granted and they've been let down too many times. And meantime my generation is working service jobs and paying down massive college debt. The feeling is one of harsh resentment, honestly."

"I understand that. But I think we have to unite to defeat Trump."

"I have friends who think Biden's just as bad."

"That's ridiculous."

"I'm just telling you what I hear. It's a widespread sentiment among young people. They don't feel like they have a stake in the system."

A busboy came over to pour water—a compact Central American with mestizo features, most likely Guatemalan. Lot of Guatemalans in the city. The first wave fleeing the civil war that lasted from the sixties into the nineties, the later ones fleeing the gangs and the poverty. Thousands at the border even now. He wondered if his father noticed busboys.

"Let's order and then we can catch up," Russell said.

The big laminated menu, which probably hadn't really changed since Jeremy was a little kid. Which had very few vegan options. The Bibb salad and the breadbasket were his inevitable meal here. After all these years his dad still acted surprised and then apologetic about the limited menu options for someone like him.

When the waitress came over, an actual French waitress, cute, with the accent, Jeremy could see his father perking up, rising a little in his seat; he ordered his usual, the steak frites. How he digested that in the middle of the day Jeremy hadn't a clue.

"I'll have the salad," Jeremy said.

"That's all?" Russell said, and then, "Oh, right, I guess there aren't so many options for you."

"It's fine, Dad. It's just food. You worry too much about it."

"It's not that I worry about it so much. I just find it one of the great and abiding pleasures of life."

"Let's not have the food discussion." For Jeremy, food was fuel. A necessity for the maintenance of brain and body. Like sleep. It was something a lot of the world's population didn't have enough of. It wasn't something to write poems and essays about.

"Okay."

Jeremy could certainly beat the drum for the ethics of a vegan diet, but he'd given up on his dad. It wasn't worth getting into it again. Not today, anyway. He was off the clock. He didn't want to get into an argument with his dad.

"Speaking of food, I hope you called or texted your sister yesterday."

"Why, did she hurt herself?"

"She opened a restaurant, for Christ's sake. This was a very big deal for her."

"Oh, right, sorry. I sent her a text." Not really, but he would. "I had my plate full in Michigan."

"It would behoove you to call her, or maybe send flowers."

"Flowers? Really?"

"Yes, what's wrong with flowers."

"It seems so, I don't know—"

"Bourgeois?"

"I don't think I've ever sent flowers."

"Well, then, it's about time. I thought we raised you to have manners."

"I'm just saying flowers and thank-you notes and hostess gifts don't go very far toward addressing the basic problems of society."

"What do you imagine does?"

"Good men acting in a virtuous fashion. I'd hoped it would start with Bernie."

"And now?"

"I'm not sure you want to hear this."

"Hear what?"

He wasn't sure how to say it, and the fact that his father wouldn't understand made it even harder to express.

"I've been reading Thomas Merton. I like his ideas about spirituality and interfaith understanding."

"Merton was a great writer, it's true."

"I thought you'd say that. But I'm not talking about his style. I'm talking about his ideas."

"Are you getting religious on me?"

"I'm just exploring issues of spirituality. Merton arrived at a place of racial tolerance, nonviolence and social equality through his faith."

"While historically faith has led to warfare and intolerance. The history of the Catholic Church should make us allergic to blind faith."

"I understand you had your struggles with the institution. But I hope you don't close your mind entirely to the spiritual side of life."

"Maybe you can carry that particular torch for me."

Jeremy almost said, I'll pray for you, but he realized that would entirely freak his father out. And the kind of people who said that out loud tended to be self-righteous. Jeremy knew he didn't have all the answers, but he felt that he was asking the right questions. Increasingly, he was drawing away from the notion that social ills could be remedied politically. He felt he was undergoing a transformation, though he was reluctant to put it into words.

10

Thursday night on the way home from work Corrine had bought a packet of light blue surgical masks at Walgreens. She'd been too self-conscious to wear one on the way home, but this morning, after reading the news and listening to NPR's *Morning Edition*, she donned one on the subway, riding to work, one of several people in the car to be so equipped, including a Black nurse in blue scrubs, who nodded to her in kinship, which reinforced her sense of doing the right thing even if it failed to ease her self-consciousness. She had tried to talk Russell into wearing one to no avail.

"It's really just cosmetic, the science doesn't indicate they offer any protection," he said. Which seemed to her to fly in the face of common sense, though that was the position of the CDC. Hell, the Japanese were always wearing them during cold and flu season. How could it not help? Airborne virus—hello?

She got a call from Casey Reynes as she was walking out the door. She realized she hadn't returned Casey's last call and took this one out of a sense of guilt, though she was already running late.

"Hey, Case, how are you?"

"I'm fine. Just finished Pilates—and who should I get a call from but Lisa."

"Oh, God. I've been dodging her calls."

"Which is why she called me. She's worried that you're mad at her."

"Of course I'm mad at her. She bugged me to come to Storey's opening and then she bugged me to add her kid and his girlfriend and then she never showed up. Why wouldn't I be mad at her? But I'm not going to lose any sleep over it."

"She's obsessing about it."

"Remind me why you introduced her into my life?"

"She was at Miss Porter's with us."

"I still don't remember."

"So, are you freaking out about the virus?"

"I'm not *not* freaking out."

"Crazy, right? I can't believe I sold the house in Southampton last year. Everybody's going out there to get away from the city."

"Really?"

"It's a mass migration."

"Well, we're stuck here. Our rental doesn't start till July. Listen, I'm about to descend into the subway."

"I can't believe you still ride the subway."

"I'm beginning to wonder why myself."

"I mean talk about a mobile petri dish of germs. Before you descend, I just want to remind you that you've promised me we'd do a dinner with Kip Taylor."

"Casey, he's barely separated from Katrina. He moved out in January."

"Exactly. I want to be first in line."

From what Corrine had heard that line was very long and plenty of supplicants had already been granted admission to Kip's bachelor bedroom in the Carlyle, where all the rich divorcing men landed when they left their marital apartments.

"Well, let's just wait till this thing blows over."

"Don't forget."

Restaurants were closing voluntarily; on Thursday afternoon Danny Meyer, who was hugely influential in the restaurant world, had announced the closure of all the restaurants in his hospitality group, and then there were back-to-back announcements from the governor and the mayor that limited bars and restaurants to 50 percent capacity, which might be just the beginning. A mass restaurant closure was going to have a major impact on their food contributions. Meantime Casey was texting: *Double date. Kip Taylor et moi et vous.* Corrine loved Casey, but in her experience, wealthy newly divorced New York men did not date in their own age bracket. How could Casey, the worldliest and most sophisticated of Corrine's friends, not know that? It was weird how Casey, who used to try to school Corrine on the ways of the world, had seemingly lost her savviness in the wake of her divorce. Or maybe it was just desperation.

At the ten o'clock meeting she decided to pull the trigger in advance of the emergency. "I think we're going to start buying food," she said. Normally all food was rescued from restaurants and supermarkets, but there was an emergency provision in their charter. "We have a budget surplus and we can go directly to donors, but if restaurants and other businesses close, we're going to see twice as many food-insecure people."

She was going to say, All hands on deck, but she started coughing.

She'd thought it was hot in the subway, but it was also hot in her office, and she suddenly realized she was congested. She'd called a staff meeting for noon to follow up on the new circumstances, but by eleven o'clock it was clear she was running a fever and coughing. Oh hell, no, she thought. She sat at her desk, willing her symptoms to disappear.

At eleven-fifteen she called her assistant director, Janie, on the intercom.

"I'm going to have to ask you to lead the meeting. I'm not feeling well." Trying to keep the panic out of her voice.

"Oh, really?" Janie said, with a trace of concern. And then, in an entirely different tone. "Oh. *Really?*"

"I'm sure it's just a cold, but I certainly don't want to take any chances at this point in time. I'll call in after I get home." Her voice sounded high-pitched and strained.

"Okay."

"Don't tell anyone yet."

Corrine's office door opened into a central office area that contained four office cubicles, each enclosed on three sides with person-high partitions. Opening her door and looking out, she saw Tawana, their PR person, Lululemoned from head to toe, returning to her cubicle from the ladies' room; once she settled in, none of her coworkers were visible. Corrine decided to make a break for it, rather than causing a panic. She would inform everyone about her circumstances once she was home. She donned her mask, threw some folders into her shoulder bag and slipped out the door. Outside the supply room she encountered an intern whose name escaped her and stepped back abruptly and pressed her back against the wall, startling the poor girl, who nodded grimly and scooted past.

And now the elevator presented a new dilemma. Even if it was empty she might germify the car; she decided to take the stairs down to the street, where she next pondered how she might get home, cognizant that she might be infectious, that she probably *was* infectious and that she would endanger many in the subway, and one person in particular if she took a cab. She remembered there was a Citi Bike station on Third Avenue and decided that was her best course of action.

When she finally arrived at her doorstep in the Village she could hardly remember how she got there. She was hot and sweaty and short of breath and she did her best to veer around Angelo the doorman. Once upstairs she collapsed on the couch in the living room. She called Russell, getting his assistant.

"He's in a sales meeting. Can he call you back?"

"Yes. Tell him it's kind of important."

She must have heard something in Corrine's voice: "Do you want me to pull him out of the meeting?"

She was about to say no, she didn't want to interrupt, and she couldn't imagine that informing him now rather than later would make any substantial difference. But she was scared, and feeling very weak and vulnerable, and she wanted to confide in Russell, and to hear his voice.

"Maybe, yes, if you could."

She wasn't sure if she waited a long time or not at all before he came on the line.

"Hey, what's up?" Hearing his voice, she felt suddenly on the verge of tears.

"I'm sick." Her voice breaking.

"Sick? Hell. You don't sound good. What are your symptoms?"

"Cough. Congestion. Fever."

"Have you called Harper's office?"

"No. I called you first."

"Do you want me to call him?" She was touched, pleasantly surprised, that he would offer. And in fact, it seemed like more than she could manage.

"Would you?"

"Sure. Have you taken your temperature?"

"No, not yet. Do we even have a thermometer?"

"God, I don't know. Forget it, I'll just say you have a fever."

"Shortness of breath," she gasped. "Also."

"Okay, cough, fever, shortness of breath. Stand by. Are you going to be okay for the next few minutes?"

"I'm suddenly realizing I'm probably infecting the whole apartment."

"Don't worry about that. I'll call you right back."

"Okay."

She wanted to thank him, but he'd hung up before she could. Tears filled her eyes. She was ridiculously grateful to Russell. Normally she considered herself very self-sufficient, but right now she just wanted to be taken care of. She wanted to find out whether she had the virus and she wanted to be told, if she did, that she would get better. People in China had died of it, hundreds of them, if not thousands. Respiratory failure. Her breathing felt increasingly labored, her oxygen intake barely sufficient. She looked around the room they'd created, or re-created, a kind of half simulacrum of their last three adult residences, bathed in the warm midday light, with furniture and artifacts stretching back to other eras of their life, this Shabby Chic sofa, the well-worn repro Mies van der Rohe Barcelona chairs from their TriBeCa loft, the authentic Wiener Werkstätte side table they'd found at a flea market in Pennsylvania thirty years ago. The collage of framed photographs and paintings and posters on the unwindowed west wall; the Berenice Abbott portrait of James Joyce; the moody, almost abstract Russell Chatham landscape they'd acquired directly from the artist on a trip to Montana; the Agnes Martin etching they'd bought after Russell's first, and only, number one *New York Times* bestseller, she couldn't remember the book now. Would she have remembered yesterday? she wondered. Her brain felt mushy, as if the fever was slowly melting it. She remembered buying the Wiener Werkstätte table on a weekend trip to Pennsylvania, the old lady who'd sold it to them with her fisherman's hat and her green rubber Wellingtons, saying that she thought her father had acquired it somewhere in Europe. They'd felt so smart, finding that treasure in rural Pennsylvania. But she couldn't remember the name of that book and she could only vaguely remember Storey's opening night. She recalled entering the restaurant, but not the later part of the night. Had she drunk too much or was her memory failing her? Had she drunk at all? A glass of white wine. Alex the somm had given a little speech about the white wine. Seventy-five dollars—that was what they'd paid for the side table, trying to conceal their excitement, Russell having recognized the Wiener Werkstätte stamp on the underside. She could remember the thrill of discovery. She could even remember the smell of manure and hay from the adjacent petting zoo. But not leaving the restaurant two nights ago.

The side table, Pottery Barn, held a collection of framed family photos, most of which looked familiar to her. Russell and the kids aged approximately six on the beach in Sagaponack. Jeremy holding Ferdie, their late lamented ferret, in the TriBeCa loft.

Corrine's late mother, circa 1990, holding a cigarette in front of her face, staring into the lens with a slightly irritated do-I-really-have-to-pose expression. Russell and Corrine and Jeff Pierce in graduation cap and gown in Providence in 1980. Russell and Corrine in formal attire at one of the Nourish New York galas, at least a decade ago, Russell's hair still uniformly dark. She'd always loved his dark mane, though she'd come to like the graying version of recent years. She had a sudden premonition of leaving him, of being taken away, and felt bereft. She wasn't ready to leave this world and the people she loved. Surrounded by these artifacts of their marriage, waiting for her husband to call her back and tell her what to do, she found herself profoundly embedded in the physical world, even as she seemed to be floating away from it.

Her phone buzzed, the caller ID showing Dr. Harper's office.

"Hello, Corrine, it's Dr. Harper. How are you feeling?"

"Not great. I have a fever. And a cough." She assumed he was going to criticize her for being so long absent from his offices; the fact is she had a bit of a phobia about doctors. But not today.

"How's your breathing?"

"Labored, I would say." Speaking seemed to be taxing her ability to breathe.

"Do you have a thermometer there?"

"I'm not sure." Illness was not something they thought much about, or were well prepared for. The kids, when they were living at home, had the usual children's maladies. They'd always taken their own good health for granted.

"Russell can get you one. I've told him to buy a pulse oximeter to check your oxygen intake. For the moment I want you to isolate yourself. Is there anyone else in the apartment?"

"No, just the two of us."

"You're going to need to keep your distance from your husband. Sleep in separate rooms of course."

"Is there a test I can take?"

"Unfortunately, we don't have access to the tests at the

moment. So we're just going to assume you're infected and act accordingly. Just rest and make yourself as comfortable as possible."

Someone was calling her name.

It was Russell. Russell was calling her name. He was standing across the room, but he looked somehow much farther away, looking at her as if across a great gulf from another realm, from the safety of another shore. What was that Merwin poem about another shore? The light from the south-facing windows had turned a milky blue-gray, casting the room into shadow.

"How are you feeling?"

"Not good. What time is it? I think I fell asleep."

"It's after five. I got a thermometer and a pulse oximeter."

She wished he could take her in his arms and hold her. "What are we going to do?"

"I think we need to get you settled in bed. Why don't you take our room? I'll sleep in the guest room."

She thought it was a sweet gesture, his giving up the master bedroom, till she realized that it might also be an act of caution on his part. But it could be both, couldn't it?

Quarantine. She would be quarantined. It was a word that seemed to stain those to whom it was applied. Unhealthy, unclean, tainted. Like purdah. A woman unclean, banished from the family space. She'd read about a Nepalese woman who'd frozen to death recently after being banished to an unheated outbuilding during her period.

"Do you think you can make it to the bedroom under your own steam," he asked. "I'm sorry, but the doctor said I need to keep my distance. I won't be much use to you if I get sick, too. Assuming I don't already have it. And assuming, of course, that you do."

"You don't have it," she said, with sudden conviction. She believed in his luck; bad things seldom happened to Russell, his native optimism seeming to serve as a kind of prophylactic, confirmed by circumstance. She suspected at that moment that her own belief in the threat of the virus, and her own vulnerability, had made her susceptible—as if she'd invited the vampire to cross the threshold. Russell never noticed the vampire outside the window. He didn't believe in vampires, and so was immune to their importunements.

"Okay, I'm going to go to the bedroom. I'm afraid I've contaminated the living room. Call me Corona Corrine." She stood up, feeling woozy, wobbling to attain verticality.

"Maybe it's just the flu," Russell said, keeping his distance.

"Who would have imagined a time when we'd hope for flu, when that would be a happy diagnosis."

He watched her as she struggled down the hall.

"Oh, hell, I forgot to give you the thermometer and the other thing. I'll leave them outside the door."

Her temperature, when she finally hobbled over to the bedroom door and retrieved the bag from the floor of the hallway where Russell had left it, and hacked away with nail scissors the plastic in which the thermometer was encased, was 102.5. Her oxygen saturation level, measured by the device she clamped onto her index figure, was 95 percent, which was, apparently, borderline. She didn't need a number to tell her she was struggling for breath; she was on the verge of panic, imagining the moment when she could not get enough air in her lungs, the drowning feeling.

"Ninety-five and up is good," Russell said. "Harper said to call an ambulance if it goes below ninety-two."

She didn't want to go to the hospital. She'd only been once, to deliver her children.

11

As soon as Storey heard her mom was sick, her first instinct had been to rush to the Village to take care of her, but both her mom and her dad told her she had to stay away. What made it worse was that she was accustomed to chatting at length, almost daily, with her mother, who could now manage only a few minutes of hoarse speech before signing off. Storey felt frightened and disoriented. Her mom was her confidant, her best friend. She couldn't even imagine. . . . She wouldn't imagine.

She realized she had to close the restaurant. Corrine had been in the cramped kitchen, cheek by jowl with the kitchen staff. She could only hope none of them were infected; she certainly couldn't risk spreading the virus to her customers. She called each of her employees to explain the situation and to apologize, saying that she expected to be closed for a week and that they would be paid until they reopened. But she'd gladly say goodbye to the restaurant and walk away forever in exchange for her mom getting better. As it turned out, her decision was mooted a couple of days later by the governor's closure of all restaurants.

"This could be a blessing," Mingus said, standing with her in the restaurant kitchen as she tried to batten down the hatches, clean and straighten out for what she hoped would be a short hiatus from service. "Pause to refresh. You were so fucking crazed working up to your opening. And your first couple days were, let's face it, chaotic. You can use the time to regroup and reflect, fine-tune the menu. Plus we can spend a little time together this week. You could cook for your boyfriend, even. And I can really buckle down to my book. This could be good for both of us."

Storey wasn't clear how a lockdown of the city would add to her boyfriend's balance of free time, since he was, essentially, unemployed.

"How are your parents," she asked. Actually, she was surprised he hadn't led the conversation with news of their health.

"My mom seems fine. Dad's not doing so well. Looks like he may have the virus."

"Aren't you worried?" She couldn't understand if he was just a little in denial or whether he was being insensitive. Nor could she understand if this was a guy thing, or specific to Mingus. Maybe the former; her own brother didn't seem nearly as alarmed about their mother's illness as she was.

"Yeah, of course," Mingus said. "But Dad's tough. He's not going anywhere. He'll get through this."

"I wish I felt the same confidence about my mom."

"She's going to be fine," he said, on the basis of exactly no evidence or medical wisdom. But she wanted to believe him. She wanted to share his optimism. That was one of the things she liked—his upbeat spirit, which reminded her of her father, and which counteracted her own creeping sense of doom. And she liked the idea of the two of them, sequestered together, waiting out the crisis. What would it be—two weeks, a month? They really hadn't had much time together lately. They would shelter in place, together, waiting for the world outside to become safe again. She'd feel safer with him than without. She would cook and he would read from the book he was writing and they would have sex in the morning and again before bed. In this light, the unfolding global catastrophe took on the color of a domestic adventure. Lazy mornings, slow-braised meats, slow kisses. Reading, watching movies. She couldn't remember the last book she'd read. Maybe they would shelter in his place in the Village, since he didn't have a roommate, and it was close to her parents. On the other hand, his place was a studio, plus it would feel a little weird to cross the river back to Manhattan. She shared her apartment in East Williamsburg with Kiki Betz, whom she'd met when they were both working in the kitchen at Lilia. Kiki was a smart, butch Lesbian, with a great pot dealer and great taste in music, who often stayed at her girlfriend's apartment in Bushwick, giving Storey some space. The two bedrooms were right next to each other, off the shared kitchen/living room, and the walls were thin. All told the apartment was a little more than six hundred square feet, and with the two of them out of work Storey wondered how full-time proximity would play out. Kiki must have wondered the same thing; the day after the restaurants closed, she sat down on the couch beside Storey, turning down the Sonos volume on Arlo Parks's "Super Sad Generation," and announced she was moving in with her girlfriend in Bushwick.

"I mean, I've paid up this month, obviously. We don't know how long this is going to last, obviously, but I was thinking this might be the time to make the move. I don't want to leave you in the lurch and all, but as long as the restaurant's closed, it's going to be tough for me to pay my half of the rent, obviously." Unspoken—though obvious—was the fact that Storey had parents who could help, whereas Kiki's evangelical parents in Alabama had disowned her when she'd come out to them two years ago.

We're a super sad generation / killing time and losing our paychecks. The first five times she heard that line she'd thought it was "losing our patience." Now the actual line seemed strangely timely.

"Don't worry," Storey said. "I'll be okay. But I'll miss you."

They hugged.

"Oh shit," Storey said, "we're probably not supposed to do that."

"Fuck that. Going to take more than a fucking virus to keep me from hugging a sister."

"I was actually thinking of taking the next step with Mingus, maybe moving in together. On a trial basis. I mean, I know he may not be your favorite person, but—"

"Well, that makes me feel a lot less guilty. Just tell him if he does anything to hurt you I'll come back and cut off his balls while he's sleeping."

Storey went out to stock up on groceries while Kiki packed. Champs Diner, the vegan mecca directly across the street, normally buzzing at this hour with diners eager for seitan Philly cheesesteak and ersatz Nashville hot wings, was eerily deserted. Underneath the DEATH BEFORE DECAF neon sign was a handwritten note taped to the glass: *See Ya on the Other Side.* She passed the Tradesman bar, also closed, decorated with antique tools, real wood paneling and imbued with a faux-proletarian vibe. She'd taken a bit of inspiration from that décor for her restaurant. The organic deli, the organic grocery and the organic bodega, around the corner, were all open, as was Dun-Well, the vegan doughnut shop. Mingus would definitely dig that, assuming they were going to use her place as their base. Storey had landed in vegan hippie heaven when she agreed to take the empty room in Kiki's apartment on Meserole Street a couple years ago. It might have been nice to have a butcher nearby, she had to walk to Bushwick to get a lamb chop, but on the plus side she was only a block from the L train, and all in all she liked the vibe, which had still seemed funky and ungentrified as recently as a year ago, when a luxury rental tower had gone up around the corner, complete with a Whole Foods at street level. On the Fourth of July the neighbors blasted fireworks from the roof of her building, pausing when the cops cruised in, and resuming the barrage when they left. The neighbor upstairs was a Chinese herbal healer whom Storey occasionally consulted. Downstairs was Mrs. Caramella, the old Italian lady whose family had been in the neighborhood for decades. She cooked a big pot of sauce every Sunday, which she called gravy, the fragrance of which wafted up the stairwell all day. And Jeremy lived next door. Storey had found the place for him, finally convincing him to move out of their parents' town house last year, when they decided to sell it.

SEE YOU ON THE OTHER SIDE

• • •

When Mingus talked about moving in together, did he mean his place or hers? He had a studio in the Village, on 10th between Fifth and Sixth, which his parents had bought for him. Her place was certainly more shareable, especially now that Kiki was gone, but he was, unlike most of his age cohort, a bit of a Manhattan snob, which she viewed as a deliberately contrarian stance on his part. His political views were surprisingly conservative, given his age and his race, borrowed in part from his dad's friend Avery Finch, though she believed that his supposed libertarianism was performative—a stance that he adopted at least partly for its shock value. When you had liberal intellectual parents, one of whom was Black, moving to the right was an easy way to distinguish your own views.

It felt weird inside the deli, kind of the opposite of a neighborly vibe, with everyone loading up their baskets and eyeing one another warily. A woman in dreadlocks and a dashiki glared at her as she passed in the narrow aisle. Storey grabbed some dried pasta, some Rao's sauce, milk and granola, bananas and paper towels. She felt like she should get more—her fellow shoppers seemed to be grabbing everything in sight. She picked up a bag of flour and a pound of butter, the last one in the dairy case.

When Storey got home, Kiki was blasting Amy Winehouse's "Tears Dry on Their Own," half dancing and half packing, her stuff spread out on the living room floor. Pots and pans, kettlebells, books. Between them they had a massive collection of cookware, most of it hanging from a steel bar above the kitchen area. Copper, cast iron, stainless, aluminum and alloy. Much of it scavenged from the kitchens where they'd worked. They hadn't actually cooked very often here, since neither one of them ate breakfast and they were generally gone from noon to after midnight. But somehow it was reassuring, having all that cooking equipment on hand. And it might come in very handy now.

"Goodbye for now," Kiki said, lifting a duffel bag and a suitcase. "I'll be back for the rest tomorrow. And to say goodbye, obviously."

"I'll be here, I imagine."

"I'll text."

"I'm going to keep my composure," Storey said, holding the door.

"God please." They kissed cheeks.

"There we go again," Storey said.

"Please, I'm never going to be okay with no kissing," Kiki said as she disappeared down the stairs.

She wasn't used to spending time alone in the apartment; it felt emphatically empty and still after Kiki left. She turned on the TV for company, listening to the local news and then the national news, all about the virus, the rising numbers, the lockdown. When the Orange Man came on, she turned the channel. She couldn't bear to look at him or listen to him. It was like nails on a chalkboard. When the news was over, she muted the TV and decided it was time to read Gabrielle Hamilton's memoir, which she embarrassingly had never cracked, despite the undeniable appeal and relevance of the widely acclaimed book by the most influential female chef in New York. And she was absolutely eating it up until she fell asleep on the couch sometime after ten, only to be awakened two hours later by Mingus, who had let himself in. He knelt down beside the couch and smothered her, smelling like cigarettes and alcohol.

"Whassup baby?"

"Hi, love. Are you okay?"

He stayed put, pressing his face into hers. She could feel his jaw twitching.

"Have you been doing coke?"

He nodded into her face.

"Are you crying?" She felt the tears on her cheek. "What's the matter, baby?"

"I'm worried," he said. He gasped, as if trying to gulp air. "Worried about my dad."

12

SIRENS AND THE 7:00 p.m. din, the defiant, celebratory clamor, shouting, banging, clanging of pots and pans, which sometimes seemed like the sound of her own body hurting and aching, her own internal plumbing ringing like the pipes in the apartment in winter. And her own raspy breathing, rising and falling. Every breath an abrasion, as if the air were filled with grit. All of this, when her lungs were constricting, closing up. Like cramps in the chest. Fever and delirium. She wasn't ready to die yet, but many had. She wasn't one of the lucky ones, for whom it was like a mild flu. *Like a cold*, their science denier in chief insisted. *A lot of people will have this and it is very mild.* The man lodged himself in your brain like a virus, his crude utterances like earworms. Not capable of speaking a grammatical sentence, the vocabulary of an eight-year-old, but he had a gift for invective. For caricature. *Little Marco. Lyin' Ted. Sleepy Joe.* She still couldn't believe it, just as she hadn't been able to believe it back then, back in '16, watching the returns with a sinking heart. Back in 2000 they said they'd move to France if Bush won, she and Russell, but sixteen years later they hadn't really considered the possibility that Trump would win, it seemed too far-fetched, and they hadn't had time to emotionally prepare. Donald Jive Trump, as Washington had dubbed him. The tabloid clown, the king of kitsch, the cartoon version of a tycoon, who had been a running joke for their entire New York life. Richie Rich . . . A symbol of garish vulgarity, of shameless self-promotion. Gilt bathroom fixtures, orange hair and skin. After the election it was like a bomb had gone off in Manhattan, like the aftermath of September 11, citizens staggering in the streets like zombies, *The Walking Dead*, Jeremy's favorite show at that moment, cold-calling their shrinks, doubling down on their meds, legal and otherwise. Drinking themselves senseless. As they were doing now, apparently, in a different crisis. Different, and yet both moments felt epochal. This a disaster in slow motion. Their friends fleeing the city for the Hamptons, the Upper East Side a ghost town, the white and wealthy mostly gone to less crowded, less infectious environs.

Russell and Corrine were hunkered down in the Village, not having the luxury of a second home in the country, the sirens wailing at all hours, like September 11 and the days after, the sirens heading downtown into the wreckage, ash-covered figures staggering uptown, away from the collapsed towers, while paper rained down from the sky like confetti on the grim parade. They'd also worn masks in those days, the refugees from the towers and the denizens of TriBeCa venturing out into the ash storm—improvised face coverings. A sudden memory of a man and his dog that day, a piebald Boston terrier with its white mask of a face and its owner with a red kerchief fastened behind his head, covering his nose and mouth. And a gray man, trudging uptown, coated head to foot, looking like an ambulatory statue commemorating the recent defeat, this rout of Western civilization, a yellow respirator dangling from his neck, who would later become her lover. Luke.

Now, Russell was trying to take care of her, sending texts and leaving food outside the door. But she had even less interest in food than usual, having lost her sense of smell, which was tantamount to losing her ability to taste. Food was just texture now. She'd told Dr. Harper about it. He'd said the condition was called anosmia and that there was literature on postviral anosmia, people losing their sense of smell after a cold or flu, though it was very rare. What little interest she'd had in food plummeted to none. At least she would come out of this, assuming she came out of it, thinner.

You've got to eat something, Russell texted, after he'd picked up another tray of uneaten food from outside her door. He'd never understood the joys of abnegation, never felt the righteousness of fasting, the spiritual nourishment of renunciation that sustained the holy man on the mountain or in the cave. Corrine knew the joy of skipping a meal, refusing a dessert. Though she would gladly forgo this particular diet if she could only feel better again.

How Russell hadn't gotten the virus she didn't understand; except that she did. He was always lucky. Lucky and heedless. It never occurred to him that he would get the virus and this was his prophylaxis. But she wouldn't wish it on him, wouldn't wish it on anyone, really. She couldn't get comfortable in bed. No matter which way she turned she felt sore and at odds with her body. Right side, left side, back. She could feel her bones, and the sheets seemed to abrade her skin, as did the waffle weave of the bedspread, which she tried unsuccessfully to hurl to the floor. Everything hurt. She'd already had two baths tonight, which eased the discomfort only slightly. It was 3:00 a.m., and she couldn't sleep, and to make things worse she had this ditty stuck in her head, the old Knack song with *corona* substituted for *Sharona*. *M-m-m-my corona*. It was ridiculous. She'd tried to watch the second episode of *Tiger King*, but when Joe Exotic removed the tiger cubs from their mother's den with a long tong apparatus she started to cry and turned it off. People could be so cruel. She could cry with even less provocation.

Another siren in the street. So many sirens. Like the bad old days in New York, when it was the ambient sound of the city, sirens and car alarms. When muggings and murders were local customs. She herself mugged for her pearls her third day in Manhattan, a man on a bike grabbing and yanking, pulling her off her feet before the clasp broke. Marla Hanson, the model, her face slashed by two assailants with straight razors; Jennifer

Levin, murdered in Central Park after a night of drinking with a boyfriend. They were just the most visible ones, the ones the tabloids could sensationalize. She was reminded of those days a few months ago when a young Barnard College student, Tessa Majors, was stabbed to death in Morningside Park, just a few blocks away from the town house they'd lived in for more than a decade. *M-m-m-my corona.* It was like a time warp, a throwback to the days of the Central Park jogger and the Preppy Murder. Just when it seemed like Harlem had gentrified and crime was a distant memory. Pretty blond girl, a freshman from Virginia, allegedly murdered by three Black teens who wanted her cell phone. It had been a long time since New York had had such a tabloid-ready, racially charged crime to obsess about. Tessa refused to give up her cell phone, put up a fight, crawled up a flight of cement steps after she was stabbed. And the boy they'd taken into custody, fourteen years old—a baby. With allegedly two baby-faced accomplices. The girl stabbed at least four times. For a cell phone.

And here she was crying again and struggling for air. She couldn't seem to get enough, couldn't fill her lungs. This vital function she'd taken for granted her entire life failing her now. She would have summoned Russell, but she was frozen, pinned to the bed by the certainty that any kind of exertion would put her in oxygen deficit, conscious that her escalating panic was doing the same thing. *M-m-m-my corona.* She tried to calm herself, searching her mind for a soothing memory, and not a moment too soon came upon one—her first weekend away with Russell, when they'd driven a borrowed car down from Providence to a borrowed seaside shingled cottage in Little Compton that belonged to Russell's thesis adviser. It was April, and chilly, and they'd walked on the beach, bundled against the wind, and afterward Russell had cooked lobsters, even then he wanted to cook for her, and she cried as the lobsters squealed in the boiling water and after dinner he built a fire and they made love on a quilt spread on the floor in front of the fireplace and he'd cried and later they tried to scrub the stain of their commingled secretions, tinged pink with the first hint of her period, out of the quilt. And the soap that they used to try to lift the stain was called Joy, and would forever after remind her, when she saw it, of that night.

When she woke, the windows were bright. She looked at her phone. It was almost eleven. She'd slept, finally, falling asleep somewhere near dawn. Just as she began to wonder if she had turned the corner, she was convulsed by a fit of coughing, which, when it finally subsided, left her feeling exhausted. Was Russell at work? She looked at her texts, finding several from him, and many more from concerned friends, sympathetic and morbidly curious, including two from Veronica—was she feeling slightly guilty about her anniversary party?—and a barrage from Lisa, who had also left several voicemails. How had she even heard?

OMG, so worried about you. Do you know how you got it? Was it at the restaurant opening? What are your symptoms? What can we do to help? Do you need anything? Can send my driver on any kind of errand. Call me.

And: *Who's your MD? Shall I put you in touch with mine. He's concierge, but he'll talk to you as a favor to me. Best in NY. Call or text me.*

And: *Now I'm really getting worried. Tried to call Russell. And texted. Is he also sick? I've heard Tamiflu may help. Do you have it? Shall I send some? Is it worse than the flu? Do you know how you got it? Call or text ASAP.*

A text from Storey which ended with a string of heart emojis. And several from Russell.

How are you feeling?
Do you need anything?
Call me when you wake.

"How are you feeling?" he asked when she called him from bed. It was becoming a tedious question. She had a sudden flash of empathy for those with chronic illness; you didn't want to be a downer, to be a drag on the spirits of your healthy loved ones, you didn't want necessarily to tell the truth, over and over, that you were terrible, that you felt as if you were dying, that you were living in a different world than they were, and yet you also wanted them to feel your pain, wanted company in your misery.

"Maybe a little better."

"That's great."

"Although I nearly coughed up a lung a couple minutes ago. Where are you?"

"I'm home. It's Sunday. I told everyone they could work from home this week. Not sure how much you're following the news, but things are getting worse. Broadway is closed until further notice, ditto bars and restaurants."

It was horribly selfish, but she felt a glimmer of satisfaction that the crisis was accelerating, that she was not alone, that this virus that had felled her was becoming general.

"Can I get you something? Some tea? Could you eat?"

"Can't say that I'm hungry."

"You've got to get some kind of nourishment. Your body needs some fuel to fight this thing." That was his answer to most problems. Feed a cold. Feed a fever. Feed corona. Eat eat eat. No, thank you. I'd rather not.

"I don't know, maybe some toast," she said. She could always flush it down the toilet.

"With butter? Jam?"

Both sounded vaguely disgusting. "Maybe some honey. Just a little. And could you bring me today's papers?" While she was lucid she wanted to get a sense of what was happening out there, but by the time Russell left the tray outside the door she'd lost interest in the sheaves of newsprint, stacked on the tray. She was tired and out of breath. The only headline that caught her attention was part of the front page of the *Post*. TWO NYERS DIE, STATE CASES EXPLODE TO 613. For a moment she thought, I'm one of those, until she realized that, actually, she wasn't. No one had counted her. She hadn't been tested. And yet, she might die of it, of something which hadn't been officially diagnosed. How many others were there, like her, sick and uncounted? Thousands, presumably.

She called him: "Could you come here, and just let me see you outside the door. Just for a minute? I really need to see you."

"Yes, of course, are you okay?"

He sounded panicked.

"I just want to see you."

Moments later the door swung open and he stood there in the hallway, looking vital and handsome and worried. She still loved the way he looked. Looking at him now, she could easily superimpose younger versions of Russell on this frame. Yes, his face had sagged and wrinkled, his hair more gray than brown, but she didn't mind. She'd been with him now for more than two-thirds of her life. She'd sometimes imagined nursing him at the end of his life, hardly ever imagining she might be the first to go. She had always imagined he would be the first to go, that she would be the one left to tend his memory.

"I wish I could hold you," he said.

"God, so do I."

"Have you checked your oxygen this morning?"

"Not yet."

"Please do."

"I'm breathing a little better," she said, suddenly remembering the panic of the previous night, which had gradually subsided until she apparently fell asleep exhausted, thinking of Joy dishwashing liquid.

Suddenly something came back as if from a dream. "Did you tell me that Washington and Veronica have it? Or did I dream that?"

"Yeah, 'fraid so. They do."

"No, really? How are they?"

"Her symptoms are mild. He's got it much worse."

"Now we know where I got it."

"I'd say so. Christine Coles is also sick. You may recall I sat next to her that night."

"That turned out to be a very hot table."

"Everyone who was miffed about their placement can enjoy a little schadenfreude. The head table was highly contagious."

"At least I know you weren't all over Christine Coles. I always thought you had a thing for her."

"Maybe a little. Once upon a time."

"But you never acted on it?"

"No. I didn't. Why are you even—"

"Not that I have any right . . ."

"Let's not get into that. You're going to get better."

"Oh, Russell. I've been—"

"You're going to be fine. Why don't you get some rest?"

"Okay," she whispered, and lifted her hand in a feeble wave as he closed the door.

She wondered if this was her long-delayed punishment for her affair, for her betrayal. She didn't exactly believe in karma, but in a general sense she liked to think, despite an abundance of evidence to the contrary, that the universe bent toward moral equilibrium, toward a balancing of debts and a redress of wrongs. She couldn't help worrying that this was her time to settle up, to pay for her sin.

That night, she thought that perhaps her time had come. She was struggling for breath, bathed in her own sweat. Utterly paralyzed. The pain in her chest was excruciating. At first she felt like she was being pressed down into the bed, and then, just when it seemed she would drown, she felt a lifting and she saw, or sensed, a figure across the room, his hand outstretched, a beautiful luminous man who seemed to be raising her up from her bed, and she realized that it was not Russell, although she felt she knew who it was. She knew him, and she was ready to go with him. She felt herself at peace. But he seemed to say, Not yet, Corrine, before he faded away and she drifted off to sleep.

13

Russell was watching the PBS *NewsHour*, which was all about the rising numbers in New York, the shortage of hospital beds, the refrigerated trucks full of corpses—all happening just outside his door. He turned it off and tried to read Jenny Offill's new book, but he couldn't get any traction on the fragments of narrative, which seemed an awful lot like her last book. A collection of shards of the quotidian. He turned instead to the daunting pile of manuscripts in his office. He still printed them all out, or his assistant did. He hated reading on-screen.

Now, he picked up a thick slab of pages bound by a rubber band and sat down on his club chair, ready to be transported, hoping to be blown away, to be carried off to a new world. It was a first novel by a writer in her late twenties, submitted by an agent he respected. She'd had a story published in *McSweeney's*, and a few elsewhere. She had buzz. Russell believed that there was a music of the spheres audible only to young people; writers in their twenties had a chance to show us a new way of hearing and seeing the world. It happened every so often, maybe once or twice in a decade, that a young writer said something new, or at least spoke the old truths in a manner we'd never heard before, made us feel the old feelings afresh, as if discovering them for the first time. He'd published a couple of these books himself, and he was ever on the lookout, but the current novel would not be among them. It was mannered and self-conscious. She sounded like someone trying to sound like someone smart and clever. But she couldn't pull it off. He could usually tell in the first paragraph, though he inevitably persisted for twenty or thirty pages. There was no remedy for a tin ear. He took no pleasure in putting the manuscript aside. But there were many more waiting. Thousands upon thousands, of which some hundred or more would land on his desk each year.

Although the audience for literary fiction had been flat for as long as he could remember, or even declining, there seemed to be more and more aspiring Franzens and Lahiris out there than ever, tens of thousands of them enrolled in fiction workshops across the country. It was heartbreaking, if you thought about all that collective aspiration, about each of those individuals tapping away at their keyboards in the library, at their kitchen tables, at the coffee shop or in the spare room above the garage. You couldn't think about it, but sometimes he did. You couldn't help it. If sincerity were talent, if ambition were achievement, they would all be Fitzgerald or Virginia Woolf. Russell was usually insulated from all this naked aspiration by the literary agents, who were the first screeners of this collective logorrhea, sifting the slush for gold nuggets. But inevitably there were manuscripts from friends of friends, relatives and friends of relatives. And it was his least favorite part of his job to tell them that he could not make their dream a reality. He tried to couch it in relative terms, to say that it was just his opinion and probably an unreliable one, and others might be able to better appreciate and therefore better promote a work which he didn't fully understand to the extent that he should were he to undertake to launch it into the world. But this was, usually, a white lie.

Once in a while, he rejected a book that he believed might find a sympathetic home elsewhere. But usually, he knew that there would be no publication, no reviews, glowing or otherwise, no book party, no author tour, no readers. Self-publication, perhaps—a kind of purgatory for unbaptized books. An ongoing struggle against the indifference of the world's readers. Even when he was able to accept a manuscript and escort it through the many tedious steps to publication, sometimes the results could be heartbreaking. A dismissive paragraph somewhere in a roundup review. A boosterish notice in the hometown paper. A bookstore reading populated by a few friends sitting amid a formation of empty folding chairs as the ambient patrons, browsing the aisles in search of known titles, glanced over, mildly curious, for a moment, before returning to their search for books by authors whose public readings drew hordes of fans.

He'd either been saving Astrid's manuscript, or avoiding it—he wasn't quite sure which. Actually, both. He picked it up now with a slightly queasy sensation in his gut and a wildly mixed set of emotions among which were excitement, anxiety, arousal and guilt. He wanted it to be good, even as he sensed that, if it were, it would open a new and complicated chapter in his life.

The novel was good. In fact it was very good. And not at all what he'd been expecting—and dreading. Somehow he'd imagined he was about to read another semi-autobiographical coming-of-age novel set in the bars and coffee shops of Brooklyn, populated by ambitious and horny young litterateurs. Which, in part, he was. Part of it was set in Brooklyn. But he'd been delighted to also discover himself reading a historical novel about one of his favorite historical characters—Lady Emma Hamilton, the muse of Romney and mistress of Nelson. Twenty-first-century Brooklyn and eighteenth-century Naples alternating chapters. His relief was tempered by the knowledge that Susan Sontag had published a novel called *The Volcano Lover*, also about Lady Hamilton and the men around her, in 1992. He hadn't been much impressed with *The Volcano Lover* when it came out, finding it a fairly conventional historical novel. He realized he'd have to look at Sontag's book again, but he was certain that Astrid's Emma was much more visceral and vibrant and alive on the page.

Astrid's Lady Hamilton was no lady—the sex was unabashed and raunchy. But then, many books had been written on the subject, and many films inspired by it, and the further he got into Astrid's version, the more he felt she was making the story her own. For one thing, alternate chapters were written in the first person, from Emma's point of view, and Russell found the voice both convincing and compelling. It had just enough flavor of the period to seem authentic, and enough sexual energy and grit to sound contemporary. Just as he had suspended disbelief and settled into the early nineteenth century, his expectations were overturned in the second chapter, narrated by a young contemporary novelist who had decided to take on the subject of Lady Hamilton and her famous lover after failing in her attempt to write a novel about herself and her older lover—a famous novelist.

His reaction was complicated, though, by his own personal relation to the material. He had always thought Corrine bore a strong physical resemblance to Emma Hamilton, or at least, in her youth, to certain of the Romney portraits. And yet, reading Astrid's book, he couldn't help feeling the presence of the author, of conflating her with both of her narrators, Emma Hamilton and her amanuensis. He was finding himself becoming thoroughly enamored. And turned on—the writing was explicit and bawdy—in both centuries.

He decided, after reading fifty pages, that he was going to try to publish the book.

He felt guilty about his commingled feelings for the author and her subject, about the excitement he felt reading passages about Emma's sexual adventures, and his urge to express his enthusiasm to the novelist. He couldn't help speculating about the contemporary story, wondering if it was based on a real love affair, wondering about the identity of the narrator's lover. He couldn't help feeling a twinge of jealousy. Apparently, he wasn't the only older man in her life. Was he part of a pattern? And was that a bad thing? Or an opportunity? Even as these thoughts played across his mind, he couldn't quite believe he was entertaining them. He was a married publisher reading a manuscript for possible publication. And yet he knew his objectivity was compromised. Well, not utterly. He still trusted his literary judgment, even under the current circumstances. The book was good. And all truly good works of literature gave him a visceral buzz, a tingling in the scalp. It was something he looked for in a novel—a quickening of the pulse, a sense of excitement and anxiety. And here he was experiencing all of that. As he read the scene, for instance, where the narrator goes down on the famous novelist for the first time in an unlocked room just off the auditorium where he is about to give a reading—which echoed a passage in the previous chapter where Emma had performed the same service for Admiral Nelson while her husband and a drawing room full of Neapolitan aristocrats waited to meet the great man. As much as he wanted to finish the novel, he also wanted to talk to its author, to hear her unmediated voice. Should he wait until he'd finished? That was probably the prudent course. But he wasn't feeling prudent. He decided to send an exploratory text.

Really enjoying the early chapters of your novel. Within moments, his phone dinged.

Oh wow really

He inferred the question mark at the end—he'd noticed she didn't punctuate her texts.

He typed out: *Very compelling.* Which sounded stuffy and editorial. He erased *compelling.*

Very sexy.

Glad you think so

He wasn't quite sure where to go next. Before he could respond she wrote:

I was hoping you would think that

As opposed to thinking it had literary merit? he typed.

I hope that too

Well, yes. I think it's beautifully written. He pressed SEND, then almost immediately wondered if he'd derailed the thread of flirtation.

Means a lot coming from you

Kind of crazy—but I've always had this thing for Lady Hamilton. He erased *Lady Hamilton* and replaced it with *Emma.* And sent. *That's why I was at the Frick last month. I like to visit the Romney.*

You have good taste in women

You have good taste in subject matter. And you've inhabited her rather brilliantly. Feel like I'm getting a chance to know her.

You will get to know her even better

Looking forward to that.

Intimately I hope

He felt a stirring in his groin, an engorgement of his cock.

He typed: *That would be nice*, and immediately erased. *Sounds intriguing.*

Doesn't it. She annotated this with a purple devil's head.

He was surprised—pleasantly so—at how aroused he had become.

Let me know if you have any questions

OK.

I can elucidate or

He waited, half knowing what was coming.

demonstrate

Jesus. Was that as explicit as he thought it was?

I will probably have questions.

Good

Will let you know.

K

He didn't want to end the exchange, though it felt like it had reached a natural ending, a point beyond which it could only become more explicit. And he wasn't ready for that. He preferred this limbo state, this heightened state of unfulfilled desire. It was enough to feel this erotic excitement, this acute feeling of awareness, after years of forgetting that it existed. He loved Corrine; he would always love Corrine. Sex was comfortable, familiar, infrequent. Neither of them seemed compelled; if anything, they seemed to feel obligated, now and again. In Russell's case the act was premeditated, since he required pharmaceutical assistance to be confident of an erection, especially after three or four glasses of wine, which seemed at this point like a precondition to getting in the mood. In fact, he wondered how sex was possible without alcohol. The better part of a bottle of Volnay and a Cialis. Repeat bimonthly.

To feel that feeling again—it was hard not to be grateful, to reach toward it and savor it. To let it warm you, without picking up the red-hot embers. Perhaps, he thought, the feeling alone was enough.

14

Russell went to Citarella Monday morning to stock up for the siege, and he was not alone, the supermarket far more crowded than he would have expected, and the shelves emptier. The meat section was picked over; he managed to find some decent-looking New Zealand lamb chops, which he could cook over the course of the next week. Likewise, the shelves of the pasta aisle were half empty, with vacant slots on the shelves representing the absence of the more conventional shapes, and there were no paper towels or toilet paper. His fellow shoppers steered around one another warily, a few of them wearing surgical masks, like Japanese commuters—he'd be damned if he was going to put on one of those things. All white people down here. He was still getting oriented to his hundred-block change of location. Despite gentrification, Harlem was much more mixed. The opening of the Whole Foods grocery store a few years before had been much commented on as the ultimate sign of the gentrification of the neighborhood. Certainly, it had been a godsend for Russell—who, with his taste for exotic European ingredients and dry-aged prime beef, was not the target demographic of the Fine Fare Supermarket on Malcolm X Boulevard, not to mention the local bodegas. He preferred to shop himself rather than relying on the delivery services.

He spent Tuesday morning on the phone with his employees after updating his kids, talking directly with Storey, who characteristically blamed herself.

"I can't help feeling she got it at the restaurant. I feel so bad. I should have canceled."

Why, he wondered, did women always seem to blame themselves?

"Honey, I'm ninety percent certain she got it at Washington and Veronica's party at Odeon the night before your opening. You heard—they're both sick."

"I know. Mingus told me. It sounds like his dad is *really* sick."

"I'm afraid so. But that's most likely where Mom got it. Have you heard of anyone else at the opening who's gotten sick?"

"Not yet."

"I was at your opening and I feel fine. So stop beating yourself up. Just focus on what you're going to do next."

"I was planning to close for the next two weeks at least, anyway, and Cuomo made it official yesterday. Bars and restaurants are closed as of last night till further notice."

"I can't believe this is happening a week after you opened."

"Imagine how I feel."

"I can and I do. Have you thought about what you're going to do about your staff?"

"I'm going to pay them for this week. After that I need to talk to you and the other investors."

"I should think some of them will be eligible for unemployment. I've got the same issue at my company. We'll figure it out. This can't last forever."

"I hope you're right."

He started the workday with a call to Jonathan Tashjian.

"We're going to have to postpone Winfield's tour," Russell said. "When was he supposed to go out?"

"His first gig was Politics and Prose in D.C. on the twenty-fifth—next week. We have him in thirteen cities over the next eighteen days."

"I doubt that's going to work."

"Why don't we push publication back a month or even two?"

"The books are already shipping. And it's already being written about."

"We definitely need to postpone the tour. Maybe six weeks?"

"But that's going to overlap with other tours and authors."

"Let me call some of the venues and see what they're thinking."

"This can't last forever."

"I hope not. It looks like my kids are home for who knows how long now that they've closed the schools."

"Call me after you've talked to some of the bookstores."

"Will do. Meantime, don't know if you've heard, but the Strokes have a new album dropping in a few weeks. Called *The New Abnormal*."

"Good to know. I'll attempt to download it." Either that or he would get Jonathan or one of his children to do so. Do albums still *drop*? They just materialize in the cloud, suddenly.

"Send our love to Corrine. If there's anything we can do . . ."

"Thanks. She seems a little better today. Fingers crossed."

While he was preparing a tray of toast and yogurt for Corrine, he dodged a call from Astrid Kladstrup, who left a message. "Hey, it's Astrid. Have you succumbed to the virus, or are you ignoring me? I was hoping we could get a drink together, but now the bars are closed. This is getting weird. We could have a drink here, at my place, assuming they don't close the bridges and tunnels. They're serving drinks to go in the hood. Call me. I miss you."

He left the tray on the floor outside the door of the master bedroom, knocking gently. He didn't want to wake her if she was sleeping, but then again, he didn't want to leave her unchecked upon. What if she'd stopped breathing in the interval since he'd spoken to her this morning? He could hardly imagine his life without her. No, that wasn't true; he could imagine it. He had imagined it, in stray moments—a speculative exercise. He would be devastated, but he knew he would survive it. He could imagine the funeral, the gathering of friends at Frank Campbell's funeral home, Washington and Veronica and their kids, Corrine's colleagues telling him of her kindness and generous spirit, Storey's friends saying how she was like a mother to them, Corrine's friends telling him to call them if he needed anything, anything at all, if he just wanted to talk. Eventually, in the not-too-distant future, running into Astrid, who had sent him a note of condolence, but had been discreet enough to keep her distance. Her creamy flesh and truffled scent. He could imagine it—and felt guilty for doing so. But that didn't mean he wished for it. Not really. He'd broken with the teachings of the Catholic Church in part over the idea of equivalency of sins of thought and deed. Thoughts came unbidden after all. Or from God. So maybe God was the pornographer.

As if to awaken himself as much as Corrine, he rapped on the door.

"Corrine, are you okay?"

Hearing a faint response, he opened the door. She was propped up on her pillows, looking not well but certainly alive—which was a profound relief. For a moment, he almost imagined that he'd killed her with his stray fantasy.

"Any better?"

"Not worse."

"Do you think we should think about taking you to the hospital?"

"I really don't want to go to the hospital," she said, her voice weak and raspy, like paper being torn. "My oxygen hasn't fallen into the danger zone the last two days and I'm much more comfortable here."

"What's your temperature?"

"Not as high as yesterday. A hundred and two last time I checked."

"I wish I could do something."

"Keep yourself safe. That's the best thing you can do for me. If we both get sick we're screwed."

She was frighteningly pale and bedraggled, as if she'd spent the night underwater, but her voice sounded a little stronger than it had yesterday.

"Try to eat something," he said. "I've got toast and yogurt and tea with honey here."

"I'll try. It's hard when you can't smell or taste anything."

"It must be connected to your corona."

"Imagine if it happened to you."

"I'd rather not."

"Have you been out?"

"Just to Citarella."

"Jesus, Russell, you can't do that. Don't you get it? Use FreshDirect or Instacart for God's sake. What's it going to take to get through to you?"

"I stocked up for the week. I thought it would behoove us to have a full pantry. Plus those services charge an extortionate commission to the stores." It occurred to him that he'd done the same thing the morning of September 11, 2001, gone out and loaded up a shopping cart full of groceries, as a hedge against things getting worse, as a thing to do at a moment when no response seemed appropriate.

"I want you to start taking this seriously."

"I'm taking it seriously. I can't help it. My wife is sick and I'm worried as hell."

And he may have been feeling guilty about the fleeting thought, imagining her gone. He wanted her to get better, to stay with him. For the first time in recent memory, he was scared. This thing was killing people. He hadn't really believed in it before, hadn't really felt that it could touch him, but he believed now.

It was a tedious crisis. Outside, the weather was stuck between seasons, the streets empty and gray except for the intermittent white ambulances, red lights strobing. Inside, they huddled around the blue light of screens and gas stoves. Watching Governor Cuomo's briefings, keeping score—counting the infected, the admitted, the intubated, the deceased. Somehow this information seemed crucial. Charts, red trend lines spiking ever upward. Hospitals nearing capacity. Bodies piling up in morgues, in refrigerated trucks parked outside of hospitals. New York, always first and most, had naturally become the center of the contagion. The city was made for the virus, with its density and its intricate and intimate webs of social connection, its stacked and packed humanity. The most vulnerable target. It had been grand, it had been a paradise, in its way, in its time—a steel-and-concrete Eden. Russell still believed in the city, believed in its resilience, having heard dozens of epitaphs, having arrived when Manhattan was on its ass, broke and decrepit and enervated by crime. He'd lived through the crashes of '87 and '08 and watched the city rebound, more prosperous than ever.

Like millions before him Russell had been drawn here to create himself, to forge an identity, to enter the teeming fray and make his mark, in the thrall of the mythology of the great metropolis, the center of the known universe with its presumptuous skyscrapers and its incessant din. The city had ultimately rewarded him, had allowed him to write his own destiny, though it had almost defeated him, driving him like so many others from his downtown home to the brink of exile. The loft they'd rented, a former sweatshop with its exposed pipes and wiring, its bedroom that they'd partitioned with makeshift walls when the kids had arrived, could not ultimately withstand the tsunami of money that washed over the neighborhood in the early years of the century. The building was sold, the interiors gutted, and Russell and his family had migrated a hundred and forty blocks north. But he'd hung on, and fought back and prospered, and he couldn't imagine himself anywhere but here, in Manhattan.

He'd seen the suburbs, grown up there, outside of Detroit, and he never wanted to return. In his mind they were utterly interchangeable—White Plains, Winnetka, Grosse Pointe, Sherman Oaks. Much as he liked Cheever and Updike, he preferred reading about the burbs to visiting them. Nor for him the wide-open spaces, the empty patches on the map. He had become a

New Yorker, early in his residence and easily. One of the things he loved about the city was its wide and indiscriminate embrace of immigrants, of which he counted himself one—an immigrant from suburban Michigan. It wasn't love—it was closer to indifference. No one particularly cared where you came from. It was irrelevant—your life before New York. Who cared, really?

And unlike many of his friends he hadn't fled the city at the first sign of contagion; he didn't have that option; unlike many of their friends and acquaintances they didn't have a country house.

He spent several days working with his accountant applying for a PPP loan to keep his workers on the payroll. He talked to most of them most days from his home office, and to bookstore owners, printers and paper suppliers. He postponed the publication of some of his books, and consoled those authors whose books were being born into this barren landscape. Jonathan was converting as much of the promotion as he could to virtual forums. Something called Zoom had become the new medium of communication.

Corrine had finally turned the corner after ten days of fever and respiratory distress. She remained in her room, but her symptoms had subsided, and he no longer woke up with a sense of dread. Veronica had almost recovered, but Washington had been taken to the hospital, where he was on oxygen, but not yet on a ventilator.

"Just checking in," Russell said to Veronica. "How's he doing?"

"He texted me an hour ago. He doesn't feel up to speaking."

"I'm so sorry."

"I'm scared, Russell."

"He's a tough guy," Russell said, feeling somewhat fraudulent. "Is there anything I can do?"

"I don't think so. Pray."

He wished he could, but that would be hypocritical, since he'd lost his faith years ago. Raised in a strict Catholic household, he'd served as an altar boy for years and struggled, in adolescence, with the conflict between his developing sexuality and the puritanism of Catholic doctrine. The idea of sins of thought seemed increasingly absurd and unfair. *Morose delectation*—the phrase used to describe the entertainment of unchaste thoughts. Not to mention the outrages against decency in Deuteronomy and Leviticus. Unlike many Catholics Russell read the Old Testament, King James Version, in part as a literary exercise and in part to test his waning faith. He sparred with his parish priest, a Jesuit, who had, it seemed to Russell, an unhealthy interest in the details of his relationship with his fellow parishioner Joan Coughlin. And in his senior year of high school he'd walked away from the Church. Veronica, however, was a practicing Catholic. He hoped it helped her through the current crisis. As for Corrine, she seemed to host a vague Protestant faith that quietly informed her life's choices.

Not for the first time he wished he had faith to fall back on. He couldn't imagine losing Washington, his best friend. It would be a lonelier world, a lonelier city, without him. He'd lost his best friend once, decades ago, and he didn't want to go through that again, not yet, not for a long time yet. And he'd lost most of the literary generation that had ruled the roost when he first arrived in the city: Norman Mailer, George Plimpton, Kurt Vonnegut, Robert Stone. Men who'd welcomed him into the fold, made room for him at their tables at Elaine's, when he was a young editor. And just a few months ago, he'd lost Sonny Mehta, a mentor, the great editor-publisher of his generation. He was starting to worry that he had more dead friends than living ones. Had he really reached that age?

Last night, he'd gotten some nice Madagascar shrimp delivered, and he'd decided to make an étouffée. He was about to call Washington to ask about the advisability of doing the roux before cooking the vegetables or adding the flour afterward. It wasn't that he didn't have an opinion himself—of course a proper roux was prepared first—just that he would have liked to debate it. It was the kind of subject they could belabor for ten minutes, though it was really just a pretext for conversing. Instead he called Storey, who quickly dispensed her answer, but seemed to be otherwise engaged. The étouffée turned out well enough; he took a tray to Corrine, which he knew she wouldn't touch, and then ate his own in the kitchen, paired with an entire bottle of André Perret Condrieu—there was no one with whom to share it.

15

STOREY AND MINGUS joined the crowd coalescing in the sunlit plaza in front of the Adam Clayton Powell State Office Building at 125th Street, gathering around the statue of Powell, the state's first Black congressman. For Storey, a return to the old neighborhood. The demonstrators seemed to be mostly Storey's age, Black and white, wearing a variety of masks, including several with the image of George Floyd's face. She was glad she was not conspicuously in the minority as a member of the privileged white majority. This was how she needed to think of herself now. She didn't want to co-opt anyone's movement. But Mingus was with her as a kind of guarantor, with his sign that read IF YOU THINK YOUR MASK MAKES IT HARD TO BREATHE IMAGINE BEING BLACK IN AMERICA. Storey was carrying a cardboard sign that said RACISM IS A PANDEMIC TOO. A group was chanting, "First degree, not third degree." The day before, Derek Chauvin, the cop who knelt on George Floyd's neck for eight minutes and forty-six seconds, had been charged with third-degree murder. These people were not mollified, though the anger seemed to be mixed with a sense of elation, a kind of joy in the warmth of the perfect spring day and the palpable sense of community after months of confinement and isolation. A few days ago, social justice required social distance and quarantine. Now it demanded the opposite.

The cops, for the moment, were keeping their distance, a thin blue line guarding the entrance to the office building. Peaceful so far. Last night in Brooklyn things had turned violent. Jeremy had been part of that protest and had narrowly escaped arrest. The cops had answered protests against police brutality with some stunning illustrations of it, and some of the protesters had answered in kind. But now the sun seemed to have reset the mood. Storey wanted to believe it would be peaceful today. As if to address her concern, the chant changed at some point to "No justice, no peace." Just when it seemed the protest was losing steam, the crowd began to march downtown along Adam Clayton Powell Jr. Boulevard, as if in response to a signal she'd missed.

"Come on, honey."

Storey joined her boyfriend, marching past the shuttered storefronts. Now, some of the demonstrators started chanting "NYPD, suck my dick," which Storey didn't think was very productive; Mingus joining in while Storey marched silently, waving her sign. At the moment, she didn't see any cops, which made her breathe easier. Spirits were running high. "Maybe they've learned their lesson," Storey said.

"Overnight? Not fucking likely," Mingus said. It was interesting to see the change that had come over him since George Floyd was killed. He'd been fairly apolitical, if not conservative in his views, but the events of recent days had energized and angered him.

Spectators appeared in the windows above the storefronts, cheering and banging on pots and pans as they'd done every night at seven for the frontline workers. At 116th Street, the marchers paused, the protesters in the lead turning back toward the others and raising their fists. Storey found it fascinating the way the crowd seemed to have a collective brain. An NYPD helicopter appeared and hovered; Storey and Mingus raised their middle fingers in concert with their fellow marchers. Someone threw a water bottle, which fell far short of its target.

They marched onward, chanting and waving their signs.

• • •

When they reached the FDR the march turned into a jog, the protesters trotting down the southbound lane, but up ahead, a line of bicycles blocked their path at the 96th Street exit. Storey wasn't sure she wanted to test the resolve of the barricading cops, but Mingus was running, and she struggled to stay abreast of him. Up ahead was chaos. The first wave of protesters had clashed with the police. The crowd around her slowed as they approached the skirmish. Screams and shouts rang out. The cops were swinging batons at the crowd. She got caught in a surge of retreating protesters, and suddenly she couldn't see Mingus, who had to be right in the thick of it. She pushed forward even as others were retreating, dropping their signs, rubbing their faces. There was a kind of stinging mist in the air—the cops spraying the protesters with something. Tear gas? Pepper spray? She was frantic. The cops punching, cursing, zip-tying protesters as they lay on the ground. What were they thinking? Storey was struggling to keep her balance as she was pushed back in the surge of the crowd, and ultimately fell to the ground, banging her head and losing consciousness.

She was being lifted and carried. George Floyd's face was staring down at her. The face was printed on the T-shirt of a Black man who was carrying her feet. "She's conscious," he shouted. Others were holding her by the arms, retreating from the melee. Her head hurt. Her rescuers lowered her to the sidewalk. A contingent of the protesters had retreated from the highway and taken refuge under some scaffolding next to a Hess station.

"Get her some water," someone shouted, and all at once a bottle of water appeared, upended toward her lips. She felt entirely helpless. A ponytailed white man with a red-and-white kerchief tied around the lower part of his face was holding the bottle to her lips, cradling the back of her head gently, while the Black man in the George Floyd shirt touched her head with a cloth.

"Does it hurt?" he asked.

"God yes," she said, pleased at the sound of her own voice, at the fact that she could speak at all. A sharp pain at the crown of her head and a deep throbbing within.

"Mingus," she suddenly said. "Where's Mingus?"

"The pigs arrested a bunch of people," said the man in the George Floyd shirt.

A man climbed up the scaffolding and started to give a speech. He had a bushy ponytail and his T-shirt read: SPEAK OUT OR SHUT UP.

"All right, y'all, we've seen what they're capable of. We gotta be smart, stick together, not scatter soon as we run up against the cops. Remember to be like water. When they try to block us, we turn the corner."

"Don't try to get up too quickly," said the man in the George Floyd shirt.

"I've got to find my boyfriend."

"Was he the brother with the sign that said IF YOU THINK YOUR MASK MAKES IT HARD TO BREATHE IMAGINE BEING BLACK IN AMERICA?"

"Yes, that's him," she said hopefully.

"They took him away."

"What? Where?"

"They put him in a van."

She felt an overwhelming flood of guilt. How could she have let this happen? She was responsible. How would she explain it to his parents? How, for that matter, would she explain it to him? That she'd let him get taken away?

"How are you feeling?"

"I have a horrendous headache."

"You probably have a concussion," said the white man with the water bottle.

"She went down on the pavement," said the Black man. "You'd better get that checked out."

"What's your name?" Storey asked. Names were important. Say their names.

"Jason."

"Thank you, Jason."

Storey struggled to her feet with the assistance of the two men. She felt dizzy but basically intact.

The man who'd given the speech on tactics was herding the remaining protesters, bobbing around the perimeter, urging them to march to the Upper East Side, that bastion of white privilege, the population of which had largely fled in March to their second or third homes in the Hamptons and Florida.

"You should go to a hospital," Jason said to Storey, before turning to follow the others.

"I don't think that's necessary," Storey said. "Be careful, Jason."

All at once she felt nauseated. She stopped walking, leaned over and vomited on the sidewalk.

The sun was still shining, warming the streets and slowly irradiating and bronzing her skin. She was suddenly conscious of her whiteness, of the fragility of the social contract, the fragility of life itself.

After she'd signed in at the emergency room and taken a seat in the waiting area, Storey knew she had to call Mingus's mom, though she dreaded doing so. Instead, she called Mingus for the fifth time, but she only got his voicemail.

Her eyes and nose still burned from the pepper spray, and she found herself wheezing, short of breath. She wondered if there was some kind of treatment for these symptoms. Noticing a young Black couple from the protest, the man holding a bloody towel to his forehead, she thought about saying something sympathetic, referencing their mutual cause, but worried that she wasn't entitled to do so, that she would sound somehow phony or opportunistic. She went to the ladies' room and rinsed out her eyes again.

Before she called Veronica she decided to call her father. She needed his advice. Hearing his voice on the other end seemed to rob her of her own ability to speak.

"Storey, honey, are you there? Is everything okay?"

"Daddy," she managed to say, before breaking into a sob.

She fell apart again when Russell arrived at the hospital, sinking into his enveloping embrace. "How are you feeling?"

"Dizzy. Sore. Better now that you're here."

Russell went over to talk to the admitting nurse while she tried to call Jeremy.

But of course, it went to voicemail. Her brother didn't answer his phone very often, but then it had to be said, neither did she. "Jeremy, it's Storey. I'm at Mount Sinai with Dad. I marched with Mingus this morning. I got a concussion and Mingus got arrested. Call me." That ought to get his attention—verifying the perfidy and violence of the state.

16

Storey went with her dad to the apartment in the Village; she didn't want to go back to Brooklyn alone. It was a little weird being in this place which held no memories for her. It had been hard packing up her old bedroom in Harlem, with its shrine to Eminem, a corner of framed photos and *Rolling Stone* and album covers; her signed photos of Anne-Sophie Pic and Hélène Darroze.

Her mom, with whom she'd talked from the hospital, was handling it pretty well.

"Have you reached Mingus?"

She shook her head.

"What about his parents?"

She had to admit she hadn't tried.

"Storey, they *deserve* to know what's going on."

"I know. It's just . . . I will."

Storey retreated to the spare room, dominated by a massive bookshelf holding a portion of her dad's library. An English partners desk with a green leather top held a collection of family photos, including the one of her with Alain Passard and the whole kitchen team at L'Arpège in Paris. That experience had almost killed her—there were days when she thought she would rather jump out the window of her tiny sixth-floor apartment in the seventh arrondissement than go back to that kitchen. She could deal with the cuts and burns, and the ache of her feet at the end of the day, if it were only that. But the ritual meanness of the pecking order and the steady onslaught of sexual harassment were hard to bear. The worst offenders were those closest in rank to her, one rung or two up from the bottom, where she dwelt. She didn't think Chef knew what happened, what the atmosphere of the kitchen was like when he was out talking to the guests, or traveling to accept awards, though he'd probably endured worse in his day. It was gladiatorial combat. But she returned, every day, six days a week, for almost three months. Maybe because—despite the malice, the jealousy, and the exhaustion—the system somehow worked, the individuals functioned as a team at the highest level of culinary endeavor. But even though she survived and made her bones, she didn't believe for a minute that it had to be that way and vowed that when she had her own kitchen it wouldn't be. Thinking of it now made her weepy again—she was a raw nerve.

She dialed Veronica's cell, thinking it would be easier to start with her. For better or worse, she picked up almost immediately.

"Hey there, Storey."

"Hi," she said or, possibly, croaked.

"What's up?"

"This is hard to say, but it's about Mingus."

"What about Mingus?"

"I think he's in custody. We were at the protest and we got separated in the crowd and somebody told me that the cops had taken him."

"Oh my God." After a pause, she said, "Are you sure?"

"I'm not really sure of anything. It was chaotic. We got separated and I got knocked down and when I came to they told me he'd been thrown into a van."

"Wait, I'm putting you on speaker. Wash got back from the hospital last night."

"Didn't he tell you we were joining the march?"

"He told me," Washington chimed in. "And I told him to stay the hell home and stay out of it." His voice was hoarse.

"He didn't tell me that," Storey said.

"And this is precisely why I told him to stay out of it," Washington said. "It's different for you. Jesus Christ, this is what the whole thing is about—racist policing."

Storey wanted to protest, point out that she had been knocked over and knocked out, but she knew what he meant. And as it turned out Washington was right. She should have kept Mingus away. It was too late now, and all she could do was give Washington what little information she had, like the location of the arrest, and tearfully apologize.

Her mom knocked and came in.

"Did you reach them?"

She nodded. "I feel like such an idiot. And I'm sure they think I am."

"You can't blame yourself."

"Yes, I can. Anyway, Washington's going to try to figure out what happened with Mingus."

After Corrine left she lay down on the bed and fell into a deep sleep, awakening utterly disoriented, in the dark, fully clothed. At first she had no idea where she was, or even what day it was. Her phone said 5:13 a.m. And then she remembered Mingus. She jumped out of bed and felt her way out to the hallway to the bathroom. Sitting on the toilet, she checked her phone, but there was nothing from him. Suddenly it seemed wrong for her to be here in her parents' apartment. What if he returned to the apartment to find it empty? She needed to be there, to wait for him. To her place in Brooklyn, she guessed, since that's where they'd been mostly sleeping. She found a new toothbrush and some toothpaste in the bathroom and gave her sour mouth a freshening. She crept out into the hall, stopped in the kitchen, opened the refrigerator and found a bottle of Snapple.

Closing the door behind her she searched her purse for a mask, a blue-green Nicole Miller tie-dye. The street was deserted. She tried his apartment first, talking her way past the sleepy doorman and taking the elevator to the fourth floor. There was no recent sign of Mingus in the apartment. She walked up University to the subway, descending to the platform, where a pair of white cops, one short and dark-haired and the other a tall redhead, were standing. Her body started to shake. The cops glanced over at her; could they see that she was trembling? She didn't want to be noticed. They stood about thirty feet away. She tried not to look at them. Only a day ago she would have been thrilled to find two cops beside her on a deserted subway platform but not now. This must be how Black people felt all the time.

"You okay, miss?" the taller one called out.

She nodded her head vigorously.

He looked at her quizzically.

"I'm fine, thank you." She wasn't even sure she'd said anything aloud, but he seemed satisfied, and turned back to his partner.

After an eternity the L rattled into the station. The cops boarded the front of the car that stopped in front of her. At the last minute she moved down the platform and stepped into the car behind theirs. A homeless man had set up a makeshift tent in the middle of the car. The subway had been running only for about an hour—for the first time in its history the system had started closing down at night for cleaning, and to roust the homeless—but this guy looked as if he'd been here for days, with his paper bags, his newspapers, his loaded shopping cart and his filthy blankets. Thankfully he was sleeping. On the seat beside him was a battered copy of *Where the Crawdads Sing*.

It seemed like she'd been away from her neighborhood much longer than twenty hours as she emerged from the subway. It was possible, for just a moment, to imagine that she'd wandered into some postapocalyptic version of East Williamsburg—the buildings vivid and angular in the flat early morning light, the street deserted and bleached out, draped in silence—until a young woman rounded the corner of Bushwick, tugged along the sidewalk by a brindle French bulldog.

She let herself into the apartment, hoping she might find Mingus waiting for her. That hope dashed, she turned on CNN and decided to clean the apartment, make it spick-and-span for his return. The news was all about the protests, here and in Portland and Minneapolis. She was sponging down the shelves of the kitchen cabinets when a key turned in the lock of the front door and he appeared.

She ran to him and crushed him in her arms.

His own embrace was tentative and weak. He smelled ripe with his own sweat and other unfamiliar scents.

"Are you okay? I was so worried. We didn't know how to find you."

He released himself from her embrace, went to the bookshelf, grabbing his stash box.

"Fucking bastards," he said.

"What happened, my love. God, I'm so relieved to see you."

He sat down on the couch and spread out his smoking materials on the coffee table.

"They zip-tied me, confiscated my possessions, threw me in a stinking, crowded cell and left me there for fourteen hours."

"Baby. I'm so sorry. What can I do for you? What can I get you? Are you hungry?"

He stopped rolling the joint and looked at her as if he wasn't quite sure who she was. "I'm starved."

"I'll make you an omelette. Did you call your parents?"

"I did. I called my mom. And then my phone died."

She couldn't help feeling a little stung that he'd called his mother before her.

"We were all so worried."

When he finally put the joint down, he said, "There were, like, thirty of us in this cell. Height of the pandemic. No food or water. No phone calls—they'd confiscated our phones along with everything else. It was like some fucking third world nightmare."

Storey folded the omelette gently, trying to put as much care into it as anything she'd ever made. "What happened? How did you get out?"

"At about five a.m. they came for me, gave me my possessions and released me with a desk ticket. I was charged with resisting arrest. Can you fucking believe that? These two cops jumped me and wrestled me to the ground. I don't know where you were at that point."

It chilled her—the note of accusation in his voice. "I was behind you. I tried to hold on to you, but one of the cops pushed me away. And then I was pepper-sprayed."

She was exaggerating a little.

She slipped the omelette onto the plate, rubbed a little butter on the top and finished it with chopped chives.

"Come, sit," she said, laying out a place for him at the kitchen table.

"I desperately need to take a shower."

"Eat first."

He sat and inhaled the omelette, eating in silence as she watched. The most elemental form of hospitality, cooking for a hungry lover.

"Better?" she asked as he finished.

"It's going to take more than an omelette," he said.

"I know, sweetie. I'm sorry."

She knew he was traumatized, but she wished he would let her help, let her in. He seemed distant, almost cold. "Why don't you take a shower," she said.

He undressed in the living room, dropping his clothes on the wood floor. "Burn those," he said. "Throw them away, whatever. I don't want to see those clothes ever again."

While he was in the shower, she bagged up the apparel and took it to the garbage can on the street.

When he came out of the shower wearing his robe, he asked, "Did you even try to find me?"

"I called your phone over and over. Check your messages."

"They took my phone away, obviously."

"I was frantic. My dad called the Twenty-Fourth Precinct, I think it was the twenty-fourth, where you were arrested, but they wouldn't tell him anything."

"Your *dad* called?"

She realized, now, how lame that sounded. She'd kind of abdicated that responsibility.

"I was paralyzed. I didn't know what to do." She threw her arms around him. "I'm sorry, baby. I'm just so glad you're home."

"Home?" he said, resisting her embrace.

"Why don't you lie down and let me give you a back rub," she said. He loved her back rubs.

"Okay," he said resignedly.

They went into the bedroom; Mingus dropped his robe on the floor and lay sprawled out on his stomach on the bed. She gave it her all, trying to break down his resistance, and she could tell it wasn't easy for him to suppress the sounds of pleasure. Finally, after twenty minutes, she rolled him over and tried to go down on him, but he pushed her away and curled up in a fetal position, facing away from her. Within minutes, he was asleep, snoring lightly, leaving her feeling anxious, alone and scared for their future. She couldn't resist feeling that something had changed irrevocably.

17

WHEN HE REALIZED that the lockdown wasn't a temporary thing, Russell bought himself a bicycle. He wasn't the first one to think of this, and by the time he went looking the only bike to be found was absurdly expensive, a Canyon Grizl SL 8, the purchase of which he rationalized against all the money he was saving not going out to restaurants or taking taxis. On that basis it seemed like a relatively reasonable purchase.

The city by bike, under lockdown, was a different city than the one he'd come to know as a pedestrian and a car passenger. The lack of automobile traffic left the roads feeling safe and open, his progress virtually unimpeded and flowing, his views long if not wide. Suddenly it was a city of architecture, of buildings and vistas, rather than a city of people. His transit through the city was usually choppy and syncopated, his views framed and partial, storefronts flashing past, landmarks truncated, the sky glimpsed intermittently. Now, there was a feeling almost of flight—a feeling that could be rudely punctured by potholes.

Tonight he was riding all the way to Red Hook, in Brooklyn, a distance of some six miles. "Having dinner with a novelist," he told Corrine, in what he hoped was an entirely neutral tone. "In Red Hook." Outdoor dining had just opened a few days before, the city having decided to allow restaurants to expand out to the sidewalks and even the streets of the city. Many had responded by building outdoor structures of varying degrees of solidity and extravagance, constructed of plywood and plexiglass, vinyl and canvas, embellished with paint and planters.

"That's a long way to go for dinner," she said.

"I want to stretch my legs, get some exercise," he said. Which was true as far as it went. He preferred not to dwell, even in his own mind, on the other reason he was going to Brooklyn, that it was her turf, that her apartment was not that far away.

He arrived at the Red Hook Tavern after forty minutes of pedaling, having stopped several times along the way to consult Google Maps, locking his bike to a telephone pole on the corner, announcing himself to the hostess on the sidewalk and taking his seat at a table in a canvas cubicle.

Astrid arrived a few minutes later, on a Citi Bike, in a sleeveless tie-dyed sundress.

"You look great," he said, standing to greet her.

She posed, cocking a hip and holding the hem of the dress. "Why thank you, sir." She took a seat across from him. "So nice of you to come to my part of the world. I hope it isn't too disorienting."

"I like to expand my horizons. I like the way you can sort of feel the waterfront from here, the way it feels like a port town."

"*On the Waterfront* was set here," she said. "It was supposed to be Red Hook, anyway. But in the end they actually filmed it in Hoboken."

The waitress came over and instructed them that their menu could be accessed by aiming their cameras at a translucent cube of Lucite embedded with what looked like a digital watermark. "It's contactless," she explained.

"Not if I touch it," Russell said.

The waitress looked baffled. "I'll get you some water," she said. "It was such a surprise," Astrid said. "Seeing you at the Frick, looking at the same painting I'd come to look at. But also, not exactly a surprise. Honestly, it seemed more like a sign. Strangely appropriate that you should be there, admiring Emma. And now that I know what an admirer of hers you are, it seems almost like fate. I'd always thought I would show you the novel when it was done. I kind of fantasized that you'd publish it. Ever since I interviewed you about Jeff all those years ago."

"I find that hard to believe," he said.

"Why? You have an amazing track record as a publisher. You've published some of my favorite contemporary novels."

"So it's my colophon that you fantasized about?"

"Partly, yes," she said. "It's a sexy colophon—the cursive, intertwined *M* and *S*, merging sinuously, with the quill pen hovering above. I'd like to see that on the spine of my first novel. But I also thought we had a certain chemistry. It felt as if something was left hanging between us. I hadn't actually intended that to sound quite so raunchy. I was speaking figuratively."

"I took it as figurative," he said, though in fact a certain image had indeed been conjured by the phrase.

"Take it as you will," she said, shrugging and batting her eyes in a manner that seemed ironic, as if she were italicizing her flirtation, as if she were allowing him to shrug it off, allowing them both to maintain, for the time being, the appearance of a professional relationship. "You're also incredibly good-looking."

"How long have you been working on the novel," Russell said, choosing, at least for now, to maintain appearances.

"On and off, five or six years maybe. But I didn't come up with the idea of the Emma Hamilton narrative until about three years ago. Before that I was flailing with the other story—the aspiring novelist having an affair with the famous novelist. Which was going nowhere, in part because I had no distance from it. It was first person, more like a journal."

Russell had been loath to ask her about autobiographical elements in her novel. But she had opened the door to that question. In general, he despised this line of inquiry, believing that the factual components of a successful novel were less interesting, and relevant, than the structural and stylistic elements. And yet he couldn't suppress his intense curiosity in this case. He wanted to know. He had to admit to himself that his curiosity was tinged with jealousy. He'd thought of himself as the charismatic older man in her life, and yet, if the novelist in the book was based on Astrid, it seemed that he had a powerful competitor. What he would have a harder time articulating or admitting to himself was that beneath the jealousy was a sense that this famous and powerful man's desire for, and possession of, Astrid valorized his own, made her that much more attractive. Assuming, of course, that this aspect of the novel was autobiographical. He didn't care to acknowledge that his jealousy as well as his desire increased proportionately to the illustriousness of his rival. The fact that his competitor might be a man of his own tribe, a man of letters, only amplified the intrigue.

"I thought I detected the lineaments of autobiography in the contemporary chapters."

"Well, yeah. I mean, aren't most first novels basically autofiction?"

Russell vaguely wondered when *autofiction* had replaced *autobiographical fiction*.

"Mine certainly started out that way, I was writing this mushy, formless novel about a struggling young would-be novelist, but then I read *The Volcano Lover* and I became fascinated with Emma. I'd read all of Sontag's criticism, I mean I devoured it, so it was the natural next step to pick up her novel. At first, I was disappointed, it seemed so not the kind of novel you'd expect from reading her criticism—so conventional and naturalistic. Like—'Hello, Sir Walter Scott.' But then I became fascinated by the story. And I started reading everything I could get my hands on about Emma and Hamilton and Nelson. This was maybe the birth of the English tabloid press—chronicling the comings and goings of the war hero and the beautiful actress-model and the happy, titled cuckold husband. Then I read their letters and there was real tenderness and love and lust there. Well, I should say his letters because unfortunately he burned hers. And I thought about scrapping my unfinished novel—I started writing a novel from Emma's point of view. But I also felt like the story had been told so many times. And I lost confidence and stopped. Then about six months later I was channel surfing late at night and I came across *Julie and Julia*, the Nora Ephron film that basically juxtaposes Julia Child's life story with the attempts of struggling young writer Julie Powell, who decides to write a blog about cooking all the recipes in *Mastering the Art of French Cooking*."

"I tried to buy that book," Russell said. "Julie Powell's book."

She looked at him with an air of incredulity. "Get out."

"True. I mean I tried to buy it for publication."

She shook her head. "Another weird coincidence."

"I was the underbidder."

"So you can see how it occurred to me to mash the two different narratives together, the contemporary story framing the historical one."

"I can indeed. And it worked."

"I can't tell you how much it means that you think that."

"You've written a beautiful book."

"So you think the two narratives are balanced? You don't think one is demonstrably stronger?"

"Honestly?"

"Yes, of course," she said, her brow furrowing with worry.

He hadn't really meant to torture her; well, maybe a little.

"I think you were right to feel neither narrative is quite strong enough on its own. . . ."

Her look of concern grew more acute.

"But the two parts make a greater whole. It's a case of one plus one equaling three. Like Lennon and McCartney." He suddenly wondered if she would get that reference, searching his mind for a more contemporary couple. Jagger and Richards might at least have been edgier. But she was nodding, smiling happily. "It's brilliant." There would be time to tell her where the manuscript needed work, where to pare down and where to build up. That could wait.

She stood up and came around the table, leaned down and kissed him, holding his face between her hands, fully engaging his lips and lingering there, probing just slightly with her tongue, transforming a spontaneous gesture into something more deliberate, before finally straightening up and returning to her seat.

He felt as if he needed to say something, but all he could come up with was "Well . . ."

"Sorry," she said.

"No, that's . . . no reason to be sorry."

"Well, I mean, it's not exactly pandemic protocol."

"Oh, that," he said.

The waitress appeared beside the table, providing an escape from further discussion of the kiss.

"We should order," he said.

"I haven't actually looked at the menu," she said.

"Actually, neither have I. Could you just give us a few more minutes?"

"Absolutely," she said. A young Asian woman—but then everyone in Brooklyn was young to Russell—with striking cheekbones that seemed accentuated by the way her hair was shaved on either side of her head.

Russell pointed his camera at the Lucite cube, to no effect.

"Let me try," Astrid said, taking his phone. A moment later she handed it back, the menu having appeared on his screen.

"The burger is really the thing to get here," she said. "It's locally famous."

"I seem to recall the first time we met we had burgers. At the Fatted Calf."

"We did."

The meal, in his memory, had elements of the bawdy dining scene in Tony Richardson's film of *Tom Jones*. The two of them eating the dripping burgers with their hands, Astrid tossing innuendo and lusty looks across the table, at one point sucking the ketchup off his fingers. That had been a near miss. Hadn't she suggested getting a hotel room? Or had he just added that detail later? He was almost sure that she had. Would ordering the burger now send a signal, cross a line? Was he ready to do so? There was something messy and primal about eating grilled meat with your hands. The juices dripping on fingers, on chins.

"Okay, burger it is."

She waved to the waitress. "Two burgers," she said. "Rare. And we'll share a wedge salad."

Russell admired her confidence, her inclination to take charge. He rather liked the idea of himself as the passive recipient of her attentions and actions, given his ambivalence—and uncertainty—about his own intentions. It gave him a certain layer of deniability, if only in his own mind. He wanted to tell himself this was all a harmless flirtation, a form of Viagra for his ego. As opposed to the actual Cialis he'd taken three hours ago.

But he felt obliged to assert himself, too. "Could we get two glasses of the Tribut Chablis. And with the burgers . . ." He scanned the list, which was short enough to yield its treasures quickly. "A bottle of the 2015 Pégäu Châteauneuf du Pape."

"Yes, sir."

"The burgers need a big bold wine."

"That sounds right," she said.

As they waited for the food, the conversation took a turn toward a neutral topic—their current reading, their mutual opinions of Jenny Offill, Rachel Cusk, Lucy Ellmann.

They'd both read advance copies of David Mitchell's *Utopia Avenue*. Russell said, "I liked it, I thought it worked, though I'm generally not a big fan of the supernatural."

Astrid remarked: "I hear you, but the naturalistic, quasi-historical sixties stuff kind of rang false to me. I mean, really, all the rock and rollers in the book are so nice, so good-natured, even the real ones who make cameos: Leonard Cohen, Janis Joplin, Jerry Garcia. Everyone's just so earnest and adorable. There's this saccharine kind of tone, it sure as hell ain't rock and roll. I kept waiting for Lou Reed or Keith Richards to show up and vomit on someone."

Russell laughed. While this critique hadn't occurred to him when he was reading, he found himself agreeing retrospectively.

"Tell me," she said. "What were your epiphanic books? The ones that made you want to do what you do?"

"I wanted to be a poet after I read Dylan Thomas. In high school I read everything from Chaucer to Lowell and I wrote a lot of very soulful poetry about my many unrequited loves. Then I read *A Portrait of the Artist as a Young Man* and I switched to fiction. I started writing short stories. When I got to Brown I took a class on Joyce and I read *Ulysses* for the first time and I didn't see how you could take the novel any further than that. Plus, I met Jeff, as you know, and when I compared my stories to his I decided that I was probably more plausible as a Maxwell Perkins than as a Hemingway or Fitzgerald."

The Chablis arrived. Russell took a sip and pronounced it acceptable: crisp, cold, dry and flinty.

"You know as well as anyone, it takes a ridiculous amount of conviction and belief in yourself to decide you're a novelist and commit yourself utterly when no one really cares. The world doesn't need another first novel or, at least, it doesn't know it does, until someone like Sally Rooney comes out of nowhere and shows us all over again that we do. I don't know, maybe it was a failure of courage. I kept writing through college, but in the end, I decided I could contribute more as an editor than as a writer."

"Well, I can't help being glad about that."

"I have no regrets. At least, not about my choice of career."

"I had a lot of doubts over the last decade. Like constant, existential doubt. Like, who the fuck do you think you are? Who gave you permission to write a novel?"

"What was the book that started it all for you. That made you want to write?"

"Definitely *House of Mirth*. I read it in high school, though it wasn't assigned. This guy I liked, really smart, bohemian, handsome—he told me to read Wharton. And that was it. I wanted to write novels, like Edith. This guy, he edited our little high school magazine. I was on the staff and I had this huge crush on him. I'll never forget the way he described Wharton—he said she was like Henry James with balls. At the time I had no idea who Henry James was, but after reading both I gotta say I think it's a great description."

"It's perfect. Who was this guy?"

"Mark Witjkowski. My first big crush. I thought he'd grow up to be our next Hemingway or Bukowski. Died in a car crash his sophomore year at Williams. Drunk. I think part of what I felt for him I transferred to your friend Jeff a few years later. Even though I never met him. Something about his writing, the author's photo."

"I'm sensing a theme—older male literary mentors."

"You're talking about the novel."

"It certainly looms pretty large there."

"That's true," she said, with an impish expression. She leaned forward and stared into his eyes. "Do I sense a question hidden within that statement?"

Russell shrugged. "Obviously I'm curious."

"You want to know if there's a real-life model for Caleb?"

Normally he didn't want to know these things—didn't want the distraction of factual details. He was no great fan of romans à clef—he thought fiction should stand on its own. He sort of hated himself for being so curious now.

"Certainly, the question is going to arise."

"And how do you think I should respond?" She was playing with him. "Should I come clean?"

Grinning, he said, "As your prospective publisher, I should probably be armed with that information, so that I can properly advise you."

"Yes, I suppose that's true." She paused, took a sip of her wine. "It's Philip Roth."

"Indeed." He nodded. "That had occurred to me as a possibility."

"He came to do a reading at Wesleyan. I managed to catch his eye at the reception after the reading. Flirting ensued, exchange of contact info. Emails, phone calls. A meeting in the city. Even if I hadn't written about it you could probably imagine the rest. Eventual rendezvous at his house in Connecticut. Trips to Manhattan. Mutual admiration, though with a different basis in each case."

"The portrait is a fairly positive one. You seem to retain a fondness for him."

"You mean he doesn't come off as a raging misogynist? All I can tell you is he was, on balance, very sweet and thoughtful. A narcissist? Probably. Self-important? Definitely. But I never encountered any misogyny."

"How long did it go on?"

"We flirted for a year before we did it. And then, together for six months, though not, it turns out, exclusively."

The salad arrived; Astrid attacked it with a knife and shoveled half onto his bread plate. He was not a fan of salad at the beginning of the meal, but he decided it would sound pretentious to say so, and that was the last note he wished to convey tonight.

They talked about the tedium of recent months, the brutality of the police response to the recent protests, Fiona Apple's "Fetch the Bolt Cutters," and the TV adaptation of *Normal People*.

"Hell, I thought it was better than the book," Astrid said. "I was positively dripping after that sex scene in the last episode. I hit PAUSE and ripped my boyfriend's clothes off with my teeth."

Registering Russell's expression of surprise, she said, "Oh, cutie, I'm sorry. You didn't know I had a boyfriend. I guess it never came up."

It was true—Russell was caught entirely off guard by the revelation of a boyfriend. It made him think that he'd misread all her signals. It certainly simplified things.

"Don't worry, that doesn't mean that I don't want to fuck you," she said. "Just that it's not necessarily going to be spontaneous."

The waitress arrived with the bottle of red wine, opening it and pouring a taste for Russell, who nodded. She poured out the glasses and cleared the salad plates. When she was back inside, Russell said, "Forgive me, but this is all . . . a bit new to me. I've been married for almost forty years."

"And you mean to tell me you've been faithful that whole time?"

"Not entirely."

"Tell me."

"I've had a couple of . . ." He groped for a word that was accurate, that encompassed two quite different situations. "Dalliances."

She tilted her head back and laughed. "Oh my God. Did you really say that? *Dalliances.* That's so quaint." After another fit of laughter she said, "It sounds like having sex with white gloves on."

Trina Cox and Trish, his former assistant. Weird, the similarity of the names. The lawyer he hired in his failed takeover of Corbin, Dern, and the assistant turned lover.

"I assure you no white gloves were involved."

"Any leather, latex? What's your fetish?"

"I'm afraid you would find me boring."

"I doubt that."

The waitress deposited their burgers on the table.

"The first time I ever saw you eat a burger I decided you would be a good lover," she said.

"Now I'm going to be completely self-conscious about eating this one."

"Just enjoy it," she said, lifting her own to her mouth, swirling her tongue around her lips, and taking a large bite.

At a loss for words, he lifted his burger to his mouth and bit into it.

"Yum," she said, licking her lips.

"If you're trying to turn me on it's working."

"Good."

Russell slugged back half his red wine—like a man putting out a fire, he thought to himself. Or else a man pouring gasoline on one.

18

THESE TWO SONS of bitches were from the Department of Transportation. To Storey they were all cops, figures in uniforms and badges wielding arbitrary authority over her attempt to reopen her business—the Department of Health, the State Liquor Authority, the fire department. She hated anyone in uniform these days. She'd been hassled by all of them in the last few days since outdoor dining had been approved, and now these weasels from the DOT were telling her that she had to take down part of the sidewalk dining structure that had been ingeniously erected by her dishwasher's cousin out of two-by-sixes, plywood and plexiglass. He'd constructed planters at either end and painted it a cheerful periwinkle blue.

One was a pudgy woman with an Eastern European accent and the other was a slight white guy with a clipboard and a Napoleon complex. The woman was wearing a navy-blue jumpsuit, bulging in all the wrong places, that may or may not have been a uniform, whereas the man was wearing khaki pants and a short-sleeved button-down white shirt and thick black glasses, the kind that might have looked cool on a twenty-five-year-old with a beard.

"You've exceeded the allowance for your frontage," the guy was saying.

"The fire department was here yesterday and they said we were fine."

"The fire department doesn't have jurisdiction over the streets and sidewalks," the woman said.

"That's for the DOT to decide," the man said.

"Your structure exceeds the statutory limit by five feet," the woman said.

"What am I supposed to do, saw the end off?" She'd basically lose one cubicle—a four-top. And one-fifth of her seating—and her potential revenue.

"Five feet. That would bring you into compliance."

"Do you people have any idea how much friggin' money I've lost these last three months. Or how hard it's going to be to break even with four tables? Does Bill de Blasio really want to put us out of business—or just turn us all into Republicans?"

Alex came running from inside, sensing danger. Her manager-beverage director was much more diplomatic than she was.

"Can I offer either of you a cool drink?" Alex asked.

The woman looked at the man, who seemed skeptical. "I might take a Coke," the man said.

"Anything for you, ma'am?"

"Maybe Diet Coke."

"Coming right up," he said.

"They want us to take five feet off the structure," Storey said.

"I think you're needed in the kitchen," Alex said. "Let me take care of this."

There was no one in the kitchen at the moment, but Storey gratefully seized the opportunity to escape. Maybe Alex could smooth talk them into some kind of accommodation.

She had never been a big fan of the city bureaucracy—the health and code inspectors who hassled restaurants for a living—but after her experience with the cops last month she'd become phobic about authority figures.

The only thing that had gotten her through the last few months was the PPP loan that her dad had negotiated for her. It had allowed her to keep her employees paid, though front-of-the-house took a big hit without their tips, and to cover most of her expenses, and her dad's friend Kip Taylor, who was her biggest investor, had negotiated the landlord down to 50 percent of the prepandemic rent, through September. She started doing takeout with a limited menu after closing for two weeks: lamb burgers, chicken potpies, osso bucco. Dishes that could travel. Comfort food for these discomfiting times. It had been a slow start, but they'd managed to build a local following. But not exactly what she envisioned when she'd dreamed of opening her own place. Hospitality was a calling, and it was about the welcome and the setting and the service as well as the food. Not about sending burgers out into the void. She didn't just want to feed people. She wanted to create new dishes, reinvent old ones, inspire and delight. If she could she would feed the world, but she believed she was doing something important in her little corner of it, something heartfelt and genuine, arousing to the senses and the soul. It was a calling. Not like the priesthood, maybe, but not so unlike that, either.

Alex swaggered into the kitchen. "I got rid of them."

"What about our five feet of shed?"

"Not a problem. But you owe me two hundred dollars from petty cash."

It took her a moment. "You bribed them?"

He shrugged. "Let's not use loaded terminology."

"And they just took the money? You can actually do that? That's, like, a *thing*?"

"It's New York City, babe. It's always been a thing."

Somehow Storey was amazed. This hadn't occurred to her as an option. She'd sort of thought of bribery as a feature of an older, dirtier, black-and-white New York. She wasn't sure whether to be indignant about the fact of corruption or thankful that the possibility still existed. She was grateful that Alex was less naïve about this sort of thing than she was. She threw her arms around him, almost tearful with gratitude. She was lucky to have Alex working with her, not least because Mingus had been missing in action lately. She didn't blame him; he'd been through a punishing trauma. But she wanted things to be the way they used to be between them, and she was terrified they might not be. She felt acutely her inability to reach him where it hurt. She understood that nothing she could say or do was going to help at this point. She could only hope that if he started writing again he might be able to write his way through this experience to the other side.

19

THEY WERE SITTING at a sidewalk table at Anton's on Hudson Street. It still seemed miraculous, this ritual they'd once taken for granted, a meal in public with a friend. Miraculous, too, that Washington was out of the hospital and up and about. Skinnier, for sure, looking more fashionable than gaunt.

"Well, the guilt should be ameliorated by your marital history. I don't mean to dredge up unpleasant subjects, but Corrine did it to you."

"Do I really need to tell you that two wrongs don't make a right."

"You are such a fucking Boy Scout."

"No, I'm just . . . I don't know. I'm contemplating the situation. I like the flirtation. It makes me feel alive. Maybe that's enough. I don't see you running around anymore. Correct me if I'm wrong, but haven't you been on the straight and narrow for years since you got caught with Casey? Didn't you choose fidelity? Or have you been holding out on me? Why are you so eager to see me fuck around when you've retired?"

"Maybe that's why. Maybe I need a surrogate. I miss the game. A libido is a terrible thing to waste. But I had to choose, you know. I knew that if I were caught even one more time, my marriage would be over for good. Veronica made that very clear. And I realized I didn't want my marriage to be over. I wanted to stay together for the kids. Yeah, that tired old cliché. But I felt it. Faced with the realities of separation and impending divorce, I realized I didn't want to be on the outside. When Veronica threw me out I realized I loved my marriage more than I ever knew. I made a promise. And I kept it. Not that it's been easy. Sometimes it's been very motherfucking hard."

"I want to stay married, too."

"I know you do. But hey, unlike me, you've got credit in the bank. You've virtually got a free pass."

"I'm not sure it works that way."

"On the other front, I'm not so sure you should publish her novel. That could lead to some serious complications."

"That had occurred to me."

"Do you think your amorous interest may have colored your judgment of the book. Of its quality?"

"I don't think so."

"You wanted to like it."

"Yes, of course. But I was surprised by how good it was. Would you do me a favor and take a look?"

"Sure, I don't have nearly enough manuscripts on my nightstand."

"Just read a few chapters."

"Yeah, of course."

"She's the real deal. I think it will get picked up."

"Doesn't have to be by you."

"Now I'm really confused."

"You're wondering if she would be interested in sleeping with you if you weren't in a position to publish her book?"

"I'm wondering why I chose to confide in you."

"Because you know I know whereof I fucking speak."

"I'll figure it out."

"Either that or you will let circumstances carry you. I know you. What you really want is to be seduced, to cede responsibility."

"I'm glad you know what I want," Russell said.

A cheer rose from across the street, where a crowd seethed in front of the White Horse Tavern, the famous last stop of Dylan

Thomas, who downed eighteen whiskeys not long before dying in St. Vincent's Hospital, which had once been a few blocks from here before being converted into luxury condos.

"Looks like a super-spreader event over there," Russell said.

"The masses are desperate to commingle and commune again."

"That was one of the first pilgrimages I made when I moved to the city. My sophomore year, I came to the city for the weekend, stayed with Kelton Thomas—"

"That preppy dick."

"Took the subway from West 72nd to Sheridan Square. I wanted to commune with Dylan Thomas and Jack Kerouac. As far as I could tell it was just a bunch of tourists like me. I visited the Lion's Head and the Cedar Tavern that same night. Both gone now."

"That wasn't the original Cedar Tavern you visited—the one that Pollock and de Kooning and Rothko hung out in—that one was demolished in '64."

"There didn't seem to be any abstract expressionists hanging out."

"What was this place before? I feel like I've been here when it was another establishment."

"I think it was a restaurant, but I forget what it was."

"What was this place before," Washington asked the waitress, who was refilling their wineglasses.

She shrugged. "Sorry, I only started here last week."

She doesn't yet know the city is haunted, teeming with ghosts, Russell thought—that there have been dozens of restaurants in this space. And tens of thousands of diners, people to whom each one was special as the site of a first date, an anniversary, a birthday, an illicit rendezvous, a breakup, a reunion. Regulars, who felt more at home here than in their own small apartments, served by familiar faces, dining with friends among animated strangers—neighbors who mourned the demise of each one. And the people whose dreams and savings were invested in each of these incarnations, some of whom prospered and more of whom failed. And now, as the city struggled to awaken from its coma, hundreds and even thousands more would disappear forever, living only in the memories of their patrons, who would someday say—What was the name of that Italian place on Hudson Street? The one with the David Salle etching behind the bar? That dive bar on 9th Street that had two coke dealers and only one bathroom? The twenty-four-hour French place in the Meatpacking District?

"Remember Billy's?" Russell said.

"God, yes. How many hangovers did we treat with Bloody Marys at those tables."

"How much of Corbin, Dern's money did we spend?"

"You were always known as a virtuoso of the expense account."

"I took Avery there the week before it closed," Washington said. "Still can't believe he's gone."

"Poor bastard. Did he ever turn in that novel you commissioned?"

"It wasn't a novel. More of a memoir. But no. Not so far. We're still going through his papers. We'll put something together."

"Alone at the end." The writer had died in the early weeks of the pandemic, attached to a ventilator in a room at Lenox Hill Hospital.

"We were all afraid that was going to be your fate."

"I've got a few more good years."

The waitress arrived with their main courses, the smell of grilled beef and the sight of her youthful flesh silencing them for an interval.

"I wonder if it would be better," Washington said, after she'd gone, "if desire faded with age."

"It probably does—eventually."

"Consummate your infatuation while you still harbor it. But forget about the book. If it's as good as you think, someone else will publish it."

"By the way, what's up with Mingus's book," Russell asked, approaching a fraught subject sideways. For "book" substitute "head."

"I don't think he's writing much at the moment. I'd say he has a case of PTSD, and I'm not talking about the pandemic."

"I know Storey's really worried about him."

"What was it Fitzgerald said—'Begin with an individual, and before you know it, you have created a type; begin with a type, and you find you have created nothing.' Right now Mingus is seeing everyone as a type. Even Storey. He's got to move beyond types, so to speak. As a person and as a writer. He's got to start recognizing individuals again."

"Is he up to it?"

"If he ever wants to be happy and fulfilled, he'd better be."

Increasingly, Russell found himself obsessed with his phone, attuned to the chime which signaled the arrival of a text. Thinking about her all too often. When he was supposed to be working. When he was supposed to be reading. When he was drinking, most of all. Becoming more and more enthralled with each glass of wine at dinner. And since Corrine had given up drinking after having COVID, Russell was inevitably drinking an entire bottle with dinner. Since the lockdown started, that had been his routine, and while he told himself that at some point he should probably moderate it, he saw no reason to do so anytime soon, given the current circumstances. Being buzzed facilitated his flights of erotic fantasy, most of which featured Astrid. It had been years since he'd had a specific object of carnal desire, contenting himself with occasional online forays to YouPorn and equally occasional bouts of marital sex, which was pleasurable enough, although it was the opposite of exciting. They had a sexual routine which had been constructed of elements pleasing to both, although it was impossible to deny that routine was the enemy of passion.

He felt himself in a heightened state of awareness throughout the day, energized by her texts, by a sense of erotic possibility. He hadn't had these kinds of feelings in years, not since his fling with Trish, who was briefly his assistant a couple of decades ago.

Somehow, in the late nineties, it hadn't seemed quite so inappropriate. He'd felt guilty as hell for being unfaithful to Corrine, but he hadn't felt like a sexual predator, like an exploiter of a power imbalance. Nor did he want to feel that way now—though he felt, if anything, more like the pursued than the pursuer in the current instance, Astrid seeming far more confident, and experienced and determined, than he. Which, he had to admit, turned him on. But Washington was right: If he published her, he really couldn't sleep with her. Which posed a dilemma. Not that they were in imminent danger of consummation, given the protocols of the pandemic and their mutually coupled status.

The glimmer of a solution arrived two weeks later when she called him at the office.

"I have a confession to make," she said, eventually.

He felt a tingling on the back of his neck, a flush of dread which must have colored his face.

"Yeah?"

"My agent wants to auction the book."

His first reaction was indignation. By her own admission her agent hadn't really been excited about the book until she heard about Russell's interest. But he quickly grasped the redeeming feature of the situation. If someone else bought the book, then the decision was made for him—and he would be free to pursue his infatuation with Astrid.

"Don't be mad."

"I'm not mad. Your agent is looking out for your best interests. And as someone who cares about you, I appreciate that. It's the smart thing to do."

"Wow. That's so . . . kind of you. I thought you'd be really upset."

Russell felt almost guilty about the subterranean motive beneath his ostensible magnanimity. But there was also a certain satisfaction in doing the right thing for the wrong reason.

"I want what's best for you and your book. And that may be publishing with me. I'm going to make the case that going with a larger publisher for a bigger advance may not necessarily be in your best interest, that I can do better for you and your career in the long run. But we'll see what happens."

"I'm going to do another draft first, so if you have any thoughts . . ."

"I have notes. Which I can send along."

"Really? Even if we don't end up publishing together? I wish I could kiss you and squeeze you and do filthy things to you right now."

"Rain check."

"When are we going to see each other?"

"Sooner or later the circumstance will present itself." At the moment the situation was out of his hands. The hotels were all closed—except for those that had taken in the homeless. Business travel wasn't happening. Spouses—and boyfriends—weren't going anywhere. Opportunity was scarce. On the other hand, he had to admit he kind of liked the slow buildup. He wasn't in a hurry. He hadn't even, if he were honest with himself, quite made the decision to cross that line. And, at any rate, until the auction happened, he would not know for certain whether he would be her publisher or not. Nor, for that matter, whether her interest in him would fade once she had a contract.

20

CORRINE'S LEAVE OF absence had extended to four months. She'd been on some Zooms, on the phone, putting out fires and giving advice, but she'd transferred the running of the organization, for the moment, to Zara Swift, her associate director. The need was greater than ever, the closure and partial reopening of restaurants immensely complicating their food supply. Everything was complicated. It was exhausting. And she wasn't up to shouldering all of it just yet. She felt as if she woke up in the morning with half of the energy she'd had six months ago, that sleep, far from recharging her, made her more weary. And most mornings she woke up dizzy. Typing was more difficult; she made constant mistakes in her emails and texts.

Waking early one morning, she went out to get bagels and the papers while Russell slept. She was standing in line when she noticed a young couple eyeing her feet and whispering. When she looked down she saw that she had mismatched shoes, a black Rothy's flat on one foot and a white running shoe on the other.

She started meditating in the mornings, and, on the advice of the doctor, she tried to walk two miles every day. One Sunday morning she walked west on 10th Street and paused on the far side of Broadway, staring at the open door of Grace Church, which seemed to beckon to her. The sign outside told her that the Sunday service was about to begin. She walked in and sat down in the second-to-last pew. The liturgy was familiar to her from childhood. For the first time in what seemed a very long time she felt oriented and safe, anchored by the familiar smell of the varnished wooden pews and the old hymnals. She went back the next Sunday, and afterward, when Russell asked her where she'd been, she said she'd been out walking.

"You'll bounce back," Russell assured her as he sliced a bagel with one of his fearsome-looking German knives.

"How do you know that?" Sometimes his optimism was really annoying. "I've become an idiot."

"Just give yourself time. Being out East will help. Sunshine, fresh air."

They were going out to the Hamptons next week. And while she was looking forward to it, she had doubts about the therapeutic benefits. On the other hand, it would certainly be less of a social circus out there than it had been in recent years. No big cocktail parties, no charity galas, no movie premieres. Lisa had left many messages saying how dull it was and asking when she was coming out. Many of their friends had moved out there in March, but they were all making a point of their abstinence from social life—there was a kind of virtue-signaling competition going on, although she knew that many were forming bubbles, small cells of friends who got together outdoors to drink and dine. Those who were quick enough had bought patio heaters to facilitate spring gatherings, but they had apparently become impossible to find by the end of April. She supposed they would find their bubble.

Kip Taylor had offered them his guesthouse in Sagaponack for a nominal fee. Kip, who was seldom on the wrong end of a deal, had managed to rent a lavish compound back in late March, before the duration of the pandemic became obvious, having ceded the use of his oceanfront house in Southampton to his wife in the negotiations over division of marital assets.

Kip's guesthouse was a more-than-comfortable shingle-style cottage with its own pool, a miniature sibling of Kip's enormous mansion, full of blandly tasteful furniture from Restoration Hardware, set a hundred yards away amid seven acres of velvety lawn, enclosed by privet hedges. The compound was a short walk from Gibson Beach, surrounded by similar homes constructed in recent years on what had once been corn and potato fields. It was a serene retreat, except on Tuesdays, when an army of workers with rackety grooming machinery descended on the compound to tend to the lawn and the gardens. All in all they felt incredibly lucky, although life in the Hamptons was more constricted than at any time since they'd started coming some twenty-five years ago. Restaurants were closed, except for takeout, and the social events which had filled their evenings in years past were all suspended until further notice. Happily, the din of construction, also a feature of life in this seaside paradise, had ceased, and with an offshore breeze they could often hear the ocean waves breaking on the beach. And the traffic which normally choked the two-lane roads in this formerly bucolic landscape had evaporated.

Rusticating New Yorkers could be counted upon to resist constraints on their social life, and, after an initial period of dutiful quarantine, small dinner parties started breaking out all over the East End of Long Island. By the time Russell and Corrine arrived, there seemed to be a sense, for some of their friends, those who weren't actually terrified of the virus, of *enough already*—an impatience with the rules of lockdown. Not long after they arrived, Kip invited Russell to a Chainsmokers concert on the beach in Southampton, but Corrine was adamant that Russell not attend. The fact that the event was for charity, with tickets costing up to twenty-five thousand dollars, seemed to serve as a social justification for many of the attendees to flout the rules of social distancing and common sense, although the concert, dubbed Safe & Sound, was billed as a drive-in experience with guests sitting in their cars. Russell wasn't particularly passionate about the music of the Chainsmokers and deferred to his wife's wishes. He did keep up, to some extent, with contemporary music, but he tended to favor guitar rock—bands like the 1975 and Cage the Elephant.

Kip took one of his girls to the concert; the next day someone posted a video of the two of them dancing in what looked like a mosh pit in front of the stage, which eventually landed him on Page Six, along with the Winklevoss twins and Ken Griffin, the hedge fund manager. In the days following the concert, social media and the mainstream press were universal in their condemnation of the event. The fact that David Solomon, the CEO of Goldman Sachs, aka DJ D-Sol, had DJed an opening thirty-minute set only served to corroborate the narrative of insensitive plutocrats partying through the pandemic.

His conscience clear, Russell felt gloriously lazy as he and Corrine basked in the warm, chlorine-tinged air, surrounded by thickets of blue hydrangea, looking out over the blue-green vista of lawn and pools.

"I mean, seriously, what were they thinking. Please tell me that your boys' wine dinner tonight is outside."

"It is," Russell said, righteously. Kip was throwing a dinner for the wine group, all of whom, with the exception of Chef Michael, had houses out here.

At seven-thirty he walked across the lawn to the back patio of the main house where a table was set for six and a uniformed waiter was filling water glasses. The place settings were four or five feet apart. Kip appeared in the doorway with Dale Cornell, who was wearing a black Pink Floyd *Dark Side of the Moon* T-shirt over cargo shorts and holding two wine bottles.

"You didn't have to dress up for me," Russell said to Dale.

"Ah, my neighbor," Kip said.

"Your tenant," Russell responded.

"Do you raise any crops here?" Dale asked, examining the green expanse.

"We sow doubt and confusion," Russell said.

"Always in demand."

"Who's coming?"

"Everybody but Chef Michael. He's trying to keep his empire afloat."

"Speaking of which..."

Dale and Kip exchanged a meaningful look.

"What?" Russell asked.

Kip looked back through the open door. "Word on the street, Provenza's in big trouble."

"How so?" Russell felt a guilty thrill at this news about his recent nemesis—the Obama hater.

"Most of his net worth is in this office tower in Chicago. He lost his major tenant at the start of the pandemic. And now it looks like he's going into foreclosure."

Bobby Cohen appeared in the doorway, trailed by Mickey Perlmutter. "Gents, good to see you. Why the long faces?"

"We were just talking about Tony," Kip said.

"I heard," Bobby said, with the air of someone who is never surprised by bad news. "The CMBS came due."

"The what?" Russell asked.

"Collateralized mortgage-backed securities. A very convenient but risky way to finance property. The loan's due and he can't pay. And it's not like a bank loan—you can't negotiate your way out."

Tony appeared, grinning, kissing cheeks, a ritual that always left Russell uncomfortable.

"Well, boys. You will all be kissing my ass when you see my contribution to tonight's festivities." He placed his leather wine tote on the table, unzipped the top and slowly withdrew a bottle; although the label was slightly scuffed and tattered, they could all see what it was—the most venerated label on the planet. It was a moment before Kip noticed the vintage tag.

"Oh my God, is that the '34? Are you fucking kidding me?"

"Yes indeed," Tony said. "Nineteen thirty-four Romanée-Conti. The ne plus ultra."

Under the circumstances, Russell was not about to mention that the 1945 might be rarer. All he could say was "Holy shit!" He suddenly felt bad for feeling a little glimmer of schadenfreude a moment ago.

"You boys remember when I bought this, direct from the cellar of Madame Lalou Bize-Leroy herself. Had to employ all my legendary charm to convince her to sell it."

"Tony," Kip said. "That's incredibly generous. I mean—"

"Hey, who else am I going to drink it with? Who else would appreciate it more than you guys."

"Well, you could sell it and buy a BMW," Bobby said.

"Hey, I've got my Lambo. Beamers are a dime a dozen."

Rufus arrived just as they were sitting down, bearing a bottle of 1996 Montrachet and advance hardcover copies of a book called *Can't Slow Down: How 1984 Became Pop's Blockbuster Year*, occasioning murmurs of delight and dissent.

"Oh, man," said Dale. "This should spur some debate."

"1984?" said Bobby. "Really?"

Gradually, with the consumption of the first flight of wines, the general mood became sanguine, and, with the second flight, positively buoyant. Tony's wine consultant Jonah acted as sommelier, carefully pouring and refilling. The wines, except for one tired, oxidized bottle, were almost uniformly excellent, and Kip's chef was doing a great job. As usual there was talk of deals, of the pandemic, of friends and acquaintances who'd caught the virus, who'd gone to absurd lengths to avoid it, about a recent large garden party of Republicans in Southampton who'd flouted the proscription of large gatherings and scorned the use of masks. The event had drawn the kind of condemnation that the Chainsmokers event had—although not necessarily from the same quarters, the concert having been heavily populated by Democrats.

When Jonah asked whether Tony would like him to open the precious bottle, Tony announced that he alone would open it. Jonah stepped back abruptly from the table. A reverential hush descended over the group as Tony slowly and surgically removed the cork from the sacred bottle, a two-part process that involved the insertion of a corkscrew, followed by a two-pronged tool which eased the ancient cork away from the glass. The extraction eventually proved successful, and Tony held up the wet brown cork for inspection.

"Yep," he said, "fully branded, Romanée-Conti 1934." A branded cork of the appropriate age was one of the tests of a genuine bottle.

Tony handed the bottle to Jonah, who cradled it in both hands as he made his way around the table, pouring an inch of the precious liquid into the bulbous glasses in front of them. The color was beautiful, a translucent crimson, tinged with a faint hint of amber at the edge.

With a sense of exhilarating expectation, Russell swirled the wine, and raised the glass to his nose, as did the others. He had read tasting notes about this wine, including one that said the perfume of the bouquet infused an entire room. In this case, Russell had to put his nose directly into the glass before he got any sense of bouquet. A hush had fallen over the table, the others, too, having nosed the wine and detected what Russell had— the faint but unmistakable smell of TCA, a moldy fungal aroma, otherwise known as cork taint. The wine was corked.

No one knew where to look. Certainly no one wanted to speak, to be the first to acknowledge the disaster.

Russell looked across the table at Tony, who appeared as if he might vomit at any moment. Finally, he put down his glass and looked around the table.

"Well, ain't that a kick in the head."

No one had even tasted the wine yet. Dale took a sip. "If you get past the nose there's a pretty amazing wine there," he said.

Everyone followed his lead. And he was correct, if somewhat optimistic, in his appraisal. It was possible to detect traces of the greatness that would have been there in the glass if not for a fungus that had infected the bark of the cork tree in Portugal in the early years of the Depression. To dispel the gloom, Kip had Jonah dig a 1985 Romanée-Conti out of the cellar, and while the wine was very good, it couldn't quite wash away the tainted taste of its illustrious predecessor. Dale was the first to leave, citing an early Zoom meeting. His Uber had arrived. He slowly lifted himself up from his chair and, when Tony rose beside him, wrapped him in a bear hug, a gesture that seemed all the more poignant given the history of tension between them.

"Take good care of yourself," he said.

"Caution has never been my strong suit," Tony said.

Perlmutter took the cue: "Got my trainer at six-thirty," he said, rising from the table.

"And you've got your wife in about thirty minutes," Kip said.

"Duty calls."

"I think the word you're looking for is *booty*," Bobby said.

"Next time *you* bring the '34," Tony said, slapping Perlmutter on the back.

"Soon as I can find one."

"There's at least two or three more legit bottles out there," Tony said.

A few minutes later Bobby took his leave, promising that he would host the next dinner at his house, and Rufus wobbled off into the night.

Tony stayed on for the duration of a cigar and a glass of Chartreuse, uncharacteristically subdued, listening to Kip, with Russell's encouragement, talk about his love life.

"Gentlemen, I think I shall bid you farewell," Tony said, rising unsteadily.

They both stood.

"Are you driving?" Kip asked. "Is that wise?"

"It's, like, five minutes on the back roads," Tony said.

"Let my caretaker drive you. You can get the car tomorrow."

"I'm fine. I'm an excellent driver. Don't let anyone tell you otherwise."

Later Russell would recall this remark; for the moment he and Tony exchanged an awkward sideways hug.

"I'm worried about him," Kip said, after he was gone.

"I don't know. He seemed okay, maybe a little more subdued than usual."

"Exactly. When have we ever seen him subdued? And the '34 RC? I mean, that was crazy. Why now?"

Russell's phone dinged with a text notification.

You still there?

"It's Dale," Russell said.

"I'll call him."

Kip put the phone on the table on speaker.

"It's Kip and Russell on speaker."

"Just you two?"

"Yeah. What's up?"

"Did Tony drive home?"

"Yeah. A few minutes ago."

"That's not good."

"It's only a few miles. I offered him a ride."

"I don't know, I hope I'm wrong, but I have this feeling. I think he was saying goodbye tonight. I mean, he's on the verge of bankruptcy and he opens a bottle of wine worth sixty K?"

"He's always lived dangerously," Kip said. "But yeah, it occurred to me, too. I'll give him a call."

Kip hung up; the call to Tony went to voicemail, as it did again ten minutes later.

Russell walked back across the lawn a little after midnight; he didn't really know Tony well enough to judge his frame of mind.

Corrine was awake, reading in bed.

"How was your dinner?"

"A little weird," he said, recounting the highlights of the evening.

Kip called the next morning. "He drove the Lambo into a tree about two miles from here on Sagg Main."

Russell wondered briefly at Kip's specificity, wondered, as he processed the fact of Tony's death, whether the distance and location were significant details.

The *New York Post* reported the next day that the car was going approximately 150 miles an hour when it hit the tree.

21

Storey was losing money on the outdoor dining and takeout and didn't know how much longer she could keep operating at a loss. Between the governor and the mayor there seemed to be no agreement about reopening indoor dining, and not even any agreement about who had the authority. Everyone hated de Blasio, it was one of the few things Republicans and Democrats could agree on—that topic could save a dinner party. Cuomo had become a sort of hero of the pandemic, with his daily news briefings, but Storey wasn't that impressed. It was easy to look smarter and less crazy than Trump. But that doesn't make you Marcus Aurelius.

"Why don't you write something," Mingus said one night as they lay in bed watching *Palm Springs*. "Like an op-ed."

"Who's going to publish an op-ed by me?"

"Maybe you could team up with a famous chef. Someone you know. That could give it more impact. Older established chef, young up-and-coming chef, speaking out together on their shared struggle."

This was actually not a bad idea. She was grateful for his input, grateful for any kind of positivity from him, since he'd spent a lot of time wallowing in self-pity and anger after his encounter with the cops. But he'd become much more affectionate and attentive in recent days. He said he appreciated the way she'd tried to support him in recent weeks. It was a welcome metamorphosis.

"Thanks, baby." She kissed him, getting a hit of musky THC.

"I can give you a hand."

"I would love that. You're the writer in the family." She suddenly wondered if *family* was too much. If she were going to scare him. He could be skittish that way.

"Your dad should be able to help place it."

Was that his way of reminding her who her real family was?

"Probably. Hey, I know, what about Suzie Zhou? Maybe I could get her to be my coauthor."

Suzie qualified as a famous chef. She'd worked her way up through the kitchens of Per Se and Eleven Madison, started her own restaurant in the aftermath of the great recession, picked up her first Michelin star a few years ago. Storey had spent a year and a half in her kitchen, working her way up to sous-chef; Suzie had encouraged her to open her own place and advised her throughout.

Suzie loved the idea. "Hey, let's give it a try. A bunch of us are planning a lawsuit against the state. Anything to get these motherfuckers off the dime."

More satisfying even than the feeling that she was engaging a righteous cause was the pleasure of working with her boyfriend, who came out of a long torpor to help her with the composition. He added a layer of stylish irony and sarcasm, which she liked a lot. In fact, the first paragraph was essentially his. He threw himself into it with genuine indignation.

"Do you realize that as of yesterday," he said, "a thousand restaurants have officially closed in New York City, and a lot more have probably closed without notice. I mean, this is a fucking apocalypse."

He did the initial research and passed along figures and quotations. She wrote a couple of paragraphs to follow his lede, and then, when she got stuck, he basically dictated another paragraph.

"Can you believe de Blasio," he said, "saying that dining out is 'a very optional activity.' What does he think about all the unemployed restaurant workers—that eating is an optional activity? So fucking myopic, to see this only from the consumption side."

She typed as Mingus ranted. She loved his passion—loved the fact that he seemed passionate about something, anything, again. And that it was her cause.

She sent a draft to Suzie, who sent it back with additions and comments. Mingus then rewrote it again and finally judged it ready for print. There might have been a time when she would have felt resentful about Mingus's co-opting a project of hers, but in fact it had been his idea to begin with, and he didn't want any credit.

SAVE OUR RESTAURANTS, SAVE OUR CITY
By Suzie Zhou and Storey Calloway

Good to know that gyms and bowling alleys are reopening in New York City. We're relieved that Mayor de Blasio will soon be able to make the long commute from Gracie Mansion to his gym in Brooklyn, sharing indoor space with other heavy-breathing fitness buffs. Meanwhile New York City's restaurants are dying, one by one, and our mayor and governor seem sublimely indifferent to the crisis. Takeout, delivery and outdoor dining are essentially bandages applied to a hemorrhage, and without some reliable projection for the resumption of indoor dining, without some concrete guidance as to the criteria for reopening, or a timely and substantial aid package, thousands of the city's small businesses will cease to exist, and hundreds of thousands of New Yorkers, the majority of them among the city's least affluent citizens, will be out of work for months and years to come.

Fewer than half of the city's 25,000 restaurants have been able to open for outdoor dining. More than a thousand have already gone out of business with more following every day. More than half of the city's 300,000 restaurant employees are collecting unemployment while thousands of undocumented workers don't even have this option. Last week Mayor de Blasio described restaurant dining as "a very optional activity, which some people do a lot who have the resources and others can't do at all because they don't have the resources." Trumpian grammatical awkwardness aside, this statement exhibits a profound lack of understanding of the daily life of this city—with its thousands of diners, pizzerias, taco and ramen joints and other local restaurants catering, pre-COVID, to millions of hungry New Yorkers every day.

Yellowfin tuna tartare is not a necessity, and no one would argue that the customers of Suzie's and other fine dining establishments are bearing the brunt of the suffering in this pandemic, but the same can't be said of the restaurant's sixty former employees, or the eighteen workers at Condrieu, unemployed since March 13. Those figures do not include the farmers and fishermen, or the employees of the cleaning and linen and clerical services who also depend on restaurants like ours for their livelihood. Those employees are highly skilled individuals who take great pride in their work, raise families and pay taxes. They are deeply offended to hear that their industry is somehow "optional." And most of them, like hundreds of thousands of others, are now struggling to pay their rent and put food on their tables. These challenges will only grow more dire in the coming months.

Most New Yorkers sacrifice domestic living space to partake of the rich social and cultural opportunities just outside their doors. Restaurants serve as their dining rooms and their living rooms, where they meet friends, relax, celebrate—and watch their fellow New Yorkers doing the same. We do not see restaurants as some kind of luxury—they are the heart and soul of New York City.

On July 20, New York City made it to Phase 4 of its pandemic reopening, weeks after other parts of the state. It was no surprise that the city, the recent epicenter of the coronavirus outbreak, remained locked down longer than less affected regions. But Phase 4 in other parts of the state included limited indoor dining—which remains prohibited in the city. Two months after most of New York reopened to indoor dining, the state has not experienced any infection spikes traced to restaurants. Last Friday Governor Cuomo announced a statewide infection rate of .65 percent, the lowest since the start of the pandemic.

So far there has been no official explanation as to why it's safe to dine indoors in Westchester or Nassau or Suffolk County, but not in New York City. Is it because city dwellers talk faster and louder than their suburban and rural compatriots? We'd like to see the science on that. Hair and nail salons, museums and zoos are open for business, with certain restrictions, and New Yorkers are free to ride subways and buses.

Wealthy New Yorkers may not want to come back to a city that's a shadow of its former self, that has few of the attractions that drew them here in the first place—restaurants chief among them. For the moment, there are outdoor dining options, but regardless of whether outdoor dining permits are extended past October, the arrival of cold weather will effectively put an end to alfresco dining. And without some kind of intervention, it will put an end to thousands more New York City restaurants that are barely holding on now as they wait for some glimmer of hope or guidance.

One of us opened her restaurant just a few days before the city closed down—the other has observed previous cycles of expansion and contraction in the economic life of the city. But the current crisis is the most profound ever to challenge our industry, and we are hurting. We believe that restaurants are the lifeblood of the city, but we are hemorrhaging. We both love New York City and we believe in its future, but the more restaurants and businesses we lose, the more storefronts that turn up empty, the harder it will be to restore the world's preeminent city to its former glory.

Storey's dad, who thought he knew as much about voice as anyone, not to mention fine dining, said he liked it, but wanted to know how much of it was hers. "It doesn't exactly sound like you."

He was right, of course, though for some reason she was slightly irritated by this observation.

"Obviously it was a collaboration," she said.

"Don't be offended," he said. "I was just curious."

"Obviously I collaborated with Suzie."

"Yeah."

"If you really want to know, Mingus helped."

"It has a certain bite."

"Well, don't you think that's needed?"

"Well, yeah, I'd say so."

"Will you help us place it?"

"Absolutely. We'll start with the *Times*."

Russell called two days later to say the *Times* had passed. "I was kind of expecting that."

"Fucking dickheads," Mingus said.

"You're on speaker," Storey said.

"Did they give a reason," Mingus asked.

"Not really. I just think they're toeing the official liberal party line. Safety first, blah blah. Any ideas about where you want to go next?"

"What about *Eater*?" Storey suggested.

"Kind of preaching to the choir," Mingus said.

In the end they published in *Air Mail*, Graydon Carter's online magazine, and got a fair amount of pickup and a lot of buzz in the industry—if not any immediate action from the city or the state. And from Storey's point of view, almost best of all was the fact that immediately after helping her finish the piece, Mingus had started writing again. And, more important, they'd started making love again.

Finally, on September 9, it was announced that indoor dining would resume at the end of the month, albeit at a severely reduced 25 percent capacity. Storey started pulling out tables and putting up partitions in preparation while Mingus toiled intermittently on a piece about his arrest and incarceration.

22

Russell took her to a shabu-shabu place in SoHo, a little jewel box with an L-shaped counter presided over by the chef, a very pretty Japanese woman in a navy smock with a tall samurai-style topknot, who bowed in greeting. There was one other party at the other leg of the counter, a trio of Japanese kids—hard to believe they were older than twenty—two guys and a girl, whispering and occasionally wafting a polite inquiry, in Japanese, at the chef.

He arrived a few minutes early; she arrived ten minutes late. He decided he could forgive her tardiness, given the obvious care she'd put into her appearance. She was wearing a form-hugging, low-cut floral dress, the bra cups of which were trimmed with mint-colored lace, which she told him was vintage when he complimented it. Along with nude stockings with a black seam up the back.

"You look—wow!"

"Glad you like the dress."

"I wasn't necessarily giving all the credit to the dress."

"I should hope not."

"The word *voluptuous* comes to mind."

"You're the editor."

"*Publisher*, if you please."

"Well, you did some very helpful editing for me with the first draft. I really appreciated your suggestions."

"When I find a book particularly compelling, I break out the old blue pencil."

"I really, *really* appreciate it," she said, putting her hand on top of his and looking at him in an almost cartoonishly seductive manner.

"Am I supposed to melt under your steamily appreciative gaze?"

She laughed.

"I mean, was that look *real*? Or was it in italics, so to speak?"

"Both," she said. "I was doing an impression of a deeply grateful damsel who would do almost anything to show her gratitude. But it was also sincere."

"Well," he said, "you could let me publish the book."

"That doesn't seem nearly as fun as what I had in mind."

"Probably not."

The auction for her book was set to take place in three days, a fact which hovered in the air between them. Russell would love to publish it, but at the same time he would love to continue flirting with Astrid and to see where it led them. Viewed this way, he supposed it was a win-win situation. At this moment, the book seemed much less interesting than its author.

"I could, of course, tell you all the reasons why I'd be the best publisher for your book."

"You already have."

"That's good—we can dispense with that."

"We'll have to find other topics, I guess."

"It would seem so."

The chef interrupted them to ask about dietary restrictions and to explain the meal, presenting the tray of glistening, extravagantly marbled, thinly sliced Wagyu beef which would constitute their main course.

"Very hot chef," Astrid said. "Is that why you like this place?"

"The food is equally sexy," Russell said.

"Does she serve *uni*?"

"As a matter of fact—yes."

"Nothing like gonads to enliven a meal, I say. Oh, look, I think I've gotten you to blush again."

In fact, he did feel a slight flush on his cheeks. "You seem to be good at that."

"It's so easy, and yet so rewarding somehow."

"What shall we drink?" he asked. "I brought a bottle of red, but let's start with something lighter."

"Sake? That sounds right."

Russell ordered a bottle he'd enjoyed on his last visit.

The chef poured it into tiny ceramic cups and returned a moment later with two small bowls. "This is first course, *dashi-maki tamago*, egg custard in dashi sauce, *dozo*."

"I love the sense of ceremony," she said. "The Japanese are good at that."

"Speaking of ceremony . . ." He raised his sake cup. "To *Admiral, My Admiral. Kanpai*." At first, he hadn't been wild about her title, but it had grown on him. He wasn't sure that Whitman was the right touchstone for such a British story. But it had a ring.

They touched their cups and drank.

"What are you reading?" she asked. "I mean, for fun. Or don't you get time to read recreationally?"

"I do. Right now I'm reading *Anna Karenina*. Rereading, that is. This damn pandemic seemed like the right time."

"That's a . . . curious choice."

"Have you read it?"

"In college. I'm sure it would be more resonant now."

"There's a bunch of sociological and theological shit that I kind of skim past, but Anna is a great character, and the love story is really powerful."

"You *do* remember how it ends?" She eyed him dolefully.

"Are you taking this personally?"

"I probably haven't told you I'm somewhat superstitious. Maybe a lot superstitious."

"At the risk of sounding presumptuous, the circumstances aren't really analogous."

"You mean *our* circumstances?"

"Well, yeah. I'm not even sure what our circumstances are."

"No?" She regarded him quizzically, then reached under the table and grabbed his crotch, squeezing hard, making him jump. "Does that help clear things up?"

He took a slug of sake. "That's very clarifying," he said.

"I mean, I know you have this gentlemanly diffidence, and I think it's kind of sweet, but let's not be *too* coy."

"Okay." It was true, he'd been attempting not to examine his motives or his objectives too closely, imagining that he was letting himself be swept up by circumstances and by Astrid's agenda rather than having one of his own. Which wasn't really honest, he realized.

As if on cue, the *uni* arrived, specifically *yuba* shabu with *uni*. "Tofu skin with sea urchin," the chef explained as she placed the mottled black bowls in front of them.

In the present company, Russell couldn't help thinking that the *yuba* shabu looked like a spiral strand of semen on its ceramic spoon, but he refrained from expressing this observation. His train of thought skipped to the *shirako* he'd eaten all those years ago with Corrine—actually cod sperm—on a tasting menu at a long-shuttered Japanese restaurant in the East Village, and he felt a flash of guilt, thinking about her, even in her admonitory mode, complaining about the dish, about tasting menus in general, thinking about their history together, before reminding himself that she had an amorous history that was separate from their own. An extramarital history.

"I like the contrast," Astrid said. "The bland tofu and the funky, briny *uni*."

"Is your boyfriend a foodie?" He felt he had to acknowledge his existence at some point.

"No, not really. He's a vegan."

"Well, that's admirable, I guess." Actually, it sounded incredibly trendy and tedious.

"I guess. I couldn't do it. Seems to me like restricting your sexual menu to the missionary position, with a condom. It's actually a bit of a point of contention. What about Corrine?"

"Not a vegan, thank God, but she's definitely not a foodie. In fact she has kind of a complicated relationship with eating."

"Anorexic?"

"She has been. In the past. Not now. But she just doesn't love eating the way I do and sometimes that can be a real drag."

"*Tell* me about it."

"Kind of ironic that she works for an organization devoted to feeding New York's hungry."

Astrid leaned forward to accept another pour of sake and not for the first time that night Russell admired the ample swell of her breasts. She caught him staring at them and winked.

"I like the sake," she said.

"I know very little about it, but I know what I like."

The trio at the other side of the counter burst into a fit of giggles.

"Why do Japanese girls always do that. Hide their mouths when they laugh?"

"Modesty?"

"It seems like such a repressed culture. On the other hand, Japanese porn is so fucking kinky."

"Watch a lot of that, do you?"

"Just enough to know. Who do you think invented bukkake?"

"The Japanese?"

"I rest my case."

Russell hoped the chef wasn't overhearing this.

Moments later she placed two more small bowls in front of them, which contained cooked abalone in ponzu.

"Still," Russell said, "you gotta love the food."

"How's your Jefferson bio doing," she asked, after he ordered another bottle of sake.

"Not bad, really. Second printing. I mean, it would be doing a lot better if we could put him on the road. Zoom promotion isn't quite the same thing."

"I've seen some pushback," she said. "Like that *Slate* piece. And the one in *The Atlantic*. It's probably not the best time to be making a case for the slaveholder in chief." The chef was now initiating the main act, picking up pieces of the pink beef with chopsticks and swirling them in a pot of gently boiling broth.

"Can we just focus on the imminent feast," Astrid said.

"Okay."

"Though I like your passion in defending your authors."

He was not quite ready to accept this compliment. But the first mouthful of Wagyu, dipped in a sweetened soy sauce, softened his attitude considerably, as did the fact that she insisted on serving the second bite personally, tweezing it between her chopsticks and raising it to his lips.

Russell leaned down, reached into his wine bag and hoisted a bottle of red wine to the counter. "For the beef," he said. "Two thousand fifteen Pommard Epenots, Domaine Clos de la Chapelle, a Burgundy." Within minutes the assistant chef had opened the bottle and poured a sip for Russell to taste. "Oh yeah," he said. "That's the shit."

"Delicious," she said, when she tasted it. "That's so cute that you bring your own wine."

By the time the last two glasses were poured, Russell was feeling very good indeed. A certain amount of physical contact had been taking place under the counter. Astrid was rubbing his crotch, pressing hard on his increasingly tumescent cock. He stopped her when she tried to undo his belt buckle.

"Are you ready for the final course," asked the cute chef.

"Can we just wait a few minutes," Russell said, thinking he would like to wait for his erection to subside.

"Tell me about this wine," Astrid said as she squeezed him again.

"Well," he said. "Pommard is in the Côte de Beaune, just north of Volnay. . . ."

"Go on."

Much as he liked the sensation he pushed her hand away again.

"Which was very fashionable in the early twentieth century."

"And."

"It kind of went into eclipse for a while. . . ."

"And now?"

"Now a number of ambitious younger producers are reviving the area."

He felt like his breathing was suspiciously labored.

"And how would you describe this particular wine," she asked as she squeezed him again.

"Fuck if I know," Russell said.

He didn't think anyone had noticed anything but he felt embarrassed nonetheless. Had she really intended to give him a hand job under the table? The chef gave him a look before turning away that made him think he'd been caught out. The trio on the other side of the counter, on the other hand, seemed oblivious.

"Are you enjoying your meal?" she asked, all innocence.

"Yeah. Absolutely. It's just that I'm probably going to have to find another shabu-shabu place."

23

WHEN CORRINE ARRIVED at the Lees' loft in TriBeCa, she found her husband hard at work in the kitchen alongside Washington, wearing his REAL MEN DON'T WEAR APRONS apron, while Washington was wearing the one that Russell had bought him some years ago, JUST HERE TO STIR THE POT. In accordance with long-standing tradition the men cooked and the women mocked their earnestness from the sidelines. Loud music was inevitably involved. Storey had stepped in briefly as a sous-chef after culinary school, but since she'd started cooking full-time, she'd scaled back to an advisory role. It was amusing to watch the boys, who imagined themselves to be serious cooks, deferring to her.

Having not been here in almost a year, Corrine couldn't help admiring anew the scale and the crisp aesthetic of the loft—a kind of perfect example of the late nineties TriBeCa conversion era, when many of the old industrial buildings had been gutted and restored to the luxury ideal of the day, with passenger elevators and doormen and gleaming stainless-steel kitchens. The Lees' loft was finished with a curated collection of midcentury-modern furniture and black-and-white photographs. Le Corbusier. Mies. Adnet. Cartier-Bresson. Mapplethorpe. It looked ready for its close-up in *Architectural Digest*. Whereas the loft in which the Calloways had spent so many years before being priced out of the neighborhood was like a museum exhibit of postindustrial starving-artist-era TriBeCa. They had partitioned off first one bedroom for themselves and then another for the kids, and updated the kitchen, but as renters they were reluctant to make major capital improvements.

Washington and Veronica lived very well, in part thanks to Veronica's salary. They'd visited the Calloways a few weeks back for their traditional election-night gathering, a strangely unsatisfying evening which had ended without a climax, if you didn't count Russell and Washington getting drunk. The electoral votes had finally come in for Biden a few days later.

Corrine greeted Veronica, fist-bumping, in keeping with the new protocols.

"Can't thank you enough for doing it here," Corrine said.

"It's no trouble, really. Except for the chefs blasting music and trashing the kitchen."

"Well, don't speak too soon. My sister is coming."

"How is she these days?"

"I guess we'll see."

Hilary had been in rehab at the start of the pandemic, when Silver Meadows discharged all patients, and she'd been on and off the wagon since, as far as Corrine could tell, based on late-night phone calls and two dinners. It was at least her second trip to rehab—Russell and Corrine had paid for the first, whereas Corrine wasn't sure how the second trip, if indeed it was only the second, had been financed. Their mother's estate was still being settled, and Hilary had been hitting Corrine up for money; she'd written a few checks without telling Russell.

She couldn't really deny her sister, who was the biological mother of her children. In retrospect she could hardly believe that Hilary had agreed to donate her eggs and her body. Or that they had been so desperate as to ask. Of course, they had paid her, but still. In the early years Corrine had been terrified that, once the children learned their origin story, Hilary might replace her in their affections—a needless worry, as it turned out. If anything, they were embarrassed, and a little ashamed of the woman whose eggs had given them life. Hilary was, in fact, terrible with kids. She was a party girl, a professional girlfriend. When she was younger her exuberance and her beauty had carried her into many rooms. In her twenties and thirties she'd dated a series of not-quite-A-list actors and rock musicians. Later she married an NYPD cop who left his wife for her, but that marriage had petered out after a few years. She'd been banished for egregious behavior from Corrine's holiday celebrations for several seasons, but there'd been a thaw in relations after their mother had died, and she'd behaved herself relatively decorously last Christmas, their last in the town house in Harlem.

She appeared at the door tonight clutching the arm of a man who looked as if he might be the bass player in a band you'd almost heard of back in the nineties, rail thin, with a floppy blond mane, in black leather.

"Hey, big sis, what's shakin'?" Hilary said. "This is Rory."

Corrine looked at Veronica, wondering if she'd been warned about Hilary's plus-one; the hostess seemed slightly perplexed. Not for the first time, Corrine wished that her sister could be more like Russell's brother, which is to say, almost always absent.

"This is Corrine, and Veronica."

"Cool loft," he said.

"Why thank you," Veronica said.

Coats were collected and hung. Hilary towed her date over to the kitchen area to greet the boys.

"I know these guys," Rory said.

Russell looked uncertain, but Washington said, "Rory Calhoun, *right?*"

"I wrote *Feathered Nests*," he said. "We used to hang out back in the day."

"Yeah, right, of course," Russell said, seeming unconvinced.

"Almost finished with my latest," he said.

Neither Washington nor Russell were able to show much enthusiasm for this prospect. Apparently, Hilary had brought a hungry writer with an unpublished manuscript into their midst. Corrine would have to get the story on him later.

"It's based on my life," Hilary announced.

"Well, babe, I mean, it's a work of fiction. But obviously I draw on life."

"I've given you so many great stories."

"I can't deny that."

Corrine couldn't help thinking that her sister would make a very compelling low-rent version of Becky Sharp or Holly Golightly.

"What can I get you to drink, Rory?" Washington asked.

"I'll have tequila and soda," Hilary said.

Washington glanced over at Corrine. He'd pointedly not asked Hilary for her order. He shrugged as if to say, I tried. By this time everyone knew that Hilary and alcohol had a lot in common with gasoline and an open flame.

"I'll have the same," Rory said.

"Actually, we brought the tequila," said Mingus, from the door, waving a ceramic blue-and-white bottle, looming behind Storey and Jeremy.

Corrine was happy to see that they'd come together.

"And I brought the stuffing," Storey said, bearing a pan covered with aluminum foil.

Introductions were made.

Mingus, shaking Rory's hand, said: "I'm just grateful you're not a cop. Hilary was with Dan the cop for what seemed like forever." Corrine could see he was a little stoned.

"What was so bad about Dan?" Hilary demanded.

"He was fine if you like gun-toting racists."

"So what," Hilary said, "you're one of those 'defund the police' types?"

"No, I'm just, like, yet another victim of police brutality." So apparently Mingus had mellowed toward Storey, but he was still angry about his detention.

"Honey," Veronica said to Mingus. "Let's let sleeping dogs lie."

"You mean sleeping pigs?"

"Them, too," Storey said.

"So you're Hilary's daughter," Rory said to Storey.

Storey looked as if she'd just been slapped. "Well, sort of." She didn't like to be reminded of her origins.

"That's so cool," Rory said. "I mean, I can see the resemblance."

"I think I just dodged a bullet," Jeremy whispered to Corrine. Corrine could have kissed him but refrained.

"Let's get a drink," Mingus said, tugging his girlfriend away in the direction of the bar, a walnut cabinet loaded with top-shelf booze and cut-crystal glasses.

Washington crossed the room with two glasses, handing them off to Hilary and Rory.

"So where did you two meet?" Veronica asked.

"We met at Silver Meadows," Hilary said.

"In *rehab*?" Corrine asked.

"Well, yeah, actually."

"My problem wasn't booze," Rory said cheerfully, holding up his glass. "I had an opiate issue."

That was not exactly reassuring.

She exchanged a look with Washington. Lovely—Hilary had picked up a junkie at rehab. "And what's your excuse, sis?"

"For what?"

"Aren't you supposed to avoid alcohol?"

"I've got it under control. Everything in moderation."

"I don't think that's what they teach you in rehab."

"The twelve-step thing is so extreme," Rory said. "It's, like, 'one size fits all.'"

"Plus it's the holidays," Hilary said, raising her glass and drinking half of it down.

Russell was fairly rigid about the timing of the Thanksgiving meal. While some leaned toward lunch and others toward the dinner hour, in Russell's family the meal had always been served in the interregnum. He could make a compelling if rather tedious case for why this was their practice, how it was the one meal a year with its own special time, neither lunch nor dinner, how an earlier meal made dinner irrelevant whereas a later start wouldn't allow for proper digestion of the feast before bedtime, but really, it was just what he had grown up with.

Today they sat down, appropriately spaced, at the Lees' sprawling, asymmetrical Nakashima table a little after four-thirty, in accordance with custom, with Russell and Washington at opposite ends. After everyone was seated, Washington rose to speak, turning down the music—the Band's eponymous album—with a remote.

"We welcome you all here for the first pandemic edition of Thanksgiving. We are thankful to be together with our loved ones—"

"Where's Nora," Hilary asked, noticing the absence of the host's daughter, if not remembering her name.

"Still in Paris," Washington said. "But she sends her love. Meantime, Chef Russell and myself invite you to serve yourselves from the bounteous buffet on the counter. All-American soundtrack by the Band, four of whom were actually Canadians. Oh, yes, and we want to thank the real chef, who made the stuffing. Chef, would you care to tell us anything about the stuffing?"

"It's an apple-and-chestnut stuffing," Storey said, "made with whole wheat sourdough that I baked a few days ago."

Russell stood up and dinged on his glass with his fork. "If I could just say a word about the wines."

Life wouldn't be complete, Corrine thought, without a word or five thousand about the wine.

"Thanksgiving wine pairing is tricky," Russell said, "given the heterogeneity of the traditional dishes. . . ." Corrine tuned the rest out, as she almost always did. Her husband could be more than a little pedantic, particularly on the subjects of food, wine, grammar and English usage.

"We might have enjoyed them even more without the speech," Corrine whispered to Washington, when it was over. But at least it was over quickly.

"That's our boy," Washington said. "It wouldn't be Thanksgiving without the wine speech. I just wish he'd told us which was higher in alcohol."

"You're probably not the only one at the table who wishes that," Corrine said, watching Hilary top up her glass. She hoped a drunken episode wasn't looming.

"Can I have your attention for a minute," Jeremy said. "I think we should express our thanks with a prayer."

"Really?" Russell said. But Corrine was proud of him.

"Bless us, O Lord," he intoned, "and these thy gifts, which we are about to receive from thy bounty, through Christ our Lord, amen."

There was an almost stunned silence around the table, which Corrine punctuated.

"Thank you, Jeremy," she said. She thought it was kind of outrageous that this crowd was more surprised at Jeremy's saying grace than they were at Rory talking about his opiate problem.

Corrine waited for the others before stepping up to the counter and picking out some turkey with a little gravy and some of the green bean casserole, and a few brussels sprouts. The Band sang: *Corn in the fields. / Listen to the rice when the wind blows 'cross the water, / King Harvest has surely come.*

Back at the table, Hilary was railing against the wearing of masks.

"First they said it didn't help, and now we have to wear them everywhere. It's all bullshit."

"Scientists do change their minds, based on new evidence," Russell said. "Not that I love wearing a mask."

"It's really only the N95s that provide significant protection," Washington said. "The others are just cosmetic."

"I think it would be lovely if we just forgot about the pandemic for the duration of the meal," Veronica said, evoking various expressions of assent.

"Are we allowed to talk about the election?" Mingus asked.

"An even more fraught topic," Veronica said.

"Surely we don't have any Trump lovers in the room?" he continued.

Corrine and several others looked at Hilary, who said, "I know you liberals will all attack if I say anything positive about him."

"You're correct," Washington said. "We would pelt you with bread and insults. Although I would be curious to hear what you could possibly say in favor of the Orange One. But let's just leave it to our imaginations, shall we?"

The resolution had come three and a half days after the polls closed. Corrine was jogging on University a little before noon on an unseasonably warm Saturday when she started hearing the horns, the shouts and the chants. Even before she heard the chants, she could guess what had happened, and she felt a rush of exhilaration, a sense of pride in her country, and her city, which seemed to be erupting with joy. A woman hung from a fifth-floor window above University banging on a pot with a spatula. Corrine continued running to Union Square, two blocks up, where, as she expected, crowds were gathering. People in pink and blue clothing, in blue and black masks, were celebrating amid the yellow trees of the park, banging on pots and tambourines. A guy in a turquoise jacket was blowing "When the Saints Go Marching In" on a huge trombone. Corrine slowed to a walk and joined the throng, finding herself hugged by a Black man in a red, green and black caftan and then by a teen girl with pink braids. She could feel herself grinning, could feel the sympathetic energy of the crowd, her own exhilaration amplified by that of her fellow celebrants. She took out her phone and snapped a picture of the crowd, sent it to Russell with the message *You've got to get up here!* Even though he hated exclamation marks, she felt that this was an exceptional moment. As she waited for her husband's response, she joined in a sing-along "Celebrate" and then *Na na na na, na na na na, hey hey hey, goodbye,* feeling herself plugged into a kind of collective energy as well as into the collective memory of her city, the nation's very first Labor Day rally,

Emma Goldman, who spoke frequently to her followers here, and those who'd gathered here after the attacks of September 11 and the killing of George Floyd to protest and to celebrate and to find common purpose and kinship and refuge from the teeming anonymity of the city.

"Could we talk about the stuffing," Veronica said.

"The best part of the meal," Russell said.

Corrine used to love the stuffing, when she was younger, before she learned about carbs.

"But can we really call it stuffing," Rory asked, "if it's not stuffed inside the turkey? Like what happened to that? When did that change?"

"Are we really talking about stuffing?" Mingus said.

His mother said, "It seems a little more anodyne than politics."

"Just because we're eating turkey doesn't mean we should emulate the ostrich," Mingus said.

"That's a total myth about ostriches sticking their heads in the sand," said Russell.

"I'm just saying we shouldn't ignore all the reasons to not be thankful today." Hilary's mood seemed to have turned dark. Which happened sometimes when she drank too much.

"Actually, maybe we should stick our heads in the sand, for just this one day," Russell said. "The holiday is called Thanksgiving."

"I'm just saying some of us have more reasons than others to be thankful," Hilary said.

"Meaning what?" asked Corrine.

"Meaning thanks to me you have these wonderful children to be thankful for. Have you thought about thanking me for that, lately?"

"Hey, what happened to Rory?" Russell said. "He's been gone awhile."

"Check the bathroom," Hilary said, jumping up.

Russell was ahead of her. The bathroom door off the living area of the loft was open, the bathroom empty. Corrine followed him into the master bedroom, where the bathroom door was locked. Russell knocked on the door.

"Rory? Rory? Are you in there?" He slammed his shoulder against the door with no effect.

Suddenly Hilary was with them. "Oh my God, is there a key? He's probably OD'd in there."

Washington appeared bearing a long thin skewer from the kitchen, which he inserted into a small round hole beneath the lock. He wiggled it around in the narrow hole.

The lock popped.

Washington muscled the door open. Rory's feet appeared on the marble of the floor.

He pushed farther to reveal the prone figure sprawled faceup. A hypodermic needle lay beside him. Hilary pushed her way inside, held a hand on his forehead. She looked slightly ridiculous, under the circumstances, holding her Vuitton purse.

"He's alive," she said, fishing in her purse. "I have Narcan."

She extracted what looked like standard nasal spray and inserted one end into a nostril.

Not feeling she was in any way needed, Corrine retreated to the dining room. Storey, who followed close behind, was crying. Mingus took her in his arms. "Don't worry, baby," he said sweetly.

"Should we call 911," Veronica asked.

After a few minutes, Rory came staggering out, supported by Hilary, trailed by Washington and Jeremy. "I'm fine, I'll be fine," he said as Hilary lowered him into a chair.

Corrine and Veronica exchanged a look of complicit bafflement.

"I thought I'd seen all the shit that could go wrong at Thanksgiving," Washington said.

"Live and learn," Russell said.

"So, tell us again what's in this excellent stuffing," Washington said to Storey, who still looked distraught.

24

THE SNOW STARTED falling a little before four, the light rapidly failing even as the air and the streets turned white. The sudden cold and the swirling flakes seemed emblematic of his interior state, of the fog in his brain and the ache in his bones, compounded by a vague sense of guilt that he'd done this to himself. He hadn't been as careful as he might have been; in fact, in the end he hadn't been that careful at all, in these latter days of the plague, after months and months of caution and observance of the rules. Sort of. Mostly? It was not in his nature to be overly cautious, certainly not for a stretch of nine months. Corrine always taxed him with recklessness, and not the least of his regrets was in confirming her opinion, of proving her right, although she'd refrained so far from saying she told him so. *And yet*, he wanted to say. *And yet.* Unless he were to lock himself up in the apartment for the duration, the chance of infection was always there. The supermarket, the bodega, the taxicab. He'd felt he'd staked a reasonable position on the scale between full prophylaxis and reckless abandon. But maybe not.

His timing was lousy—the FDA had just approved the Pfizer COVID vaccine, though it would probably be months before it would be widely available.

Outside the snow was starting to accumulate, the terrace garden disappearing, turning white, softening the edges of the metropolis, even as he felt himself slipping into a cloud of blurry somnolence. He thought of Gabriel Conroy, in Joyce's "The Dead," watching the snow fall outside his hotel room window while his wife slept in the bed beside him, having fallen asleep after telling him for the first time about her first love, Michael Furey, who had died after walking through the rain in winter to come and see her, though he was already ill. Russell, like Gabriel, had a wife who had loved another—who had loved two others. Jeff, like Michael Furey in the story, his wife's long-lost love, who also died young. And that other one, that fucking Luke. He wondered if she thought of them often. He wondered suddenly about his primacy in her heart. When she breathed her last, would she think of Jeff? Or Luke? Did she still think about them now? He realized that no matter how close we may feel to another, we never really know the secrets of their heart.

He had a headache, a cough emanating from deep in his chest and a fever. What he feared more than almost anything, after death, was losing his sense of smell. Without it, food and wine were tasteless, pleasureless. Sex would be seriously compromised, too. He knew people for whom the condition had lasted months, and he didn't think he could take that. By now he knew the list of possible long-term effects—cognitive, cardiac and respiratory impairment, memory loss. He'd watched Corrine suffer and struggle with her recovery. Now he was the one quarantined in the master bedroom. He'd tested positive yesterday after visiting the urgent care on 8th Street the day before. It was a strange feeling, getting confirmation that you had an illness that had killed millions around the world. On some level he was scared; on another level it didn't seem real. He oscillated between these two emotional poles throughout the afternoon after his diagnosis. He just read that Giuliani had it, too. Sort of embarrassing to have the same disease as that dildo. Hard to believe he had briefly seemed like a decent guy—*America's mayor.* Hard to believe now what it was like in those days and weeks after the attacks of 9/11. Rudy the steady captain of the smoking, listing ship, as opposed to the clown who'd held a press conference at a landscaping business across from a sex shop in northern Philly, bloviating about election fraud moments before Pennsylvania was called for Biden. Not that he hadn't always been a dick. But they needed a hero in those early, scary days as the acrid smoke poured off the site of the towers, when they thought nothing would ever be the same again. And yet, the feeling faded and the hero degenerated into a stooge. And they all gradually resumed their lives as if nothing had happened, most of those resolutions gradually forgotten. And this crisis, too, he supposed, would gradually fade into the background of quotidian life in a few years, except for those who'd lost their cherished ones. . . .

Although Corrine was presumably protected by the antibodies from her own infection, they decided to err on the side of caution and have her sleep in the second bedroom. That night they watched *Leave Her to Heaven* together, occupying opposite ends of the couch. Russell considered it a good sign that he was dazzled by Gene Tierney, despite the fact that she played a murderous obsessive. He couldn't be that sick, surely, if his aesthetic and erotic faculties were intact.

"She really is beautiful," Corrine said.

Russell decided against seconding this sentiment. It was never a mistake to refrain from praising another woman to your wife. Instead, he said, "You know, I've always thought she looks a lot like you." And it was true—there was a distinct resemblance in the cheekbones and the eyes. They shared, in his mind, a certain patrician aspect.

"You know she went to Miss Porter's?" Corrine noted happily.

"Really?" He was surprised that this was the first time he'd heard this.

"Yep. And she was a deb. Her parents wanted her to be a society girl."

"So my instinct was correct. She really was a blue blood."

"You know she had an affair with JFK," Corrine said.

"Not exactly a rare distinction."

"She wanted to marry him, but he said he couldn't because of his political ambitions."

"I think if I were him, I would have just changed career goals."

Russell felt a sudden surge of love and attraction toward his wife, and shabu-shabu regret.

Storey texted them that night to say *You MUST watch My Octopus Teacher*, which they dutifully streamed the next night. *Call me after you've watched it*, Storey texted. Russell found himself unexpectedly moved by the film, with its depiction of the relationship between a small female octopus and a depressed filmmaker.

"Aw, look at you," said Corrine. "You're all teary-eyed."

Russell wanted to deny it, but he really couldn't. He attributed his reaction to his weakened state.

"Let's call our daughter," Corrine said. She dialed and put them on speaker.

"Wasn't it amazing," Storey asked.

"It was. Your father got very emotional."

"Right? Me, too. So Dad, here's what I want to ask you. Will you ever eat octopus again?"

"That's a good question," he said.

"I know I won't."

"No, I don't think I will," Russell said.

He'd been scheduled to have dinner again tomorrow with Astrid. The auction for her novel had taken place a few days ago; bidding had been spirited and Russell had bid in earnest, going up to two hundred for world rights, but he was left in the dust by the big publishers, and the book had eventually gone to Knopf. He was happy for her, and possibly for himself. He certainly had his doubts about the book earning back Knopf's half-million-dollar advance. As part of a massive publishing conglomerate, they could afford to be optimistic. And if he had been relieved, on the one hand, to have been absolved of any possible ethical complications, given his interest in the author, he couldn't help wondering, on the other, if her interest in him would survive the neutralization of his power to advance her career. In the event, she had, if anything, increased the frequency of communication, soliciting his advice and asking when they could get together again.

How r u feeling

Not too bad. Like the flu. Cough, congestion, fever.

Worried about u

Fingers crossed it doesn't get worse. I can still smell and taste.

Still got erectile function? ED has been cited as symptom

Jesus, really? Haven't heard that. And haven't tested the equipment.

Maybe I should send visual aids

Maybe you should.

The nude photos she sent were efficacious in ruling out that particular symptom.

25

"Have you got your vaccination yet," Lisa asked, without prelude, when Corrine answered her phone.

"No. I'm not eligible yet. I'm happy to report that I'm under sixty-five, and as far as I know I'm not a frontline worker. Why, do you have yours?"

"Oh God, yes. I got mine weeks ago. Of course, my husband's a doctor. But all my friends have gotten it. Except for a few anti-vaxxers. But even *I'm* not that right wing."

"There are a few of us still waiting in line."

"Let me see if I can fix you up. I've got this great concierge doctor."

"I can wait."

"Don't be ridiculous. I'll get you a shot. Meantime, I was hoping you could get Chad a reservation at Storey's restaurant for Valentine's Day. How crazy is it that they're reopening indoor dining on the busiest night of the year? Bill and I have a table at Le Bernardin, but my kids seem to believe that Brooklyn is the only place to dine."

"I can check. I know she's been swamped with requests."

"I would consider it a huge personal favor. He tried on Resy, but it's sold out. Apparently, your daughter's restaurant is hot. I told him I could get him into Daniel, but that wasn't hip enough."

"I'll call her, but I wouldn't hold my breath if I were you."

"I'm sure she saves tables for VIPs and friends and family. I mean, everyone does."

"With the seating restrictions she's only got five or six tables to work with. But I promise I'll try."

"Call me back. Love to Russell."

After she hung up, she considered Lisa's proposal. Would she jump the line for the vaccine if she could? Not that she really believed Lisa would come through. But she supposed it would be satisfying, if baffling to her friend, to turn down the offer if it materialized.

Corrine did talk to Storey, who said, "Mom, are you insane?" She was fully booked, with a dozen on the wait list.

"I'm glad you're fully booked. So I take it you will not be celebrating Valentine's Day. How's Mingus?"

"I haven't really seen him much in the last couple of days. He's been in the Village working. I've been working pretty hard to get things up and running again. He's writing up a storm. And I take it as a good sign I haven't heard much from him. If he's blocked he calls me constantly, so he must be really into it."

"Seems like you guys are getting along much better."

"It's true."

Corrine sent Lisa an email explaining that Storey was fully booked, and then some, and dodged the multiple phone calls that came in response for the next hour.

For their own Valentine's Day celebration they went to Odeon, their former neighborhood joint, site of many Valentine's dinners. Most of the restaurants in the city had booked up within hours of the announcement about indoor dining, but they were fortunate to have a history, and the private number, there. It was a little weird, seeing the tables set so far apart, and only a fraction of the diners that usually populated the room. But she was grateful to be back. Corrine felt, on the one hand, a warm glow of nostalgia and, on the other, a sense of melancholy for the years that were gone and the loss of youthful ardor, remembering earlier dinners imbued with passion and, once upon a time, an impatience to return home and tangle up together beneath the sheets. But she felt that Russell, after seemingly losing interest in sex during most of the lockdown, had lately become more amorous. In the last couple of months he'd pounced on her several times, as if newly inspired.

After ordering two glasses of champagne, Russell started poring over the wine list, as was his habit. Corrine didn't approve of phones at the dinner table, particularly in public, but she felt justified when Russell buried himself in a wine list. Thankfully Odeon didn't have a dedicated sommelier, so she wouldn't have to endure that conversation.

She scrolled through several work emails before coming on one from her former lover.

Just thinking of you on Valentine's Day. Hope you are healthy and thriving. Love, Luke. It had been, what, four or five years since she'd heard from him? She looked up abruptly, guiltily, to see if Russell was watching her, but he remained absorbed. What had prompted this sudden communication, she wondered. She couldn't help being happy to hear from him, even as she remembered how the revelation of their affair had been catastrophic and had nearly ended her marriage.

"I'm thinking we should splurge," Russell said. "I ended up having a very good year. Sales up eighteen percent on last year. Not to mention your inheritance. I think we can afford a grand cru Burgundy."

"I'm not sure my inheritance justifies anything too grand," she said. After taxes, splitting it with Hilary, it had come out to about half a million, most of that money having come from the sale of her mother's house and a small Winslow Homer canvas that had been passed down from her maternal grandparents.

"Yes indeed. I think we start with a Bâtard-Montrachet for the first course."

"Are we really ordering two bottles?"

"It's Valentine's Day."

"I'm just saying if you want your wife to remain conscious till the end of the night . . ."

"That would be desirable."

"You may have to drink the lion's share yourself."

"I think I'll manage."

She suddenly wondered about his intentions tonight, whether he was thinking about having sex and, if so, if he had taken a pill. She had recently discovered a bottle of Cialis in his Dop kit. She hadn't really meant to snoop; she had been looking for nail clippers. At the time it hadn't occurred to her to count the pills left in the bottle, she'd already felt guilty enough about finding them. The prescription was recent—it had been filled in November. If he'd ever used it before she hadn't been aware. In fact, he'd had a few failures of tumescence in recent years. Perhaps this was in response—apparently erectile dysfunction was a symptom of age.

"I think I'm going to start with the oysters," Russell said. So maybe he was planning to get lucky tonight.

"And the strip steak." He said this as if it were the result of long deliberation, although it was what he almost inevitably ordered. "What about you?"

She, too, almost always ordered the exact same things. But she tried to inject some drama into the announcement. "I think I'll get the salmon tartare . . . and the salade Niçoise."

She would have happily settled for just the salad, but she knew it disappointed Russell when she ordered only one course, and she didn't want to debate the issue. He seldom complained when she didn't finish what she ordered. He just wanted to have a partner in dining. It was an almost sacred ritual for him, the evening meal, preferably eaten at a restaurant. She tried to indulge him in this. The pandemic had been hard on him in this regard, whereas she'd been secretly relieved that the restaurants were closed. Except for Storey's, of course.

They talked about the kids, about work and about Hilary.

"How long do you think it will take her to run through the cash from your mom's estate?"

"I'd rather not think about it. Is there any chance she might conserve and spend it wisely?"

"How long have you known her?"

"At least she won't be hitting us up for a while."

"Don't count on it."

"I used to worry that the kids . . . that they . . . that we'd made a mistake."

"With Hilary's eggs?"

She nodded.

"I think nurture has trumped nature. Our kids don't seem very Hilary-like. Although I'm frankly worried about Jeremy."

"I don't know, I think it's partly a generational thing."

"That doesn't necessarily make me feel better."

"I like to think he'll find his way. Look how passionate he was about the Bernie campaign."

"And how disillusioned he is now."

"Actually, I think he's moved on." She knew, in fact, that the stridency of his political convictions had softened and that his reading had taken a turn toward religious subjects. She talked to him more often than Russell realized.

"When I was his age, I'd been working at Corbin, Dern for four years and married to you for two."

"You can't judge him by the standards of a different time."

"I don't see why not. Aidan's son is teaching political science at the University of Chicago."

"If you compare yourself to your brother, I think you'll come out ahead in the long run. You know Jeremy has a new girlfriend."

"So you said. Do we know if she has a job?"

"She's a massage therapist."

"Is it wrong of me to wonder why he and his friends all seem to work in the service sector?"

The wine arrived. Russell examined the bottle, nodded his approval and watched impatiently as the waiter opened it. She, too, was eager to see him get some wine in his glass, since she knew his mood would soften. The waiter poured a splash into his glass. He raised the glass, examined it, swirled and sniffed it. As he always did. Finally, he tasted it, made a slightly noisy slurping sound as he sucked it through his teeth.

"Very nice," he said.

At least he wasn't one of those assholes who regularly sent bottles back. It pained him to do so.

"Now we can relax," Corrine said.

"I'm relaxed."

"If you say so."

She could almost see the tension lifting from him as he took a second sip. She sipped her own glass and wondered why Luke had suddenly thought to get in touch after all these years.

"I wonder how many Valentine's nights we've spent here."

"Eight," she said.

He looked surprised.

"I counted while I was getting dressed."

Russell drank two-thirds of the white wine and ordered a red for the main course. He was definitely getting buzzed, but in a good way. Fortunately, he was by and large a happy drunk, and it seemed, tonight, that he was also a horny drunk. She was shocked when she felt his shoeless foot pressing beneath her legs under the table. It had been years since that had happened. He grinned, crookedly, at her.

"It seems you've lost your shoe," she said.

"I've found a better place to put my foot."

She decided to roll with this. She swigged a glass of wine in order to get herself in the mood. Might as well take advantage of this unexpected attack of amorousness on Russell's part. They finished their dinner without further incident; Corrine excused herself to go downstairs to the ladies' room, where she removed her panties, placing them in her purse. She'd done this once before in this very bathroom, years ago. She only wished she had some lube in her purse, although she was a little wet.

When she returned to the table Russell was signing the check. He slugged back the rest of his wine and pushed back his chair. Outside he held her hand as he waved down a cab. He preceded her into the cab, sliding across the seat, and gave their address to the cabbie before leaning over and kissing her. He kissed her passionately, and squeezed her thigh. She took his hand and guided it between her legs.

He pulled away as he touched flesh and grinned at her. She pressed on his hand and he pressed his middle finger inside of her. She moaned as he found his rhythm, as he found her clitoris. She tried not to respond too vigorously or audibly, conscious of the cabbie in the front seat. As if reading her mind, sensing her restraint, Russell said, "Don't worry, we have the partition between us."

She allowed herself several muffled exclamations.

And all at once they were home. She straightened her dress as Russell groped for his wallet, opening the door and stepping out into the street, walking to the sidewalk and waiting as he paid. He joined her and they walked to the door as if it were just another night in New York, greeting Rafael the doorman, entering the elevator. Russell attacked her again inside the elevator; she pointed to the camera.

"Fuck it, we're married," he said, groping her and kissing her till they reached their floor.

They almost tumbled inside. Russell drew her into the bedroom, where they frantically disrobed. Russell sat down on the bed, pulled her toward him and put his tongue inside of her. She could hardly remember the last time he'd done this. She'd almost forgotten how good it could feel.

She was on the edge of orgasm when he pulled her down onto the bed and climbed on top of her. She came within moments of his thrusting inside of her. He seemed possessed, inspired, manic. It felt good, except that it also hurt; she felt a dull pain at the back of her vagina. But mostly it felt good, and it was over quickly.

"I don't know what's gotten into you, but I like it," she said, eventually, after he had rolled over on his back.

"It's Valentine's Day," he said.

"Well, let's not wait a year to do that again."

She lay on her back listening to his heavy breathing subside, holding his hand, her happiness tinged with melancholy as she contemplated how rare this kind of passion, once the norm, had become in their life together and because she realized that she'd been excited by Luke's email. She wondered if Russell ever thought about anyone else when he was making love to her.

26

THE PANDEMIC WASN'T done with them, but they were done with the pandemic. Russell and Corrine had gotten their first shots in late April, more than a year after the virus arrived in New York, driving out to the Native American reservation in Southampton after a friend alerted them that the clinic there had extra doses. Astrid had finally gotten hers.

Let's celebrate
Okay, where and when?
My place, tomorrow night. Tom out of town

The phrase *out of town* seemed freighted in more ways than one. It seemed almost archaic. Nobody had really gone anywhere in a long time, had they? More crucially, it was pretty clearly an invitation to consummate their relationship. Russell found the idea thrilling and daunting in equal measure. Tomorrow was . . . so imminent. Was he really going to cross that line? Or had he crossed it already?

What say

He hesitated, his thumbs suspended over the keypad.

Okay. Tomorrow.

He had done it. Or, rather, he had committed to doing it. He felt giddy. And slightly queasy. Excited. And anxious.

She texted him the address and suggested they meet at seven-thirty.

I'll have cheese and wine and music & & &

Sounds very tempting.
I hope so

That night Russell and Corrine went to the old-school Italian red-sauce joint next door to their building, a restaurant so quaint and unfashionable that Russell took a kind of ironic delight in its every kitschy detail—the elaborately framed repros of old religious paintings and still lifes, the sloped silver-plate wine cradles—in the fact that it had been serving pretty much the same food since the Beat era. Occasionally, you wanted a slab of lasagna more than anything else in the world—and he appreciated the fact that they let him bring his own wine. There was a pair of younger New York chefs who had polished and updated this formula and sold it back to hipsters and finance bros who were desperate to pay fifty dollars for a bowl of penne alla vodka, charging twice what the old-school red-sauce places did.

They were greeted with elaborate deference by the owner and seated at their regular table, or rather what had become their regular table since the resumption of indoor dining. They no longer had to show their vaccination cards. Corrine was gratified by the convenience of the location, "the coziness" of the setting.

"I just talked to Veronica," Corrine said, after they'd ordered a couple of Americanos. "She invited us over for tomorrow."

"Oh, hell, sorry, love. I've got a work dinner tomorrow." He felt a kind of tightening of his facial muscles as he enunciated this lie. It hadn't occurred to him he might have to justify his absence.

"I thought you told me this morning you were free tomorrow night."

"Sorry, this just came up." He was trying to concoct his story on the spot—why didn't he work this out earlier? Apparently because he wasn't practiced in the art of deception.

"Dinner in Brooklyn with an Irish novelist we're publishing in the fall." He *was* in fact publishing an Irish novelist in the fall. But it sounded phony to him as soon as he uttered it.

"How did he manage to get into the country? Or is it a she?"

Fuck, he'd forgotten about the travel ban. Was this an innocent question, he wondered, or was Corrine suspicious?

"She's Irish, but she's been here in the States for the duration." Of course the Irish novelist he was publishing hadn't been anywhere near the United States for at least a year.

"Is she attractive?" Corrine asked.

Russell was momentarily flummoxed by the question. "She's, umm, no, not really. I mean she's not unattractive."

Corrine laughed. "That was a pretty tortured answer."

"Well, it was kind of a loaded question," he said, seeking to regain the high ground.

"I was just messing with you. And it was kind of fun to see you get all flustered. But now I'm starting to worry."

"It's just another business dinner," Russell said, trying to adopt a weary, not defensive, tone.

The waiter arrived with their drinks, thankfully punctuating this exchange. Russell took a grateful sip of the bittersweet cocktail, realizing that he was not a very good liar, hoping that he would not be called upon to prevaricate again tonight.

"Did Storey text you today?" Corrine said.

"Don't think so."

"She wants us to watch another documentary." Corrine picked up her phone and scrolled. "It's called *Seaspiracy*. Apparently about the horrors of the international fishing industry."

"She's already got us off octopus. Is she going to stop serving fish at the restaurant? And if eating fish is immoral, what about birds and mammals?"

"I admire her passion. I think it would behoove us all to think more about what we eat and where it comes from."

"I'm not sure that behooves her as the proprietress of a restaurant that caters to omnivores."

"More and more people are going vegetarian and vegan. Especially young people."

"I think I'm feeling an irresistible urge for the veal."

"You know that's not allowed."

He'd agreed some time ago not to eat veal, though he broke the rule sometimes when he was on his own.

By the end of the meal, after most of a bottle of wine, Russell was feeling a warm glow of affection for his wife, and a buzz of guilt about his earlier lie about his plans for tomorrow night.

The next morning Russell took extra care with his toilette, showering, shaving carefully and rejecting several outfits before settling on a camel Lacoste polo and jeans with a blue blazer. He hadn't fully decided what he was going to do, but he decided to be prepared. He took a ten-milligram Cialis and tucked a second one into the coin pocket of his jeans. After Googling the drug, he'd decided to take a booster in the late afternoon. He saw no reason to take any chances. His digestive system was in turmoil even before he took the drug, which he attributed to nerves—to guilt and uncertainty.

He found himself frequently distracted during the workday by a sense of moral dilemma. He could plead illness, of course, though that seemed wimpy, and would only delay the matter. The half of his staff that was working in person trickled out after six. A little before seven, he took his second Cialis and summoned an Uber. He tried to read a manuscript in the car, but after scanning the same paragraph several times over, he put the thing back in his messenger bag. He watched the city flash past: the kitchen appliance and lighting fixture stores along the Bowery, and on Delancey, past Orchard Street, the discount clothing bazaar, where he and Jeff Pierce had once hunted out bargains on the weekends. As he passed the old Essex Street Market, where he had sought out culinary treasures, and ascended to the Williamsburg Bridge, Corrine called.

He eyed her name on the screen of his phone, uncertain whether to answer.

"Hey, babe. What's up?"

"Just wanted to check in. I'm going to grab a bite with Veronica."

"Sounds good."

"Are you in Brooklyn?"

"Almost. On the bridge."

"Have fun. Tell me all about it."

How, Russell wondered, could a conversation be so mundane and yet so fraught?

Her voice, so bright and upbeat, was a reproach.

He couldn't go through with it. He wouldn't. He realized, with a keen pang of regret, that he loved his wife. Not that he had doubted it before. But he hadn't always felt it the way that he did at this moment.

After he hung up he thought about telling the driver to turn around, but he felt it would be cowardly. He would keep his date with Astrid and just be honest with her. Tell her he had changed his mind. He owed her that much.

The car dropped him in front of a tan brick, five-story industrial building constructed in the thirties, which had, in the last twenty years, become notorious as a sort of bacchanalian post-graduate dorm, site of all-night rooftop parties and raves, as well as a ground-floor strip club. Russell had texted her a few minutes before arrival, as instructed; her buzzer was out of order. She was waiting just inside the door for him. Her smile seemed to him to light up the dingy lobby. They kissed. She probed his mouth gently with her tongue, looking at him quizzically when he failed to return her enthusiasm, then took his hand and led him up a flight of stairs and down a hallway.

He looked around the high-ceilinged room with huge windows and a sleeping loft attached to a steep ladder. Two bikes and several skateboards hung on the walls, along with half a dozen framed artworks: a blown-up portrait of a very young Zelda Fitzgerald; a reproduction of *Lady Hamilton as "Nature"* from the Frick; a *Goodbye, Columbus* poster with Ali McGraw, signed by none other than Philip Roth; an Interpol tour poster. A long lime-green vintage couch dominated the center of the room. She took his head between her hands and kissed him again. He failed to kiss her back. It was tempting, but he had made up his mind.

"What's up, cowboy," she said, holding him at arm's length and scrutinizing him.

"I'm just not sure I can do this," Russell said. "In fact, I'm pretty sure I can't."

"Let's just take it slowly," she said.

He nodded, not wishing to be too abrupt, although he was determined not to sleep with her, that nothing would happen. He looked around the room for signs of the boyfriend, as if to bolster his resolve, but the art and décor were pretty gender neutral.

"Let's just start with the cheese and charcuterie that I so thoughtfully arranged on a plate for us." She beckoned him toward the coffee table in front of the couch. "And, of course, the wine. I'm afraid I was unable to find a Pommard, but I bought a bottle of Chablis that the cute clerk at the wine store insisted was not unworthy of a connoisseur such as yourself."

She walked over to the kitchen area beneath the sleeping loft, retrieving the bottle from a refrigerator that was either very old or else a retro repro.

She poured two glasses and carried them over, then brought the tray of food over to the coffee table in front of the couch.

"Actually," she said, leaning forward as if to display the cleavage beneath her square neckline, "I have something else we might indulge in, if you're in the mood." She reached into her bra and pulled out a small plastic zip-top bag filled with white powder.

"Coke?"

She nodded.

It had been years since he'd indulged. A decade or more. Coke had once been a part of his life, the great social lubricant and love potion, the fuel of late nights on the town, the fairy dust of his youth. Along the way, over the years, it had lost its magical powers, its returns diminishing, its warm glow becoming harshly fluorescent. Eventually, he remembered, came the great betrayal, making him wildly horny even as it robbed him of his abilities to act on his desires. A couple of lines tonight, he reasoned, would surely decrease his ability to perform, even with the Cialis. Yet, his Pavlovian response was a warm tingle of anticipation. His body remembered the good old days, rather than the declension. Still, he wondered if he should resist.

She fetched a mirror in a silver frame which had, to judge by the smudges on the glass, been employed for this purpose before, and poured out a small pile of the coke. She chopped it up with her Delta SkyMiles card, crosshatching the pile vertically and horizontally, before separating out eight neat, uniform lines on the mirror.

"I think you've done this before," he said.

"A few times," she said. "Do you have a bill?"

Russell removed a crisp twenty from his wallet and rolled it into a tight cylinder and handed it to her. That had been the denomination back in his day. Maybe it was a hundred now, although probably not in Brooklyn.

"Go ahead," she said.

"No, please. Ladies first."

"You really are old school. Would you hold my hair?"

"Of course."

When he'd first met her it wasn't long enough to hold. He gathered her hair behind her head as she leaned down and snorted first one line and then another. She shook her head and lifted it slowly.

"Whoa!" she said.

"Good?"

"I think." She handed him the bill. Her expression was one of puzzlement.

"You okay?" he said.

"Not sure."

Her eyelids were drooping—which was not the typical reaction of a person who'd just snorted two lines of coke. Her head started to wobble. He dropped the rolled bill and put his hand beneath her chin, which was clammy.

"Astrid? Astrid, look at me."

Her pupils were pinpoints.

"Jesus Christ. Talk to me. Are you okay?"

She opened her mouth as if to speak, but only a faint gurgling sound emerged.

Her eyes were almost closed now. She gradually slumped back on the couch cushions.

He couldn't understand how this was happening, until it clicked: *fentanyl*. He'd read about dealers mixing it with coke, which had struck him as counterintuitive, but he hadn't thought much about it, since cocaine was no longer a part of his life.

She was overdosing on fentanyl.

He grabbed his phone and dialed 911, exclaiming, when someone picked up, that he had a friend suffering an overdose, at least he thought it was an overdose, giving the address as he held her arm, feeling her turning cold. "Hurry, please!"

Her lips were turning blue, as were the tips of her fingers.

What was he supposed to do? He was vaguely heartened to remember that Rory had bounced back from his overdose at Washington's, but unlike Hilary he didn't have the antidote.

"Astrid, wake up. Can you hear me?"

He put his hands on her cheeks and shook her gently.

"Wake up, Astrid. Please."

He held his hand under her nostrils. She was breathing, but barely. He pinched her nostrils closed and blew into her mouth; he continued this, on and off, alternating with chest compressions, until he finally heard the siren up the street.

He considered the possibility of flight. Now that help was here, his continued presence couldn't possibly make any positive difference, could it? Whereas he was in a heap of shit if he stayed and became a part of an official inquiry. He stood up, stared at the door and looked at Astrid, sprawled helplessly on the couch. He froze. Later he would question whether his remaining there reflected indecision, or a desire to do the honorable thing.

When he heard a clattering commotion in the hallway he ran

to the door and held it open. Two firemen in full gear were waddling down the hall, a chubby white guy and a smaller Hispanic man. They were both carrying axes.

"In here," he said, holding the door wide, pointing to the couch.

The big guy laid down his ax, bent over her and checked her pulse. "What did she take," he asked.

"It was supposed to be coke," Russell said.

"Looks like your dealer cut it with fentanyl."

"Not my dealer," Russell said, reflexively, standing a few feet back.

The other guy uncapped a plastic tube and bent down over her, shoving the tube into her nostril. Russell thought he saw her head move.

"Is she alive?"

The fireman was checking her pulse. "Barely."

"Wait a minute and give her another one," said his colleague.

Two uniformed paramedics entered, pulling a gurney behind them.

"What's the situation?"

"Overdose, probably fentanyl. Barely responsive. Administered one dose Narcan."

"Let's do another one." The big fireman administered another dose up her nose, then stepped back to observe her as a paramedic placed an oxygen mask over her face.

"Are you the boyfriend? Husband?"

"Just a friend."

"We talking intravenous?"

"No. She snorted what she thought was cocaine."

"How long ago?"

"Maybe fifteen minutes. I did CPR while I waited for you guys."

"Was she responsive?"

"Not really."

"Let's get her to the ER."

The paramedics lifted her onto the gurney, just as two cops waddled in the door, bottom heavy with gear. Two bored-looking white guys.

"What've we got?"

"OD. Unresponsive. We're taking her to Wyckoff Heights."

Russell had no idea what he was supposed to do.

"Is she going to be okay?"

"Who are you?" asked one of the cops.

"A friend."

"You witnessed the incident?"

He felt his body tensing. "Yes. She thought it was cocaine."

"Where did she get it?"

"I don't know."

"I'm going to need your name," he said, taking out a notepad.

Russell tried to think of an alias, considered the risks of giving one, but in the end couldn't manage anything but his own name and phone number.

Down in the lobby a crowd had gathered, a dozen or so curious young onlookers, among them his son.

"Dad, what the hell?"

"Don't ask." Russell watched as the paramedics loaded the gurney into the back of the ambulance. Should he go? Was he wanted? Was he allowed?

One of the paramedics climbed in the back with Astrid; the other closed the doors.

Russell looked back at Jeremy, who was holding hands with a pretty young woman with tiger-striped hair. "I'm Samantha," she said, holding out her free hand, which Russell shook limply.

"Who was that?" Jeremy asked.

"An author."

"What happened to her?"

"I think she OD'd."

"Jesus, am I going to read about this?"

"I hope not."
"You'd probably better go home."
Russell nodded.
"Nice to meet you," the girlfriend said, waving as he staggered off into the night.

27

Russell appeared in the bedroom doorway, looking frightened, looking as if he'd just swallowed something that, even if it weren't necessarily fatal, was having profoundly uncomfortable gastronomic effects.

She couldn't help asking him what was wrong.

He walked over and sat down on the edge of the bed, perched precariously. The lapel of his jacket stuck up from behind.

"I'm not sure where to begin."

"This sounds serious."

She sat up and hugged her knees.

"As you know I was having dinner with this author."

"A female author."

"Yes, a female author."

She already knew where this was going and she was already feeling the impact, realizing that Russell had been unfaithful, though come to think of it she'd felt it in recent months, felt his furtive attachment to his phone, seen the guilty looks, interrupted at least one suspicious conversation. And then there was the Cialis. So many little things, she realized all at once. She'd known, even if she hadn't really known she'd known.

"Her name is Astrid Kladstrup."

"That doesn't sound Irish."

"Not exactly."

"That's what you said."

"For God's sake, Corrine. I was lying."

Kladstrup? Why did that sound familiar? Hard name to forget. An ugly name. "The girl at Storey's opening? The cute brunette?"

He nodded sheepishly.

"Anyway, she sent me her novel, and it was good, very good. I wanted to publish it, but there was a bidding war, and eventually it went to Knopf."

"But in the meantime, you started flirting, sending increasingly suggestive texts."

"That's . . . well, yes. But I mean, that's all it was. It was the lockdown."

"If that's all it was we wouldn't be having this conversation."

"No, true. We had a couple of dinners."

"Is *dinner* a euphemism?"

"No, it's not."

"Then what?" She was trying to decide how angry she was going to become, she who, after all, had herself stepped out on her husband. "Why don't we fast-forward to tonight."

He seemed to be taking stock, considering how to frame it.

"I went to her place in Brooklyn for a drink."

"*A drink*. A euphemism, if I've ever heard one."

"I admit, it was inappropriate. And I was considering . . . well, you know. But I decided before I got to her place that I couldn't do it. I couldn't do it to you. After I talked to you on the phone on the way, and I realized how much I loved you."

"So you lied about the author dinner?"

"No, actually. She is an author."

She ceased commentary, having decided to let him hang himself.

"We had a drink. And then she asked me if I wanted to do some coke."

She nearly repeated the word out loud; it seemed so preposterous. Did people still do coke? Weren't the bright young things into other drugs now? She thought of cocaine as an extinct pleasure, as the late-night music of her own youth. It was always there in the background and it had been great fun, really, until it started to be less fun, and eventually to be a problem for some of them, including Washington and Russell, who were coming home in the middle of the night and going to work later and later in the morning. And doing God knows what else. Although in Russell's case she'd somehow imagined he was faithful. He had finally promised to quit, and as far as she knew he had, long ago.

"I know, I know. I haven't done it in years. But I didn't want to be a killjoy."

"No, of course not. God forbid."

"The crazy thing is that after she chopped the lines, she offered it to me first. And I said—'Ladies first.'"

This part was believable. Russell was always a gentleman, faithful to the codes of his class, chivalrous to the end. If not necessarily *faithful*.

"I'm just realizing that now. It could have been me. I mean, if I'd done it first . . ."

"What? What happened?"

He looked genuinely stricken. "She overdosed."

"On coke?"

"It was cut with something. Probably fentanyl. I've read about this. She started gurgling and turning blue. It was terrible. I called 911 and then I started CPR. I have no idea how long it was before the firemen came. Followed by the paramedics and the police."

"Is she alive?"

"I don't know. The paramedics administered Narcan."

Oh, hell, she thought, imagining the ramifications if she were dead, the humiliations to come. She knew she should feel sorry for the girl, and of course she did, she hoped she was alive, but she couldn't help feeling sorry for herself and her family in the event that she wasn't. She couldn't help being furious at Russell for putting them in this position.

She slapped him, hard, in the face, startling him and herself.

"All right," she said, when they had both somewhat recovered from the shock. "That's it. I'm disappointed and I have expressed that. I'll stand by you and defend you if necessary. We'll stand together. I hope it's not necessary and I hope the poor girl is alive, but regardless, I'll play the wife and be by your side."

He nodded, rubbing his reddened cheek. "Thank you."

"Did you give your name?"

He nodded.

She felt sorry for him. It was almost laughable how he'd been punished for his clumsy attempt at infidelity. Especially if he was as innocent as he claimed.

Her mind turned to the practicalities. "Why don't you text her?"

"Is that wise?"

"Presumably no one can get into her phone. But if she's alive she'll look at it as soon as she's able. And you've already given the police your name."

"I guess I should mention that when I came downstairs to the lobby with the EMTs Jeremy was there."

"What? What the hell was Jeremy doing there?"

"I think he's dating a girl who lives in the building."

"Jesus, what did you say?"

"I don't remember. Not much. I said she was an author."

Jeremy's knowing made it even more real. He wasn't stupid. He would have read all he needed to know on Russell's face.

"God, I hope she's alive," Corrine said, realizing as soon as she said it how selfish the utterance was. She couldn't have cared less about the girl; she was thinking only about herself and her family.

28

HIS TROUBLED DREAMS were not specific to the events of that night. Instead, he dreamed about his mother, whom he'd not thought about in months. She was calling for help. She was in her bedroom, calling out to him, but he couldn't reach her. The door was locked. She was calling out for her morphine. And he couldn't get to her. She was dying. She was in pain. But somehow the door was locked and impassable and there was no one else around. Russell called for his father, but there was no response. He went outside and somehow climbed the side of the house, looked in her bedroom window. But it was not his mother lying in the bed—it was Corrine. She was calling out to him, still in his mother's voice, saying, Help me Russell, I'm in here. Some unknown barrier prevented him from reaching her.

This was the only dream he remembered in the morning, though he'd woken several times in the night. Looking over at Corrine, he half expected to see her writhing in pain, drenched in sweat, as in the dream. But she was sound asleep, looking unconscionably serene. It was he who was drenched in sweat. Just as he started to feel relief that his dream was only that, he remembered the events of the night before, and his sense of dread rebounded.

He checked his phone for messages or texts; there were none. No response to his text to Astrid. He wondered what hospital they'd taken her to. Had they told him? Had he asked? The minutes before they put her in the ambulance seemed to be shrouded in mist. He remembered seeing Jeremy. Fuck. That on top of everything else.

Saturday. The old rhythms of prelockdown life were returning, if somewhat less audible, less insistent, than before. He wished it were a weekday, with the distractions of work to ameliorate his sense of foreboding and anxiety. He got the papers from the hallway, turning first to the *New York Post*, half expecting to see something about Astrid, thumbing through the first twenty pages of the tabloid, right up to Page Six, which was actually on page 22, but of course it was too soon, and Astrid's was not a boldface name, though her recent book contract might render her newsworthy. The combination of a drug overdose, a pretty young woman and a six-figure book contract would definitely be *Post* worthy. Throw in the whiff of a sex scandal—a married, age-inappropriate publisher—and you had all the makings of a classic tabloid item. But there was nothing this morning, the gossip pages populated with reality TV stars, rappers and social media influencers whose names were largely unknown to Russell.

Back in the day, Page Six had been studded with the names of his own friends and acquaintances, and indeed he himself had popped up from time to time as an attendee at a party or as the publisher of a particularly noteworthy title. For many years, decades, he was conversant with contemporary music; he went to the film premieres and the book parties. The culture producers—film directors and novelists and artists—were his peers. When someone would ask him how he knew Oliver Stone or Matt Dillon or Julian Schnabel, he was apt to shrug, as if to say, Doesn't everybody? His brother loved to mock his acquaintance with these luminaries, but they were denizens of his ecosystem, citizens of his Manhattan social strata. They went to the same restaurants, the same art openings. He published some of them, sold the movie rights for books he had published to others, did coke in the bathroom at Odeon with one or two of them. He was still intimate with the literary scene, although he couldn't quite help feeling as if it were passing him by or in decline. Norman Mailer had once said to him, at a party, that Faulkner and Fitzgerald and Hemingway had been the figureheads of the golden age of American literature, that he himself was the king of the silver age and that Russell's peers and the authors he published were representatives of the bronze age. At the time Russell had considered this the sclerotic refrain of an aging lion, but now being, if anything, older than Mailer had been when he made this declaration, he could sympathize with the sentiment because it echoed his own sense of cultural decline, even as he could imagine the counterargument—that he'd become an old fart.

He looked at his phone again—no texts.

The Saturday *New York Times*, which arrived to subscribers with many of the Sunday sections intact, could normally absorb a couple of hours of his attention. This morning he was hard-pressed to concentrate. He turned to the Book Review and scanned the table of contents but couldn't summon any interest in the titles.

He pushed the papers aside and took the elevator downstairs, stopping first at Madman Espresso, where he ordered a double latte for himself, and a matcha latte for Corrine, stooping to pet an inquisitive goldendoodle who was leashed to a pretty young woman wearing a tight black Interpol T-shirt. He wanted to talk to her, to say, I love Interpol. I heard them at the Mercury Lounge in . . . '02, '03? But he held back, remembering the poster in Astrid's loft last night, and not wishing to be the creepy older guy, concentrating his attention instead on the dog, who was delighted by it. His owner seemed suspicious and tugged him away. Russell walked across the street to the deli, where the counterman, seeing him, asked, "Breakfast burrito, hot sauce?" Russell nodded, liking that he and his preferences were known here, loving his routine, appreciating it even more on this grim morning when it seemed that his life might come crashing down around him. Yesterday he walked through his morning ritual almost unconsciously, whereas today it seemed miraculous. Stepping outside, he placed a five-dollar bill in the cup of the panhandler who camped out there, who wore a black puffy parka summer and winter, and no socks.

Back upstairs, he placed the matcha on Corrine's bedside table, grateful that she was still asleep, grateful for the image of himself as the thoughtful husband. What had he been thinking these last few months? He felt he'd suffered a bout of temporary insanity. He loved Corrine. He needed her. He'd spent two-thirds of his life with her and he hoped to spend the rest of it together. He was not really eager to face her yet, although she had taken the revelations of last night with more grace and understanding than he could have expected. He checked his phone fruitlessly. A minute later, as he sat down again at the kitchen table, it buzzed. He grabbed it, only to find a text from Jeremy: *What the hell was that about last night.*

Long story.

I bet

Why don't we talk? I'm calling now.

"Dad?"

"I thought it would be easier to actually talk."

"That was pretty fucked up last night."

"Yeah, I guess. It was all extremely awkward."

"So you were with that girl?"

"She's a novelist. We were having a drink at her apartment."

"It must have been a hell of a drink."

"She decided to do a couple lines of coke. And I guess it was laced with fentanyl."

"So you were just innocently doing coke with this girl in her apartment?"

"She's a friend. I've known her for . . . ten years." If you counted that first encounter about a decade ago.

"Does Mom know about this?"

"She does now. I told her everything last night."

"So are you sleeping with this girl? I mean, were you? Do you even know if she's alive?"

"In answer to your question, no, I was not . . . sleeping with her. And I don't know if she's alive. I haven't heard anything yet. Do you have any idea what hospital they would have taken her to?"

"Maybe Wyckoff Heights."

"I'll call there."

"Good luck, Dad."

"Thanks, Jeremy."

"Let me know if I can do anything on this end, Dad. You know I love you. I'll be praying for you—and her."

He tried the Wyckoff Heights Medical Center and two other nearby hospitals with no success, an exercise in futility which consumed an hour and a half, most of that on hold. While he was arguing with a receptionist at Jamaica Hospital, Corrine wafted in and out in the Frette robe he'd bought her for Christmas, picking up several sections of the paper to take back to the bedroom. Finally, he dialed Astrid; the call went straight to voicemail.

"Any news," Corrine asked when he joined her in the bedroom.

He shook his head and tried to gauge her mood, reading her demeanor as neutral, if not amiable.

"I don't know what to do."

"You must feel hellish."

"It's awful."

"I'm sorry."

"No, Jesus, I'm the one who should be sorry."

"You should be and you are. But you didn't buy the cocaine and you didn't force her to do it."

"Why are you being so nice?"

"Because I can see that you're punishing yourself. I don't want to add to your misery right now. That doesn't mean I'm not angry at you. Or that I won't be angry later. I reserve that right."

"Not knowing is the worst. I don't know what to do with myself."

"I would say pray. But sadly, that's not an available option for you."

"No, I'm afraid that would be supremely hypocritical. But why do you say 'for you'? I mean, last I checked you were just as agnostic as I am."

"I've been working on my faith, if you must know. Trying to find my way back."

"Since when?"

"Since I was sick, I guess."

He looked at her in wonder. It seemed amazing that his wife might be a believer. It was as if she'd just told him that she had a secret life, about which he was ignorant. He'd noticed her reading *The Confessions of Saint Augustine*, but he'd naturally assumed she was interested in its literary merit. Russell and Jeff had plucked a phrase from the book as their faux motto, back in their days at Brown: "Lord, save me. But not yet." To two skeptical, intellectually arrogant young men, it had seemed hilarious forty years ago, the idea that you could live as you wish for as long as you wish and eventually repent.

"So would you say you believe in God?"

"I would say that I am inclining that way. Maybe I'm just taking up Pascal's Wager on my own terms. There's more to be gained believing than not believing. I don't necessarily mean avoiding hellfire. It's more a question of inner peace, of feeling less alone in the universe."

"But do you actually feel it? Or is it an intellectual thing? Is it a wager? Or a leap of faith?"

"I guess the latter. I'm still working it out."

"Wow."

"I know it must seem strange to you."

"Why didn't you tell me?"

"I know you. You would have been skeptical if not downright scornful. But maybe not so much now."

"At this moment I kind of envy you. But as you said in the beginning, I can't just suddenly call on God because it's convenient."

"Well, I can pray for you."

"Really?" Again, he was astonished, as if she'd just promised to mix up a potion with dragon's teeth and tongue of newt. "Well, thanks."

"You should probably tell Storey about this, before anything comes out. You don't want her to read about it in the *Post*. And Jeremy, of course. How much did you tell him last night?"

"I talked to him this morning."

"How did that go?"

"In the end he was kind of sweet. He said something that struck me as odd. He said he'd be praying for me, and her."

"Good for him."

Too awash in anxiety to work or even to read, Russell called Storey, asking her out to brunch, offering to meet her in Brooklyn. Happily, she was free. They agreed to go to Marlow & Sons, the Williamsburg bodega-café-restaurant that was the mothership of the postmillennium Brooklyn dining boom. Its DNA could be seen in Storey's and a hundred other restaurants in the borough.

When Russell arrived, Storey had already secured an outside table under the green canopy and was chatting up her server, a boy with long brown hair on one side and a shaved scalp on the other. His earlobes were distended by two large black hoops.

"Hey, Dad. This is kind of cool. When was the last time we had a father-daughter brunch?"

Russell struggled to get his balance on the rickety chair.

"Prelockdown for sure."

"What's the occasion?"

"No occasion, really."

"Really? You sounded kind of tense on the phone."

"Well, I was hoping we could start with some nice small talk."

"What did you do?"

"Why do you assume I did something?"

She stared at him implacably. "I'm listening."

He told her the story, much as he had told it to her mother last night, watching her face modulate through expressions of skepticism, disapproval and concern. He hoped that in retelling it he might discover some ameliorative fact, some sliver of hope.

"Oh my God—did she die?"

"I don't know. I've tried calling around to the hospitals."

"Jesus, Dad. You realize it could have been you?" Thankfully, this seemed to be the salient point for her. "You said she offered it to you first?"

He nodded.

"Your famous outmoded patriarchal manners may have actually saved your life."

Storey had openly objected to Russell's chivalrous gestures—holding the door, standing when a female stood up or sat down at a table—and mocked him for it.

"I mean, I hope she's okay. I'm glad that you are." Tears welled in the corners of her eyes.

"I feel hideously guilty."

Storey swiped her tears away. "Does Mom know about this?"

"I told her last night."

"How did she take it?"

"Better than I expected."

"Well, it's not like she couldn't relate." Storey had been the one who discovered her mother's affair, and had, it seemed, never entirely forgiven her for it.

"Do you think infidelity is inevitable?" she asked. "I mean, is there such a thing as a happy marriage?"

"Your mother and I have been pretty damn happy on balance. I thought of that while I was in the cab riding to my planned rendezvous. And I realized I couldn't go through with it."

"I mean, come on, Dad. She cheated on you with that rich guy. What's his name—Luke. And it wasn't a one-night stand. It was like a year or something. We don't even know."

"But we survived that crisis. And maybe in some way we came out stronger."

"Dad, that's a stupid cliché. Are you saying that you feel the same way about Mom as you did before you found out about her affair? That she didn't wound you?"

"No, that's not what I'm saying. But I wasn't perfect, either. I had my dalliances."

"Really?"

He hadn't meant to admit that. "Flirtations. Whatever." He couldn't believe he was using Jeremy's millennial word, though he saw how it could be useful. *Whatever.* "Anyway, I forgave your mother. And now she seems to be willing to forgive me for this."

Storey had been very hard on her mother after learning about the affair with Luke McGavock, had hardly been civil to her for months after finding out. Russell was grateful that, for whatever reason, she seemed not to be taking his news the same way. His mind drifted to Astrid. He was filled with dread: Was she dead or alive?

"Dad? Hello? Are you listening?"

"Sorry, what were you saying?"

The waiter came to take their order.

Storey chose a salad.

"Do you want some wine?" he asked her. He was not a daytime drinker, normally. But he felt like a little alcohol might ease the feeling of wanting to jump out of his own skin.

"I can't help wondering," she said, "whether Mingus is going to be like all the married men I know, his dad in particular? Or not."

"As regards what?"

"You know. As regards fidelity. Come on, Dad. We all know Washington was like this major player. We know he fucked around for years. It wasn't lost on Mingus."

"Are you worried?"

"Of course I'm worried."

"I think eventually you'll need to talk about it if your relationship is going to move forward." He looked down at his phone again, hoping against hope, though it hadn't dinged. Nothing.

"I can't imagine how you must feel."

He put his phone down on the table. Normally he would have put it in his pocket. Russell considered it rude to leave a phone out on the table, but this was hardly a normal day.

"It sounds as if you're contemplating a future with Mingus."

"Contemplating, yes. I suppose I can't help it."

"Maybe you two will do better than we did." That was the dream of all parents, that their offspring would be better, happier, richer than they had been themselves.

He conversed with his daughter through the lunch, although he was only intermittently conscious of the details of the conversation, his mind returning time and again to the events of the previous night, and the dark possibilities of the future.

The Uber ride back to the Village was a blur; the driver had to alert him to the fact that he had arrived at his apartment. Corrine's greeting was tepid.

"Any news?"

"No, unfortunately."

"How was lunch?"

"Fine. Under the circumstances. I told Storey what happened. She seemed to take it in stride."

Corrine raised her eyebrows in skeptical fashion, and he realized that while she was being as understanding as possible, there were two sides here, and they weren't on the same one.

"I mean, she was obviously disappointed in me—"

"But she probably reminded you that her mother had been unfaithful."

Russell shrugged.

"I thought so."

Knowing he was incapable of focusing, Russell changed into workout gear and went down to the gym with the intention of distracting and punishing himself. He made a point of doing extra sets of the exercises he liked the least.

Back upstairs, he stood under the hot shower until his fingers began to prune, and spent the rest of the afternoon watching episodes of *Jeeves and Wooster*, with Stephen Fry and Hugh

Laurie, in his home office. P. G Wodehouse had diverted and delighted him in some of his darkest moments, though in this case the exercise was only partially successful. Corrine, who had never really appreciated the genius of Wodehouse, stayed in the master bedroom, which, apparently, he was no longer supposed to call the master. What was the new term? The *primary suite*? Something like that. Corrine had promised to support him, but he could see that she would do so from a distance.

Cooking was always a welcome distraction; he scrolled through the recipes in his box on Newyorktimes.com, deciding to make shrimp and grits, in part because the recipe came via Julia Reed, a writer friend who'd died less than a year before at the age of fifty-nine—a great southern raconteur and bon vivant who had drunk him under the table on several occasions. As much as her death had shocked her friends, it also seemed like a cruel anomaly—cancer in the era of COVID. He suddenly remembered a drunken make-out session one night at a dive bar in New Orleans, when he'd attended a literary conference—a memory he would have preferred not to confront on this of all days. But there it was.

He went downstairs to the gourmet grocery on University, picking up the ingredients, and busied himself in the kitchen for almost an hour, occasionally sensing the Sword of Damocles above his head, before opening a bottle of Meursault and calling Corrine to the table.

The call came as he was clearing the plates. He almost dropped them when he saw the name: Jack Shea, *New York Post*. Shea sometimes covered the publishing industry, but he was also a reporter for Page Six. Russell had had mostly friendly dealings with him over the years.

"Oh fuck," he said.

"What?"

For a moment he considered not answering. But he realized

that wasn't an option. However bad the news was, he needed to face it.

"Hey, Jack," he said, in a voice that sounded like someone else's.

"Russell. Sorry to bother you on a Saturday night. But I don't think this can wait."

"What's up?"

"Well, I don't mean to be the bearer of bad news, but were you aware that Astrid Kladstrup died of an overdose last night?"

"No," he said, finally. "God, no."

"Yeah. You really didn't know?"

"Not until now. No. Jesus. This is . . . I'm devastated."

"I can imagine. I'm sorry. But I have to tell you, my source tells me that you were present at the scene. Would you care to confirm or deny that?"

"Can I go off the record here?"

"If you must."

"I was there."

"Can you tell me what you were doing there? I gather you're not actually her editor."

"No. We're just friends. I mean, we were."

"And you were . . . visiting?"

"Yes."

"And doing drugs together?"

Fuck.

"She . . . had some cocaine. I hadn't done it in years. Obviously, I didn't do it last night. She snorted a couple of lines and then her breathing became labored. I called 911 and started CPR. The paramedics arrived . . . I don't know, I'm not sure how much time passed. When they took her away, I didn't know if she was still alive. Jesus, Jack, is there any way you can leave me out of this?"

Russell racked his brain, trying to dig up some piece of information that he could trade. That was how it worked. You could often get a story killed by providing a bigger story. But this was huge, and he had nothing.

"I don't see how I can, really. And it's not as if I'm the only one who's going to be on this story. I'm happy to print any kind of statement you want to make. That's the best I can do."

"Fuck, man."

"Sorry, Russell."

"Can I call you back? What's your deadline?"

"I can give you thirty minutes."

29

CORRINE HAD BEEN listening attentively, raptly, to the conversation, which Russell had conducted on speaker.

Putting the phone down on the table, he looked ashen. "I don't know what to do."

He seemed to be looking at her across a vast distance. She lived in another world, a safe world.

"Do you want my input?"

"Yes, please." He looked at her gratefully, hopefully, as if he imagined she might be able to save him.

"Either you say nothing and hope that your name appears in a single short sentence. Or you come up with a statement that makes you sound like something other than a horny old lech."

"I can't imagine what that would be."

"I think you can only approach this obliquely, praise her work and her talent. Divert attention from your presence at the scene to your role as an early believer in her talent and a loyal friend."

"Well, which way do you think I should go?"

"Let's try to draft a statement."

Twenty-five minutes and four glasses of Pinot Noir later, they had it. Russell called Jack, who agreed to print it.

It had felt good to work together, to be in the trenches,

on the same team. She was still angry at him, and she would undoubtedly be angrier when the paper came out tomorrow, but she rather enjoyed the position she found herself in—the strong, supportive wife of a wayward and contrite husband. She felt terrible that this poor girl was dead, but she couldn't help acknowledging a sense of relief, now that they finally knew her fate.

They finished the bottle of Pinot Noir and agreed on a movie—*Pride and Prejudice*, the Keira Knightley 2005 version, even though they had already seen it, or perhaps precisely because they had seen it already, although this time there was no joking around about Russell's crush on the starlet. There was comfort in knowing, already, that the romantic drama would be happily resolved in the end. Afterward Corrine washed her face and moisturized, took half a Xanax to guarantee a decent sleep before the storm hit in the morning.

Russell's side of the bed was empty when she woke a little before eight. She found him at the kitchen table with the papers spread out around him. He greeted her, nodding gravely.

"How is it?"

"You read it and tell me."

Rising literary star Astrid Kladstrup was pronounced dead at Wyckoff Heights hospital in Brooklyn, the victim of an accidental drug overdose. Kladstrup had recently signed a half-million-dollar deal with Alfred A. Knopf for her novel *Admiral, My Admiral*, which reportedly detailed an affair with an older man, a prominent literary figure. According to police, the victim apparently consumed cocaine laced with fentanyl at her apartment in the McKibbin Lofts, a bohemian housing complex in Bushwick notorious for wild parties, which once housed a strip club. Russell Calloway, editor in chief of McCane, Slade, who was visiting

Kladstrup, called 911 after she lost consciousness. Reached at his home in Manhattan, Calloway said, "My wife and I are deeply saddened by the loss of Astrid, who was a brilliant writer and a close friend of our family." Page Six was unable to reach a spokesperson for Kladstrup's publisher, Knopf.

Corrine was rather proud of the phrases *my wife and I* and *a close friend of our family*. These had been her formulations. She felt that they sanitized what otherwise seemed like an entirely inappropriate relationship. But what the hell was this about her novel being about an affair with an older man?

As if reading her mind, Russell said, "Son of a bitch really screwed me by mentioning the subject of the novel."

Corrine was doing the math. "Exactly how long have you known this girl?"

"The older man is Philip Roth. Not me. But you'd never know that by reading the item."

She read the piece again. "You're right. That is a nasty touch. But I think it could have been worse."

"It would have been much worse if you hadn't come up with that *friend of our family*. I'm really grateful for that. *Really*."

"Let's see what the fallout is."

"Oh my God, look at this."

"What?"

"On Page Six. Bill and Lisa Sherman killed in a collision on the Long Island Expressway. Socialite and prominent plastic surgeon. Jesus."

Later, Casey would call them with more details. Drunk driver in the wrong lane. They might have survived if they'd been with their driver in the Escalade, but they were in Bill's Ferrari. It was a spur-of-the-moment thing. On their way to a dinner party in Manhattan. Which, of course, Bill had strenuously objected to, before giving in to his wife.

• • •

Storey checked in a little after 11:00 a.m., calling Corrine first. "You okay, Mom?"

"It's not the best day of my life, but I'll be fine. Your father will be spending a significant stretch of time in the doghouse."

"I know he feels really bad."

"We will recover. Unlike that poor young woman."

"Mingus says he's never doing coke again."

"Maybe some good will come of it after all."

Lisa would have been calling repeatedly, if she were still with us, Corrine thought. She felt bad for Lisa, also, of course.

She did take Veronica's call. Veronica, of all people, could empathize.

"What are people saying?" Corrine asked.

"I've had a few calls, people trying to find out what I know. Which of course is nothing."

"Honestly there's not much to tell. Russell says it was a long flirtation that was never consummated, though it almost certainly would have been, that night."

"Washington's been creeping around the house with a guilty look on his face. I think he's suffering a kind of sympathetic PTSD."

On Monday afternoon Russell called Corrine from the office. "You're not going to believe this."

"Try me."

"An ad hoc committee of six of my young female staff wants to meet with me to discuss the situation and to initiate a broader discussion about gender politics and patriarchal structures in the workplace."

"You're right. I don't believe it." Corrine found herself sympathizing deeply with her husband. She hated this kind of language and this kind of victim culture. Russell often found himself on the defensive with the younger members of his staff. Actually, it was all too believable.

"What did you say?"

"I haven't said anything yet. I wanted to get your perspective."

"You know how I feel about this kind of politically correct, crybaby feminism."

"I do."

"Is telling them to go screw themselves an option?"

In fact, back at the height of the Me Too hysteria, Corrine had often found herself on the politically incorrect side of the argument, while Russell was reflexively in favor of the female perspective. Russell was willing to subscribe to the motto Believe Women, whereas Corrine knew that sometimes women lied. She'd been harassed herself, and she'd always remembered how to say no.

"I don't see what Astrid's tragic death has to do with gender politics or the patriarchy."

"That's because you don't work in publishing in 2021."

"All I can say is good luck, honey. Don't give away the store."

That night he informed her he'd scheduled the meeting for Friday. He asked about her week, and she almost told him about her appointment with the gynecologist the next day but decided against it.

Waiting room indeed. This was one of the reasons she hated going to doctors; they inevitably kept you sitting long after your appointed time, as if you had nothing better to do. Plenty of time to worry about the symptoms that had brought you here, and the possible diagnosis. And here in the ob-gyn unit at Weill Cornell the periodical reading matter was absurdly banal and suburban: *House Beautiful; Modern Bride; O, The Oprah Magazine.* As if possessing a vagina entailed an interest in sewing, baking and daytime television. In her hurry to get out of the house she'd forgotten to bring her novel, Ann Patchett's latest. Thankfully she had her phone with its news feeds, although she always kind of hated joining the herd of screen addicts, the digital sheep.

Finally, her name was called, and she was ushered into a smaller room, where a nurse asked her to don a paper gown.

Another thing she disliked—that crinkly, flimsy blue paper. She was struggling with the ties when the doctor appeared, a pretty, slender, fortyish blonde who had apparently replaced the ancient Dr. Levy. Nice to have a woman gyno.

"Hi, I'm Dr. Feldman. And you are . . ." She looked at her clipboard. "Ms. Calloway."

"Corrine Calloway."

She squinted down at the clipboard.

"Do you know when you were last here?"

"I'm not sure, it's been a while."

"It looks as if it's been four years, unless you've been to another practice in the meantime."

"No, not really. I mean, no."

"Well, that makes you about three years overdue for a physical."

Corrine shrugged. "I didn't realize it had been that long." She felt a little like a delinquent child.

"So, tell me why you're here today."

"I've been having a certain amount of pain and discomfort."

"Where, specifically."

"I'm not exactly sure. My uterus?"

"And when do you notice it?"

"All the time. Frequently."

"Are you sexually active?"

"Well, somewhat. I've been married for thirty-seven years, so we're definitely not doing it every night."

"And is the sex painful?"

"Yes."

"Well, that can happen. If you don't use it you lose it."

Was that a joke? Well—she was smiling. Maybe a little ob-gyn humor.

"What does it feel like? Is it a sharp pain, a dull pain?"

"More dull. Except maybe during sex, when it's a little sharper."

"Is there anyone in your family with a history of cancer?"

"Cancer? God, do you think it's cancer?"

"I have no reason to think that at the moment, but I just want to be thorough. Any change in your bowel habits? Do you get constipated? Any change in appetite?"

"I sometimes feel bloated. And I haven't been very hungry lately."

"Nobody likes this part, but I'll try to make it as gentle as possible," she said as she donned a pair of surgical gloves. "Take a seat on the exam table, put your feet in the stirrups and scoot your butt all the way to the edge of the table. The first part of the exam is with the speculum. It's going to be a little cold and uncomfortable."

Corrine did as she was instructed, lay back and closed her eyes. Ouch, definitely cold and uncomfortable.

"It hurts. That's it."

"Okay, this next part is a little less uncomfortable. I'm going to put two fingers in your vagina. And one hand on the lower abdomen." She inserted the fingers, moving back and forth and moving her hand from one side to the other.

"I can feel that your uterus is a normal size, but I feel something else that's enlarged."

"How big is it?" At this moment it felt way too big.

"About the size of a nectarine. This may be what's causing you pain. I need to send you to have some imaging. I'm going to order up an ultrasound. We'll have some answers in the next twenty-four to forty-eight hours."

"What do you think it is?" Corrine asked, suddenly scared.

"It feels like something in the ovary, but it's difficult to know till we get imaging. It could just be a fibroid. We'll know more after the tests. If you have time now, we can get you in for a CAT scan and I'll have my nurse draw some blood."

Corrine tried to read her doctor's face, but she was inscrutable, her expression neutral. She was attractive, in her blue scrubs and with her dirty blond hair and olive skin. Corrine found herself thinking that she would make a suitable companion for Russell, should the news be bad. Definitely his type. He would probably like the fact that she was more buxom than his deceased wife. She found herself strangely calm, contemplating her own demise. This woman would care for her in her dying days, and she would do her best to comfort and reassure Russell and then Corrine would give them her blessing.

30

He assumed she was fuming on her side of the bed, brooding over the indignity of his recent misadventure, and the public disclosure. He had already engaged in damage control, put it out there that the older literary figure in the novel of the deceased ingenue was Philip Roth, the recently released biography of whom had created its own shitstorm of sexual innuendo. That should be in the *Post* and elsewhere tomorrow. He could only hope that would help mollify her and draw attention away from himself. Roth was a big deal, a boldface name. Russell Calloway was not.

He looked across the bed and saw the grim set of her mouth, and he found himself filled with remorse.

"I'm sorry, Corrine."

She shook her head. "It doesn't matter anymore."

He kneaded her bicep, which she always liked.

"I have ovarian cancer," she said, her voice calm and steady.

"What? You have . . . Are you kidding?"

"No."

"I . . . how do you know?" he said, as if he might disprove this theory.

"I went to the doctor."

"He could be wrong."

"*She.* I've been tested. CAT scan, blood test."

"Jesus."

"No need to indulge in blasphemy."

"You're serious."

"Yes, I'm serious."

He could see, looking at her, that she was entirely serious. But how could this be? Surely this wasn't possible. He looked over at her. She looked back at him, with sympathy, but without mercy. Behind her, their Harry Benson tableau of Andy Warhol snapping a photo of Bianca Jagger seemed suddenly out of place.

"There's got to be something we can do. I mean, it's curable, right? Surgery, chemo?"

"You can come in with me tomorrow. We'll get an idea of the options."

"Of course I'll come."

"I'm sorry, but I don't think I have it in me to comfort you right now," she said. "I'm going to read a little longer, okay?"

"Of course, my love." He kissed her cheek, but he lay awake beside her, with his eyes on the ceiling as she continued to read, hoping that she might need him, somehow, for something, that she might have something more to say. Finally, she turned off the light. He rolled over and donned his sleep mask, but he lay awake long after she turned off the light, taking a trazodone after she'd fallen into a lightly snoring sleep, wondering what his life would be without her, fabricating scenarios of miraculous remission, of himself in bedside vigil, in heartbroken, dignified mourning. No—of remission. Corrine miraculously recovering, Russell nursing her back to health, taking her to their favorite island, unvisited since the plague, her own recovery mirroring the rebirth of the planet, her illness receding like the disease, the two of them enjoying a personal, romantic and social renaissance, friendships revived from desuetude, rituals of romance restored and renewed. Champagne corks susurrating, glasses clinking, the hubbub of the crowd. Rebirth. She couldn't die, not now, just as this long collective nightmare was ending, just when he had realized how much he loved her and needed her.

The next morning, after a night of little sleep, he informed his assistant he would not be in and had her put one of those messages on his email account saying he would not be responding to emails till further notice.

"Please, don't creep around me as if I'm an explosive device," Corrine said, after spending a few minutes with him in the kitchen.

It was true, he supposed—his gait and general demeanor.

"Sorry, I just—"

"I know."

"Would you like some breakfast?"

"When have I ever wanted breakfast?"

"Good point."

"I wonder how it is you imagine that food can fix anything."

He gingerly, but not too gingerly, placed a mug of black coffee in front of her. "Hundred percent Kona peaberry from Hawaii, medium roast."

She smiled up indulgently. "I'm glad you have your hobbies, your coffee and your cooking and your wine."

"Jesus, don't say that." It sounded as if she were already saying goodbye.

They both took N95 masks in their pockets; their Uber driver, Mohammed, wore a little blue disposable. At the hospital they took the elevators to the Department of Obstetrics and Gynecology. Russell was reminded of their long reproductive quest, when they had visited half a dozen specialists. The visits more or less blurred together now, and he found it hard to believe that the pursuit of a child had once consumed them entirely. Corrine had undergone two rounds of IVF, Russell shooting her up with hormones in various Manhattan bar and restaurant restrooms, the two of them appearing to fellow patrons if they noticed them at all like a couple who had cohabited a bathroom to share sex or drugs or both. After two failed rounds the ritual had shifted to involve Hilary, Russell trying to think pure reproductive thoughts as he injected her with progesterone that summer they'd all shared the house in Sagaponack while they were coordinating their menstrual cycles and Russell was sticking a giant needle in Hilary's ass filled with a substance distilled from the urine of menopausal women. "It's not natural, what we're doing," Hilary said one night, drunk and probably coked-up after having stayed out half the night, rebelling against the strict regimen of temperance and injections they'd been observing all that month.

Russell drew the line at adoption, so after several failed attempts with her own eggs, Corrine had devised the plan to plant Hilary's in her own womb. The fertility doctor had said, "Well, theoretically it's possible." At the time they were at the frontier of reproductive medicine. Russell could only hope that now they'd be at the frontier of oncology. He had to hope that medicine had advanced far enough to save his wife.

Eventually they were ushered into a small examination room, where they were greeted solicitously by the hot doctor, Dr. Feldman—it was all right to think of her as the hot doctor because that was how Corrine had described her—and a male colleague whom she introduced as Dr. Kolman, the Doogie Howserish gynecologic oncologist, who appeared to be somewhere well short of his fortieth birthday and wore a thin brown beard as if to lend himself authority.

Russell shook hands with both.

"Dr. Kolman is the expert here," Dr. Feldman said, "but I wanted to be part of the consultation."

Dr. Kolman was balancing his laptop in his lap—he turned it and himself toward the two of them. Russell tried to interpret the image of darker and lighter gray blurs. The doctor took up the task, pointing with a green pencil.

"So, this," he said, "is an eight-centimeter solid and cystic mass on the right ovary with septations and ascites."

"*Septations* means the cyst is divided," Dr. Feldman explained. "*Ascites* means there is more fluid than is expected."

Dr. Kolman nodded vigorously, approving of the translation. "There's also a four-point-five-millimeter cyst on the left ovary. That's cancer."

"We're sure it's cancer?"

"The bloods confirmed it," Feldman said.

"The CAT scan shows that she has widespread cancer," Kolman continued. "There is metastatic spread of the disease. Throughout her abdomen. There is a thickening of the surfaces that line the intestines and lesions of the liver. And there is carcinomatosis."

"What does that mean?" asked Corrine.

"It means that the cancer has spread to other parts of your body, that it's not just localized in the ovary."

"What are my options," Corrine asked, calmly.

"Ultimately you will need surgery," said Kolman. "But we can treat with chemotherapy first to see if the surgery will be more feasible."

They were all silent for a moment. Then Corrine said, "No."

"No?"

"I don't want chemotherapy."

"You should take some time to think about it, talk it over with your family."

"I've seen people linger and languish with chemo, half dead. And then die anyway."

Her own mother, for instance. As Russell had seen his mother, decades ago, suffer the dread leading up to the treatment, the misery that followed along with a brief respite before the dread set in again. All, ultimately, for nought.

"I support Corrine in whatever course she wants to take," he said, his voice breaking.

"How soon can we schedule surgery," she asked.

"Probably within the week," Feldman said. "Dr. Kolman will need to check his schedule."

Russell squeezed her hand. He couldn't quite believe any of this.

There was the question of how, and when, to tell the kids.

"We have to tell them at the same time," Corrine said, "or there will be hell to pay."

"How're we even going to get Jeremy across the bridge?" Russell asked.

"Leave it to me," Corrine said.

He wasn't certain how she did it, but two nights later they both appeared at the apartment in the Village, simultaneously and unescorted, having shared an Uber from Brooklyn. Storey, in particular, seemed excited, as if this family reunion marked a happy occasion, though her mood turned darker when she realized that Russell was making their favorite childhood dish, which he adamantly refused to call chicken tenders, as it was known in most quarters; he'd actually been known to tell waiters that *tender* was not a noun, unless it referred to a boat that was used to ferry people and supplies to and from a yacht. But it was certainly not a part of the chicken. The kids would use the term just to wind him up, to hear Dad launch into his tirade. He was willing to call these fried strips of breast meat chicken fingers, as long as it was understood by the kids that this was a fanciful association. Now that Jeremy was a vegetarian, tofu and sweet potatoes took the place of chicken on his plate. Whatever they were called, Corrine hated it when he made it for them, because the batter making and the deep-frying made for disaster in the kitchen.

"Wait, why is Dad making chicken fingers?" Storey asked.

"We haven't been ten years old for some time," Jeremy said.

"What's wrong?" Storey said.

"Why does something have to be wrong?" Corrine had hoped to have everyone sitting down at the meal, to have the conversation somehow meander to its painful center.

"This is what you do when you have some big announcement."

She should have realized that sometimes ritual should be circumvented to minimize drama.

"We already know about Dad and the dead girl," Jeremy said. "Don't we?"

"Are you guys getting divorced?"

"We're not getting divorced."

"Is Dad getting prosecuted?"

Russell laid a plate of crudités on the kitchen table. "I think we should all sit down and chat calmly."

"We're obviously not calm anymore."

"Well, let's sit anyway."

"I'm sorry," Corrine said. "I just need to talk to you guys about something."

The two kids sat at the table simultaneously, regarding her with mild dread.

"It's . . . oh, the hell with it, I have cancer. Ovarian cancer. Which has metastasized to other parts of my body."

"Jesus, Mom."

"You're going to be okay, though. Aren't you?"

"I'm going to have surgery. Probably next week."

Both kids were tearing up.

Suddenly, she saw it through their eyes, saw her own ordeal collectively, saw that it was almost worse for them, and for Russell, than it was for her.

She reached over and took Jeremy's hand. He was trying hard not to cry.

"Hey, there's a good chance she'll pull through this," Russell said.

For a while, Corrine thought, maybe. But she kept the thought to herself.

"I can't believe this," Storey said. "You of all people."

"Why not me," Corrine said.

"You're, like, the best person in the world," Jeremy said.

"Even if that were true, God doesn't dole out these burdens or spare us according to virtue."

"Should I go ahead and start the chicken," Russell asked.

"Screw the chicken, Dad. Nobody's hungry."

"Your dad is," said Corrine. "I don't think he's ever lost his appetite for anything."

"Only that time he had food poisoning in Saint Barth's," Storey said.

"Somebody needs to eat in this family."

"We're very grateful, Dad," Jeremy said. "Every family needs a rank materialist."

"Every family needs a man like your father," Corrine said. "Let's not forget this is just as hard on him as it is on any of us, even though he'll try to cover it up."

"It's hardest on you, for Christ's sake."

"No," Corrine said. "That's where you're wrong."

Russell stood up and walked over to the stove. He reached a hand in the bowl of batter and smeared it all over his face and his hair. He walked back over to the table and sat down, beige batter obscuring his features.

Both kids started to cry. Corrine herself was too flabbergasted to cry; it was the first time that Russell had really surprised her in years and now, all at once, he'd shocked her.

31

Aside from a brief text at Christmas, Russell hadn't spoken to his brother in more than a year. As kids they'd been close, but had grown increasingly distant since their mother died. Aidan had felt that he carried the burden of that ordeal, that Russell had spent too much time in New York while the youngest was left to hold the bag at home. In fact, Aidan had felt the same about their father, who died more than a decade ago. For some reason he resented the fact that Russell had relocated his life as a young man and especially, it seemed to the older brother, that he had chosen to move it to New York, New York. Aidan was one of those people who genuinely hated Manhattan, who thought that it was the center of everything rotten and corrupt and hyperbolic and self-serving about the republic, who believed that it attracted the greatest blowhards and exhibitionists and crooks on the planet. The fact that he and his wife had once been mugged in the city not long after Russell and Corrine moved there in the eighties only affirmed his loathing. He expected Russell or a member of his family to be shot at any moment. And sometimes almost seemed to hope for it.

Aidan had stayed in the Detroit suburbs, had joined GM management after graduating from the University of Michigan at Ann Arbor, which was the height of aspiration for their father's generation of Michiganders, who would have barely heard of Russell's East Coast Ivy League university. He seemed to Russell to be permanently resentful of the relative glamour of his brother's life in New York, his friendships with name-brand authors and cultural figures, his casual worldliness. And most inexplicably, in his weakest moments, Russell secretly concurred with him. In times of crisis and self-doubt, Russell agreed with his brother, felt his midwestern soul quailing and recoiling from the artifice and ego and excess of his adoptive home and of his own adaptive strategies of citizenship. Aidan was right. Russell was an impostor. Even when he most hated his brother, he believed in his inherent decency. He was Russell's last link to his humble origins.

Aidan was surprised to hear from his brother. "To what do I owe the pleasure? One of your authors won the Nobel?"

"Wrong season. Just wanted to check in, see how you were doing."

"Color me flattered."

"No, actually, I'm lying. I need to talk."

"Well, hell, you dialed the right number. What's the matter, bro?"

"It's Corrine. She's sick. Really sick. I think I may lose her."

"Jesus. Cancer?"

"Ovarian cancer, but it's spread everywhere. She's always hated going to the doctor; she was three years overdue for her appointment with her gyno."

"What's the prognosis?"

Aidan himself had undergone a carcinoma crisis ten or twelve years ago—was that right? Time was all fucked up after the pandemic. Not long after their dad died. His prognosis had been bleak, but he'd followed through on the treatment stoically and persevered, which was one of the reasons that Russell called him.

"Bad. Just really fucking terrible. She's going under the knife next week, but the doctors aren't even a little bit reassuring."

"They weren't real upbeat about me, either."

"I remember."

"Do you want me to come out?"

"The fact that you're even offering is kind of making it seem more dire."

"It sounds dire. And I'm your only brother."

"Let me think about it. You're almost the first person I've told. The kids of course."

"How are they taking it?"

"As you'd expect."

"Should I call them?"

"I don't know. You've always been closest to Storey."

"What day is the surgery?"

"Next Tuesday or Wednesday."

"You'll tell me as soon as you know?"

"Yeah."

"Too bad we can only talk when things are grim."

"Well, maybe we can work on changing that. At least you didn't blame the cancer on the New York City air pollution."

"Doesn't mean I wasn't thinking it."

"Fuck you."

"Right back at you, bro."

32

THE SECURITY GUY at the entrance, empowered by his blue uniform and silver badge, was sullen and suspicious.

"Goddamnit," Russell responded to his query, "we're going to the ICU so that she can have life-or-death surgery tomorrow morning. Does that sound like a legitimate reason to be here?"

The guy pointed to the admissions desk as Corrine gently tugged Russell's arm. "He's got a thankless job," she said. Normally Russell would have been conscious of that. That was one of the things she loved about him—his sympathy for waiters and drivers and cleaners and valets.

A wheelchair and a porter were summoned for Corrine, who was slightly embarrassed as they passed the scolded security guard in the line and proceeded to the elevators, resisting the urge to apologize.

The nurses, when they reached the ICU, were all sympathy and solicitude. Two of them—Tiffany and Janelle—eased her into the hospital bed from the wheelchair.

The room was unequivocally a hospital room, white and gray, studded with screens and dials and aluminum fixtures, but it was private and relatively spacious, with a padded reclining chair in the corner which would serve as Russell's bed. She felt bad for him, but he'd insisted that he would sleep there, a privilege, if such it could be called, of her critical status.

"I'm sorry," Janelle said, wrapping a rubber tourniquet around her bicep, "but I'm going to need to draw some blood."

"Don't be sorry," Corrine said.

Russell busied himself with the TV, quickly finding MSNBC, with Rachel Maddow, who competed for attention with the beeps on the monitor to which Tiffany had just attached Corrine via a blood pressure cuff. Rachel was revisiting some scandal that had recently resurfaced from the waning days of the Trump presidency.

When they had finally stopped prodding and poking Corrine, a young Hispanic woman appeared bearing a tray of food. Russell waved her away as if she were the devil.

"Thanks, but I ordered a delivery."

"Always thinking of me," Corrine said. The idea of any kind of food, especially the kind of fancy stuff Russell liked, nauseated her. She hadn't eaten anything in three days.

"Do you think we could watch something a little lighter and frothier. I just don't feel like I'm in an MSNBC mood."

Although she was not a television person in general, she thought the distraction would be good for them—certainly for her. She did not want to talk about what was happening tomorrow, nor did she want him dwelling on it.

"What do you want to watch," he said, flipping through the channels with her remote, which also contained the call button.

"There, stop, perfect," she said as he landed on *Modern Family*. "I know, it's a little silly," she said. Or maybe not. Maybe this was more substantial than Rachel Maddow and Donald Trump. *Family*. With that actor who used to be on *Married with Children*. *Marriage, children*. More important than Rachel. Maybe she was just getting sappy toward the end. She didn't use phrases like *the end* with Russell, but she felt strongly that she didn't have too much longer on this earth. A year? She tried to remember the lyrics to the Doors song, besides the repetition of the word *fuck* which had mesmerized her and her Miss Porter's roommates after they'd discovered the song when the Doors experienced a revival. Somehow Jim Morrison, dead for almost a decade, had become part of her quest to understand sex back then. She and her peers had pored over Doors lyrics in the dorm that winter, swooned over shirtless photos of the lupine singer. She was a late bloomer, by the standards of the times and her friends, only finally losing her virginity in the summer after her graduation, with Chad Palmer, in a musty boathouse on his family's compound in Wellfleet. They were in love—her first real love, and he had waited patiently for more than a year. She cried afterward; only later did she realize that he had a remarkably small penis and that she'd been spared the physical pain. She could still smell the stale funk of that room, the nautical relics and enclosed air intermingled with the baked-Brie scent of Chad's spunk. She'd never smelled semen before then. Chad died the next year after a concussion on the rugby field at Amherst, of a subdural hematoma, during Corrine's freshman year at Brown. It all seemed like a cliché now, like something out of *A Separate Peace* or *This Side of Paradise*, but it hadn't then.

She tried to remember him—his smell and the feel of his lips on hers, his laugh—but he was more of a story than a person to her now. There was a time she told herself she would have died for him, and now he was a memory, someone she remembered fondly. Special, because her first. She wondered if she would see him again, in what form. He forever twenty-one, she an aging lady? Would his earthly memories of her be fresh and intact? And what about all the others? The people she'd once known. The ones she didn't even remember? Not lovers, there'd only been—how many? Six of those. Even with Russell, did she remember the important moments? Or was that the definition of *important*, that they were remembered? Suddenly she was full of mourning for all she had forgotten, for the diminution of people she'd once known. Russell had been in her Romantic Poetry class sophomore year and she remembered thinking of him as Shelley, or sometimes Keats. *Adonais*. Jeff and Russell sparring in that class, as if competing for the title of doomed genius, back when they were both twenty, and twenty-six seemed old. Then a long hiatus, until, in the midst of a spat with her long-term boyfriend, Kurt, they'd run into each other at registration and ended up going to lunch, talking for hours, ending up in his room.

It was the talking she remembered the most, it seemed they didn't stop talking for five days; if she were honest, the sex was filling in lacunae in the conversation about poetry and prose recitations. He read her the entirety of Molly Bloom's soliloquy from *Ulysses*, concluding with its triumphant *Yes. Yes I said yes I will Yes.* Of course, she remembered the first time, the first time they made love, but only vaguely. It was neither *her* first time, nor would it be her last. The second time she remembered more clearly, when they went away for the weekend. With her period and the Joy. Then Jeff, poor beloved Jeff, who'd almost spoiled her marriage before it had begun. God, she'd been crazy about him, as one can be only about a doomed creature.

Russell was her soul mate, but Jeff was the great mystery that rendered her alive. Jeff was her Jim Morrison, her other, the dangerous one, the one not entirely of this earth. Russell felt it, too, was attracted to it, to Jeff's excess and his lack of terrestriality. Russell liked to say that the road of excess leads to the palace of wisdom, and he admired the people who could commit to that path, though he never could—or precisely because he never could. He accepted his role as the handmaiden of genius. Jeff and that southern kid he published and maybe the girl, Astrid.

What was it Spender wrote? *Born of the sun, they travelled a short while toward the sun / And left the vivid air signed with their honour.* All gone, the ones whose flames consumed them. While Russell abides and fans the embers of their legacies. She remembers the first and only time with Jeff as if it were yesterday. In his drafty loft in SoHo, the wavy windows rattling in their frames, after her very first lines of cocaine, her skin and every fiber of her being alight as she kissed him and lay down beneath him. He slid inside of her and came, and then three more times over the next few hours. It was just that one time, but they could never forget it. Even now—thirty years after he'd been gone, though never really gone. She'd lived with his book, which was really about the three of them, for three years while she wrote the screenplay, his words in her head, his cock never entirely forgotten.

With Luke it had been more complex—a midlife crisis, a national emergency, love amid the smoking ruins of the Twin Towers. But in the end there was Russell. Who had persevered and abided. Who, Ulysses-like, had come back for her. Who had forgiven her her sins. She could almost reconcile herself, at this moment, to the woman who would replace her. For someone would, though not right away, of course. She looked over at him, his attention switching between the TV screen and the book on his lap: *The Short Stories of Ernest Hemingway*. Funny that he'd chosen that, a book he probably hadn't looked at in thirty years. Intimations of mortality? The comfort of familiar fare? All the literary men of his generation and the ones before it empowered by Hemingway's masculinity, the hunting and boxing and marriages, and now suddenly embarrassed by it. Now it was probably more fashionable to like Ronald Firbank.

Hemingway was a bastard, and her husband a decent and generous soul. Russell would have a hard time for a while, but eventually he would find a companion. He would resist initially. He would worry about the kids' reaction, and when the kids freaked out he would try to suppress his desire, and then he would hide it for a while. But eventually he would give in. He would be thrilled and guilty at the same time. He would rediscover sex. Someone would caretake him for her, until she saw him again, as she knew she would. He needed people. Whereas she had her faith. It had crept up on her first when she was sick last year, when she had thought about dying, and had grown almost inexorably, and though she had not spoken of it to Russell until very recently, she had discussed it with Jeremy, who for all his foibles was profoundly spiritual. Just this past week they had prayed together, something she could never do with Russell. They prayed for her recovery, of course, but they also prayed for the family. It was true—there was something about a mother and her son. Only Jeremy knew how she felt, and while Jeremy was terribly worried and afraid, he understood why his mother was not. Or not in the same way that his father would be.

Storey would be distraught, of course, and she would feel terribly guilty about all the disloyal things she'd felt and thought about her mother over the years, but that would fade. And she had Mingus. Corrine worried that he was a Jim Morrison, but somehow imagined that he might stick around, that he might grow up to be the kind of man that his father had become after so long, only sooner. She would be sad not to see it, to leave them at the beginning of their story, and she would be sad for their sadness. She still loved the things of this world, more than ever as she realized they were fleeting—the sunrise over the barrel-shaped water towers of the East Village, the smell of her bath oil on her skin, York Peppermint Patties, the feel of Russell's scratchy chin on her cheek. And Russell. Russell himself. He was the abiding joy of her life.

He had apparently enjoyed his food from Jean-Georges, which she had waved away, and now he was reading, sprawled in his uncomfortable chair.

"What are you reading," she asked.

"'The Snows of Kilimanjaro.'"

"Isn't that the one where the husband dies of gangrene in the African bush?"

He nodded.

"Do you ever regret that you didn't go for it as a writer? Do you think you would have tried if we hadn't decided to get married?"

"Why would you ask that?"

"I remember the husband in the story is a failed writer."

Russell closed the book on his lap. "I never thought of it that way. I did what I was best at doing. I didn't think I had the talent and I knew I didn't have the conviction. You need to know. You need to believe in it more than anything, including love. Most who try to live outside the margins fail, and even those who succeed, like Jeff—they seldom have long and happy lives. Which is what I've had with you so far."

"Really? Despite everything?"

"Stop getting morbid. You're going to get through this."

"I'm a little scared."

"Only a little? I'm terrified."

"I wonder if I'm going to be punished for my transgressions."

"What transgressions?"

"Mostly those against you."

"If I forgive you, who the hell is God to not forgive you?"

Janelle came in, pert and pretty in her long tapering braids and her blue scrubs.

"Sorry to bother you."

"That's okay."

"Tell me your name."

"Corrine Makepeace Calloway."

"Where are you?"

"Weill Cornell Medical Center, also known as New York Hospital."

"Can you tell me the date today?"

"Is it before midnight? July fourteenth, 2021. Bastille Day."

"Very good. I'm afraid I'll be back again tonight, but just so you know the surgical team has informed us they'll be operating at seven-thirty, so someone will get you about seven-fifteen. Can I get you a blanket," she asked Russell, who nodded.

Russell struggled with his chair, extended the legs as far as they went and thrashed around. Never a peaceful sleeper at the best of times. She watched him from the hospital bed. Maybe he was right. Maybe they had another year or two together.

Corrine dozed intermittently. She dreamed about her parents, who were still together in her dream, who were helping her build a sandcastle on the beach. Corrine was worried that her blue bucket was missing. Then they were waking her. It was time to go.

Russell held her hand as they pushed the bed toward the door. His mouth was set in a kind of stern rictus, as if he were expressing his anger at the disease. "I'll be waiting here."

She tried to think of a farewell that would not seem too final;

she looked into the deep blue pools of his eyes. All she could come up with was "I love you." She realized she was no longer afraid.

Apologizing for bumps along the way, they wheel her into the fluorescent operating room, where six or seven scrubbed assistants are clattering metal against metal. Her surgeon isn't here yet. The anesthesiologist is a very young-looking Asian man. He seems very kind.

"I want you to count down from one hundred and think about your favorite beach," he says, placing the mask over her face.

She thinks about a deep blue hole off the coast of their favorite island, a place they probed but never fathomed, a warm bottomless portal into the earth. She sees Russell's blue eyes. Ninety-seven, ninety-six. She swims down into the blue.

Then she is back in the operating room, though she is no longer in the bed. There is an air of panic among the blue-suited occupants of the operating room, a sense of urgency and helplessness. Some of them are looking at her and some are staring at the monitors. Then she sees herself on the bed, motionless. She wants to tell them not to worry, that everything will be all right, everything will be as it should be, as it must be.

Her mother is watching from nearby, her hand outstretched. Then the doctor says, "She's gone."

33

As soon as they saw the surgeon's face, they knew.

Storey shrieked.

Russell was shocked, speechless.

"I'm sorry," the doctor said.

"What happened," Jeremy asked.

"She suffered a pulmonary embolism on the operating table. It's a blood clot that blocks the flow of your blood from your heart to your lungs. If you have a massive one you die. We were measuring the gas exchange. When your CO_2 levels drop your gas exchange isn't working."

What the fuck are you talking about, Russell thought. Gas?

"The cancer had spread throughout her system. It was worse than we anticipated."

Storey was sobbing. He stood up and walked over to hug her.

Later, when he thought back on that day, it came to him in flashes. Signing papers. The blue turban of the Sikh Uber driver. The communal table at Au Bon Pain, where they had finally retreated for coffee and croissants, although for once Russell was unable to finish the latter. He had finally lost his appetite. The solicitous expression on Jeremy's face, the fact that he seemed genuinely concerned for his father's well-being, the brief feeling that he might finally, someday, grow up and take his place in the world. He remembered reading the next morning, in the *Post*, that there would be a memorial service for Astrid at the Center for Fiction Café and Bar in Brooklyn, and feeling guilty that he would not attend, weighing the guilt he would feel if he did.

For the time being Jeremy moved into the spare room in the Village apartment, a fact for which Russell was quietly grateful. He couldn't deal with the texts and phone calls and the emails and most of all with those who offered to visit. Jeremy fended these off.

Jeremy was especially helpful arranging the memorial service at Grace Church, the 1845 landmark that stood just a long block away on 10th Street and Broadway. It was a place, Corrine told him last week, that she'd been visiting ever since they moved to the Village and where she was in fact in training to become a docent. It still astonished him that his wife could have had this secret, pious life of which he'd been ignorant. Some days it seemed like a betrayal. The Opiate of the People. Religion was for the weak and the dim and the profoundly needy. He could understand the impulse, but he didn't subscribe to it. Now he was divided. He was glad that Corrine had that comfort at the end, he could even crave it himself. But it wasn't something that could be merely wished for. You couldn't just say—Hey, I think I'll believe now. Or so he believed.

Somehow it seemed fortunate that Jeremy shared Corrine's faith. He commandeered Russell's address book—a leatherbound relic of the analog era which his father had stubbornly maintained for decades, and coordinated it with Russell's AOL email list. And he reached out to her colleagues at Nourish New York. Russell was uncertain whether there was a vaccine requirement for the funeral, but almost all of the mourners wore masks, which perhaps made it slightly easier to deal with the emotions, and his own, somewhat hidden as they were.

Russell had to edit the speaker roster down to a manageable number—so many people offered to speak. Storey and Jeremy and two of her colleagues spoke touchingly; Casey, who alluded as much to her long-ago divorce as to her friend's death, and

Washington, who, seated next to Russell on the podium, was magnificent. Two hundred and sixty-seven people, not all of them known to Russell, signed the guest book. He had thought about speaking but had demurred. He doubted he could hold it together and doubted that his eloquence would be equal to the occasion. In the end he'd read a short poem, "Travelling Together," which she had singled out when he'd given her W. S. Merwin's collection *The Rain in the Trees*, for her birthday in 1988.

If we are separated I will
try to wait for you
on your side of things

your side of the wall and the water
and of the light moving at its own speed
even on leaves that we have seen
I will wait on one side

while a side is there

He remembered the funeral only fleetingly; much more vivid was the wedding, exactly a year later, of Storey and Mingus, at Grace Church. Russell was absurdly happy to be allying himself with his favorite family. Deep in his heart he was realistic about the prospects, conscious of the possibility that this might not be the union for the ages. But he liked to believe that the example of their parents might prove inspirational. Storey and Mingus had grown up together and already survived significant storms. He believed happiness should be seized even if fleeting, and he'd learned to live with a certain amount of doubt.

"Who're you bringing to the wedding?" Wash asked.

"No one. I mean, seriously, I can't do that."

"I get that."

Russell had had a few dates, but he couldn't really take anyone seriously. And the wedding was no time to start. Jeremy, for sure, would not approve. As for Storey, she was living in a bubble that he was loath to burst, a romantic cocoon from which she would eventually pupate into a bride and mother. She and Mingus had decided to get married after she discovered she was pregnant.

Storey had no intention of quitting her job, though she would obviously need to adjust her schedule. Her restaurant had recently received a glowing two-star review in *The New York Times*, and business had exploded. Russell had joked that it would have been a three-star review if she'd only laid down a dirt floor, the *Times* critic being notoriously sympathetic to the rustic, the unpolished or the proletarian vibe. They'd removed the most expensive wines from the list, and the caviar, when they learned that he was coming in.

Mingus had just collected the second tranche of his advance from his long-overdue memoir for Knopf—which now culminated with the story of his arrest and abuse at the hands of the police. *The New Yorker* had just published a second excerpt, and film producers were circling. Which was both wonderful and worrisome; Russell had seen what overnight success could do to the most stable individual, and he was not sure how Mingus might react.

The rehearsal dinner was at Lilia, in Williamsburg, where Storey had once worked as a sous-chef. Storey's kitchen staff helped prepare the dinner. The cocktail hour was intimate and raucous, composed mostly of Storey and Mingus's contemporaries—recent graduates of Brown and Yale, many of whom Russell knew by sight if not by name, although they introduced themselves: Madison, Mason, Olivia and Ava, Justin and Dylan and Liam, Jessica and Sebastian. They seemed an exuberant and confident group, and skewed artsier, more bohemian, than a random selection of Ivy Leaguers.

Zora had flown in from Paris a couple of nights ago with a Frenchman on her arm. "I waited till the last minute," she said to Russell. "You know, just in case."

"Just in case?" Russell asked.

"Well, you know how plans can go sideways with my bro."

"You realize you're talking to the father of the bride."

"Hey, you've known him as long as I have."

Washington rose and waited for silence after they'd taken their seats.

"As the father of the groom, I would like to welcome you all to this celebration of the union of two special people, and I would like to welcome Storey to our family, although it seems she has in some sense been a part of it since she was born. Nothing could feel more natural or welcome than officially uniting our family with the Calloway family, although I have to say that you could have knocked me over with the proverbial feather when I realized that romance had sprung up between these two. I mean, *how the hell did that happen?* It was both surprising and yet fitting. We held our collective breath, wondering if this was too good to be true, as I'm sure Storey's father will confirm. But here we are. I'm not a religious man, but I have to confess this seems blessed and miraculous—these nuptials and the upcoming birth of our first grandchild. The moment could only be sweeter if Storey's mom were here to be a part of this."

Washington sat down, surprising those who, like Russell, were expecting something a little spicier, a little more risqué, from the father of the groom. He was feeling a little shaky, hearing Corrine mentioned, but he realized that someone had to do it, and he didn't feel up to it himself. He didn't want to break down in front of Storey and her friends, and he was pretty sure he would if he got up to toast. It had only been a year.

Happily, Mingus stepped into the breach.

"Hey, everyone. Groom here. I just want to follow up on what my dad said. I'm so lucky to be marrying Storey tomorrow, and I know that part of my good fortune stems from Storey's mom, who was an incredible lady. My first really vivid memory of Corrine—I must have been six or so, and my parents were having a dinner party and I came out and wanted to see what was going on, and my folks not surprisingly told me to go back to bed. For some reason I was really upset by this and I sniveled my way back to my bedroom and Corrine came in and started talking to me. I remember her telling me I wasn't missing much and that she wished she could go home and go to bed. And she just talked to me for ten or fifteen minutes until I fell asleep. She was an incredibly empathetic person. She was my mom's best friend, but I think there were three or four others who felt the same way. They say if you want to know the daughter look at the mother. Well, I did. And I loved what I saw. So I'd like to raise a glass to Storey's mother."

After a respectful interlude in which it became clear that Russell was abdicating his toast, the kids rushed in.

"Hi, everyone. I'm Ryan Coughlin, a classmate of Storey's. I'm thrilled to celebrate the joining of these two. Others can speak for the origins of Mingus's gift for writing, but I thought I would tell you the little-known story about Storey's love of cooking, which originated with a cartoon called *Dexter's Laboratory*. If you look on the menu, you will see that the first course is *omelette du fromage*, although no such course actually appeared. The sticklers among us may point out that the phrase is grammatically incorrect—that *omelette au fromage* is the proper phrase."

"Somebody got the joke," Storey called out.

"As a fan of Dexter, I have to say that Dexter employs this phrase to great effect, using it for all occasions. In fact it is the only thing he can say after he wakes up having spent the night listening to a learn-French recording which gets stuck on that phrase. And where do you suppose that Storey first got inspired to pursue a culinary career? I submit to you it was from watching Dexter. And what do you suppose she was asked to prepare for her audition as a *stagiaire* at L'Arpège in Paris? An omelette of course."

Russell remembered watching the cartoon with Jeremy.

"We were all sorry when we heard that Storey was leaving Brown," Ryan said, "but at this point she's probably the most successful member of our class so far. And the fact that she survived in a three-star French kitchen for three months demonstrated that despite her diminutive frame and ladylike demeanor she is one tough chick. So watch out, Mingus. She's not going to put up with any shit."

"Yeah, she was also a fan of the *Powerpuff Girls*," Mingus called out. "Which is probably how she learned to stand up to French line cooks. And to me."

Russell remembered *that* cartoon, too—three squeaky-voiced little girls who KO'd the villains that were always threatening their fair city. He saw himself sitting on the couch of the old loft in TriBeCa with Storey, watching the show, and felt KO'd himself by the distance between then and now, by the immense span of time and everything that had filled it. He told himself he was going to hold it together, but he missed that little girl on the sofa almost as much as he missed her mother. He tried to focus on the guests, most of whom were Storey and Mingus's cohort. Ryan, the speaker, was a politico, worked for the mayor's office in some capacity. He was engaged to the beautiful redhead with porcelain skin. Russell couldn't remember her name, but, of course, Corrine would have. She was so good with that kind of thing. Names, birthdays, anniversaries. As was her daughter.

"Good-looking kid," said Casey, Corrine's probably best friend. "He's like some matinee idol from the black-and-white days."

"Nice kid," Russell said. He was a little bit leery of Casey, who seemed to be trying to leverage her relationship with Corrine into increasing intimacy with Russell. "He came skiing with us a few years back." Was it a few years back? Probably further back. The pandemic had totally screwed up his sense of time. He was trying to remember the girlfriend's name. He remembered she was an editor at *Air Mail*, the online weekly.

The kid who stood up next Russell remembered seeing somewhere and, luckily, he introduced himself after banging on his wineglass.

"Hi, everyone, I'm Jackson Palmer, Mingus's New Haven roommate and best man." Not for the first time Russell wondered why Yale men thought it was somehow less pretentious to name the town rather than the college. Brown people never said, When I was in Providence. "First off, I'd just like to say it's nice to be here because I've never been able to get a reservation at this fucking place. Not for lack of trying. I mean, come on, it's pasta for God's sake. So thanks for that, Storey. I'd love to tell you stories about Mingus's college days, but I don't want to be responsible for sabotaging a marriage in advance. And if you Google *wedding toasts*, it will tell you in no uncertain terms not to mention exes or previous love interests. So . . . I can say I never knew him to hand in a paper on time. But he was the only guy I know who published in *The New Yorker* as a sophomore. And he managed to graduate summa cum laude. No small deal. Nor was getting a book contract as an undergraduate. Which was, what, eight or nine years ago. Speaking of procrastination, he missed more deadlines on his book contract than Truman Capote for *Answered Prayers*." Russell thought about Victor Propp, a novelist who'd strung along his publishers, Russell among them, for three decades or so with the promise of a book that never arrived. But no one remembered Propp, once a revered literary figure, now forgotten and unread. Those early glorious days in New York now half forgotten even by him.

"I hope for your sake, Storey, that his, how you say, *endurance* as a writer is matched in other areas of life."

This brought a slowly escalating cascade of laughter from the group.

"No premature, uh, publication for Mingus. But I am happy to announce that he has, allegedly, actually finally finished the damn thing."

This prompted applause.

"Apparently, he was very slow to tell Storey how he felt about her, too. I mean, it only took him about twenty-three years. But he finally made his move. And we know he finished at least one other big job. We can't wait to welcome a new little Lee into the world. So let's raise a glass to Mingus and Storey and their forthcoming offspring."

Russell's brother Aidan gave a toast with jokes about the city and its unsuitability for marital life, in which he compared the bride to her mother. Russell drank too much Chianti and intermittently lost control of his features. He remembered fending off an offer to share an Uber with Casey, but not much else about the end of the evening.

The kids designed the wedding ceremony with the minister. Emily, the pale redhead, took the first reading. First Corinthians, naturally. Jeremy, who had recently moved to Washington to work as an administrative assistant for Hakeem Jeffries, the New York congressman, recited the inevitable Sonnet 116 by Shakespeare. To rail against this cliché and point out that the whole sequence was essentially homoerotic was one of those causes that Russell had ceased to pursue as he grew older. His children believed that he had become less rigid with age, that, if anything, he had taken on some of those qualities that their mother possessed, in her absence. He'd started observing meatless Mondays, and he volunteered once a month at one of the food-giveaway stations for Nourish New York. He'd adopted a rescue from the ASPCA, a woodchuck-sized bitch of indeterminate lineage. He published a book about effective altruism that Corrine had urged him to take on. It seemed to them he lectured less and listened more. He quoted their mother frequently and sometimes used the phrase *when I'm gone*, which made them crazy. He tended to judge things through her eyes, as when he would say, "Your mother would have loved this" or "Your mother would have thought that was ridiculous." A part of her seemed to live on in him. And watching his daughter recite her vows, he liked to think that a part of Corrine lived on in her.

34

A YEAR AFTER THE wedding, his first thought was to wonder what Corrine would think of the city in its burnt-orange glow when he stepped out into the fragrant early afternoon of June 7. Wildfires in Canada had clouded the sky with an ocher haze which obscured the view of distant landmarks and made the looming foreground eerie and unfamiliar. The next day, or the day after, the city would be rebuilt, block by block, the sky showing blue above the gray rectangles, but for now it was dissolving. Ghostly pedestrians appeared suddenly from the mist, wearing N95 masks, as in the earliest days of the pandemic. "Can you believe this," said one man as he paused on the sidewalk beside Russell, who wished Corrine were here to see it. He did a double take; for a moment he could swear the man looked and even sounded like Jeff. Within moments the man had disappeared in the near distance, walking away with that same rangy carelessness as his long-lost friend. He knew it couldn't be and yet he could have sworn, for a moment, it was him.

Looking out into the twilight afternoon he thought of Yeats's phrase from a poem he'd sometimes cited to Jeff, *A terrible beauty is born*. It was ominous but undeniably beautiful. Would it remind Corrine of that morning of September 11, when the city stopped and looked up at the sky in fear and wonder, when it seemed that time itself had stopped? History had seemed to come to a standstill that day. And she had gone down into the acrid smoke to help. That was her impulse—to help.

Somehow the veil between worlds seemed to be dissolving in this atmospheric soup. He felt that she was out there, close by, just beyond sight, that if he tried hard enough, he could step forward into the lovely murk, saying, I'm coming, my love. I'm on my way.

ACKNOWLEDGMENTS

I would like to thank Angie Mar for allowing me to observe her kitchen at Le B., Maisie McInerney for sharing insights garnered from her time in restaurant kitchens, and Barrett McInerney for sharing his observations about the political propensities of younger left-leaning voters. This is the fourth novel in a tetralogy about Russell and Corrine Calloway, written over the past thirty-six years. I'd like to thank Gary Fisketjon for his careful editing of the first three books, Erroll McDonald for his astute editing of the last, and Binky Urban for her support and advice throughout the writing and publication of all four. Thanks also to Morgan Entrekin for his publishing world insights, and to Anne for indulging the weird hours I keep when writing.

A NOTE ON THE AUTHOR

Jay McInerney came to prominence in 1984 with his first novel, *Bright Lights, Big City*. He is the author of seven further novels, a collection of short stories and three collections of essays on wine. He lives in New York City and Bridgehampton, New York.

A NOTE ON THE TYPE

This book was set in Janson, a typeface long thought to have been made by the Dutchman Anton Janson, who was a practicing typefounder in Leipzig during the years 1668–1687. However, it has been conclusively demonstrated that these types are actually the work of Nicholas Kis (1650–1702), a Hungarian, who most probably learned his trade from the master Dutch typefounder Dirk Voskens. The type is an excellent example of the influential and sturdy Dutch types that prevailed in England up to the time William Caslon (1692–1766) developed his own incomparable designs from them.

Typeset by Scribe,
Philadelphia, Pennsylvania

Designed by Casey Hampton